MIDWAY
a novel

Brent Mason

GALLEON

Midway: A Novel

© Brent Mason 2024
All rights reserved.

First Galleon Edition, December 2024
ISBN 978-1-998122-141

Published by Galleon Books
Moncton, New Brunswick, Canada
www.galleonbooks.ca

Cover artwork by James Jensen, "The Leap." Used by generous permission.

This is a work of fiction, if that wasn't already obvious. Any resemblence to Midways real or imagined, or to persons in Midways real or imagined, is entirely due to the author's superb ability to render such Midways and carnival personae in a believable manner. Such is the skill of talented authors like Brent Mason, who, by the way, is an equaly talented musician.

Check out www. brentmason.ca.

The author acknowledges the financial support of ArtsNB.

Library and Archives Canada Cataloguing in Publication

Title: Midway : a novel / Brent Mason.
Names: Mason, Brent (Musician), author.
Description: First Galleon edition.
Identifiers: Canadiana 20240537033 | ISBN 9781998122141 (softcover)
Subjects: LCGFT: Novels.
Classification: LCC PS8626.A79858 M54 2024 | DDC C813/.6—dc23

To my aunt Marion, the first person to show me that it was possible to do creative things no matter where you were from.

The remnant asphalt heat still shimmers at 3 a.m. It emanates off the blacktop, from wrist-thick power cables that snake their way throughout the grounds, from the corrugated metal skin of the rides that have sprung from the lifeless earth. It is felt and seen, on the ramps that lead to the Ferris Wheel; on the synthetic blue-and-red fur of the hanging, plush bears jammed tight under the cover of rope-tourniquet canvas; on the undulating, shape-shifting mirror that casts its reflection from the House of Fun.

There is the *shk-shk-shk* of Old Joe's long-handled broom, audible from the west entrance, pushing the wrappers and butts and the rough cardboard French fry containers into piles that he'll sweep onto his flat shovel. There is the detritus of smaller prizes poking out of the little trash hills he's made on the blacktop: the plastic arm of a superhero, the shards of a broken Jack Daniels mirror, a torn blacklight poster of a rat giving the finger to an incoming bird of prey. The shine is off in the wee hours; there is no value, and no pretending.

It's that quiet. You can hear his broom above the occasional car hissing by in the other world. The gaping maw of the Clown at the main entrance is bolted shut; Joe has a key. He makes sure he locks it behind him, coming and going. He's warned every day to be careful and make sure, because you don't want them coming in from the outside, stealing things, breaking mirrors, vandalizing rides: someone could get hurt, right? You don't want to lose this job, Joe. Joe will nod, his eyes down, keep everything to himself, including all the money he finds out there in the tiny hours.

The Doppel Looper and the Ferris Wheel creak in the breeze that comes in from the west, a weary metal groan.... The cacophony emitted by the wide-eyed throughout the day has dissipated, swallowed by the dark sky. The blue and red and yellow lights that blink to the beat of the thirty-song loop below are dormant, and it's impossible to tell which ones are burnt out and need replacing. Under the unblinking sun there's never the will, and the busy, heart-pounding night allows no time for such trivial concerns. Maybe at the end of the run, or more likely, once the next season begins, when all are as full as a tick with hope for another beginning. Out of sight, under the counter where the tickets are taken, there's a hammer, a small pile of chrome vanadium wrenches, a can of WD-40.

The games—the joints—are lined up in perfect rows of painted wood, canvas and cotter pins. All closed tight for the night, some with ropes brought taut from the inside by hands that couldn't be completely cleaned in the washroom under the bandstand over by the racetrack. There are horse races every night this week, with special events and the Queen's Cup on Sunday.

The hot plush bears are humped up under the roof. The canvas covers on the joints come down like the lid of an eye 'round midnight. Someone is snoring. A sneakered foot sticks out from under the cover of the Milk Can game, twitching like a dog lost in a dream, under the boards where hands have thrown down dough all day, beating on them in excitement, frustration, anger. There's just enough room to stretch out in a sleeping bag, a cocoon. Cheap, at least, and there's a shower under the bandstand available in the morning if you can get in before the gates open, or the jockeys arrive...

Beyond the rides and the game lines, around the edges, RVs and campers of various size and status circle the wagons, back to front, an Airstream moat that separates the worlds. If you could slip under the lines and slide up to the side of one of the Big Boys, peek in under the cover of night, there would be piles of elastic-wrapped bills to see, broken down in hundreds, fifties twenties, tens and fives, stacked on a round, bumpered table. An overflowing ashtray beside half a carton of Marlboros, a half-full bottle of Johnny Walker. A cheap mirror from one of the joints with a weed leaf on it; white, dusty residue all that's left of the day's pick-me-ups. There's a manicure kit on the counter by the bathroom sink. A blow dryer. A Rolex is off its wrist on the nightstand, ticking....

You couldn't know there are a couple of hundred people nestled in bed in trailers, curled up under the game boards, or laid out on the floor of the House of Fun, the Haunted Castle, behind the Yeti-image facade of the Himalayan Express. Love is being made, cards are being dealt, lines are being drawn, dreams are waking up. There's no indulging of self now, no wallowing in the mud of insignificant things such as pain, hope, fate or fault. None of that matters in the exhausted pre-dawn, and matters even less, if that is possible, when the Midway is heaving with humanity. All that matters is that the flaps are up, the lights are on, the music is loud, the cotton candy is twirling, and the Clown gate is open. As a thin, pink dawn emerges, Joe's broom is done pushing the remains of the previous day into piles. He makes for the gate and locks it behind him.

...

1

Wyatt stood on the edge of the Red River Exhibition Fairgrounds for a long time. There were trucks and trailers with a black-hatted, bullseye-eyed clown face on an orange background pulling into position on the tarmac, horns honking, diesel engines humming. There were men yelling, knots of people hanging around trailers, massive metal frames shining in the sun. A line of RVs was forming far to the left of the bandstand in the distance. Wyatt was hot, hungry and tired but couldn't bring himself to walk the final few hundred metres.

What if he turned around? Where would he go and what would he do? He'd said goodbye to the past, right? The paralysing sadness of the east that had finally propelled him. The meditative sanctuary of Salt Spring Island? Done. The California dreaming? Done. All those boxes were ticked, so here he was—empty as a pocket, broken as a promise. He rocked back and forth in his hiking boots, wishing he was someone else, somewhere else. He counted breaths, trying to calm down and reel in the panic; the shadow over the shoulder. There was no choice left, or if there was it had been made long ago. He watched his right foot fall forward, and followed.

He wanted to disappear.

No one paid him any mind as he wandered around the grounds. He stepped high over the black power cables spread like arteries on the tarmac. There were piles of metal waiting to be assembled into rides. Exoskeletal, with numbered seats lined up on the side. He recognized a Scrambler and a Tilt-a-Whirl from when he'd been a carnival-going kid, flashing briefly on a memory of an old girlfriend stumbling off the ride and puking on a pile of sawdust outside the livestock stables. A small smile appeared for a moment, then went back inside. Larger rides were farther away; the beginnings of the Ferris Wheel looked like a giant meccano set. Several semis were unloading what appeared to be a roller coaster.

Dozens of people were striding purposefully back and forth across the blacktop. "Over here!" "Back it up. Stop, for fuck's sakes!" "Hey, go get the sledgehammer." Yelling, cursing, laughing and familiar ribbing—"Don't tear your panties, Jackie boy!"—rose and fell in volume and intensity on a bed of rattling diesel-engine noise. Clanging and crashing. Parts were moving everywhere. Funhouse, Haunted House, House of Mirrors…. Transport trailers with sides getting propped up and swung wide to reveal giant caricatures of clowns and demons. It was hard to isolate a scene amidst all the movement; it was a military operation, or how he thought one would look.

A clown-face-emblazoned white trailer at the far end of the tarmac had "Guest Relations" in big black letters, so he pulled his way up the stairs and in. The woman bent over the desk didn't look up.

"Yeah? Whaddya need?" A painted-nail hand reached for a smoke in an urnlike ashtray.

"Hi. I'm supposed to start working. Looking for Jonah Jensen. Any idea where he might be?"

"Nope. Most of the rides got here this morning, but the games aren't going up for a while. Haven't seen him." She hauled on the smoke, set it back in an overflowing ashtray, and kept plugging numbers into her calculator. He backed out and down the stairs.

Wyatt wandered over to the bandstand to find some shade. The sun was high and an image of an ant under a magnifying glass crept into his thoughts. "What if it was all bullshit? You never know, right? What if…?"

He did his best to tamp down the panic rearing up within. If there was no job, well…what exactly was he supposed to do? He couldn't come up with one plausible option. East was out. West was out. School was out. He did a quick inventory of burned bridges. His heart picked up its pace, his palms suddenly tingling with sweat. Please, not a goddamn migraine! There was a cinder-block washroom building on the edge of the grounds. Once there, he stripped off his sweat-soaked shirt, lathered up with hand soap and cleaned himself up as best he could, splashing the tepid water from a rust-edged tap onto his face over and over.

2

Nowhere else to go, he set his pack against the back of one of the permanent buildings on the site and sat down. He closed his eyes, the cacophony of the carnival slowly thinning away.

He came to reluctantly, winched out of the quicksand of a dream. "Hey…Wyatt. Wake up." A man's voice, a hand on his shoulder. Who? His eyes slit open. Jonah's head was haloed by the sun. A firm hand pulled him off the ground.

The sense of relief rolling over him was enormous.

"You made it, eh? Wasn't sure if you'd show up. Then again. I'm never sure if anyone is coming until they get here."

Jonah laughed, a moment that brought Wyatt back to the bar when they'd met. One of the first things he'd liked about him was that laugh. It didn't take itself or anyone else too seriously.

"Lots of talk out there, less action!"

Jonah grabbed Wyatt's pack and tossed it to him.

"C'mon. We're not gonna be setting up in a while, but we've got to be ready. There's a whole lot of 'hurry up and wait' happening. We'll get to it later than sooner." He'd already turned and was heading toward the games on the other side of the exhibition grounds. Wyatt cantered to catch up with him, falling in lockstep. They slipped out of the heat between the lines of trailers.

A couple of guys were waiting for them at the end of a row of trailers. "Scott. Bruce. This is Wyatt. Right on time." They extended their hands.

Scott was tall, pale and pudgy with bushels of long, dirty blonde hair sticking out from under a tweed flat cap. He gave a nod and reluctantly released some cigarette smoke. Bruce looked a bit like Buddy Holly—horn-rimmed glasses, short, curly dark hair and a big smile out in front. A truck horn honked, drowning out his greeting. Jonah rolled a Drum cigarette as he surveyed the action all around them.

"Slowly getting there," he said, nodding to a man on the tarmac. The man had a measuring wheel with a long handle and spray can. He was marking orange Xs on the asphalt. He had expensive sunglasses hanging from a lanyard, a pink Polo shirt and leather shoes, which struck Wyatt as incongruous in this setting. He also had a good tan. Wyatt had forgotten about the Florida connection; the Midway kicked off the season there before making its way north. Jonah left them to go over and talk to the man.

"That's Greg," Scott said. "He's the face of the Clown on the ground. In charge of the set-up in each city, all the stuff to do with the venues. When to set up, what goes where. Public relations. He's the main man, Wyatt." They watched Jonah and Greg nodding and gesturing.

"He's got the spray paint to mark where the games go." Wyatt looked around and saw dozens of orange markings spread out on the asphalt as far as he could see—angled marks with numbers and letters. More method to madness than he would have expected.

Jonah ambled back over to them, flicking his cigarette on the ground.

"Okay, good to go. You two go to the Birthday Game trailer for line two." He nodded to Wyatt. "We've got the Milk Can for Line 1."

Scott blew out a cloud of smoke and walked away through it. Jonah pointed to Wyatt.

"We'll get started on the Milk Can. There was a problem at the border, so the plush isn't getting here until tomorrow." He noticed the quizzical look on Wyatt's face.

"The stuffed animals. Maybe they were looking for coke, I dunno. Maybe condoms full of blow in Bart Simpson's belly or up a stuffed-elephant's ass." They all laughed. "So, let's go. The sooner we get the joints up, the sooner we can get out of here."

Scott and Bruce walked out of the shade.

Wyatt followed Jonah to the end of the trailers, where they got in line in with the other carnies, taking turns wrestling long, blue-enamel-painted boards out the door, along with plywood, some huge and heavy, rolled-up red canvas and a sack of nuts and bolts. They carried everything to the other end of the grounds and dropped them by an orange mark. A dozen trips at least. He had to hurry to keep up with Jonah, who moved with casual intensity.

Wyatt did his best to help, but he mostly he hauled, lifted, or held things as Jonah assembled the game. He marvelled at the efficiency with which he snapped the pieces of lumber into place, hooking metal clasps, brass hooks and beams and boards. In a couple of hours, the joint was erected, with power outlets ready to go. Together, they hoisted the canvas up over the top, putting skin on the skeleton. Wyatt went and got some long, heavy spikes and a sledgehammer from the trailer and pounded them into the asphalt on each corner so that Jonah could tie the joint down with thick rope. It felt good to be able to do something on his own.

"Never know when a tornado's gonna come blowing through!

Wizard of Oz-like witch-wind howling!" Jonah quipped.

They stood back to admire their work. Wyatt saw that most of the empty spaces on the line were now filled up with joints in various stages of construction, in perfect alignment with each other. "Let's go see how they're doing with the Birthday Game. They're not done yet, I bet."

He was right. Most of the wood was still in a matchstick pile. Scott was standing in the middle of it, looking frustrated. Bruce was sitting on a canvas roll, smoking.

Scott broke the uncomfortable ice.

"Fuck, Jonah. I thought I had it down. I can't get the cross-pieces right. Sorry, man."

Jonah didn't say anything, just looked at him for a second with eyebrows raised, stepped over the wood and started snapping pieces together. The rest of them hustled to get him what he needed; it felt like a competition to Wyatt, trying to grab Jonah what he wanted before he asked for it. There was a need to please. Another hour and they had it up. Jonah didn't say much beyond what was necessary. His impatience was palpable. Scott swore to do better next time.

3

Jonah had a brown VW Westphalia that got them off the grounds and across town to where they'd be staying. It was his parents' house, but they were away for the month and had offered it to him for the ten-day run in Winnipeg. Scott and Bruce got out, and Wyatt and Jonah continued to get food and beer. They pulled into a pub, the Coach House, that offered "world-famous wings." Wyatt was skeptical of the claim. When they'd sat down across from each other, he saw the Jonah he remembered from the recruitment session at the bar back east in winter.

"So. How was that? Welcome to the Midway!" He leaned forward. "What do you think?"

"Well, it's a fuck of a lot bigger than I thought. That's a military operation! It comes all the way from Florida?"

Jonah lit a rolled smoke and leaned back.

"Yeah. We always start the season there with a big fair in Dade County. The owners, the twins, live there. You'll see them soon enough. They're the grandkids of the guy who started it back in the thirties. It was classic carny action back then. Freak shows. Bearded ladies, midget tossing, haha. Siamese twins, hermaphrodites. The whole deal. It was all in sepia. Ever see that Calvin and Hobbes strip about that? Where the world was black and white before colour cameras? Strippers and tricks turned at night after the crowds left. And crooked as a crowbar. The games were *all* rigged. He grew it from one small show. Started buying and merging with others. He stumbled onto the Canadian circuit kind of by chance. He ran it all the way across the west and got the contract for the CNE in thirty-seven. That was a big deal back then. By the time his son took over in the fifties it was the largest Midway in North America. They'd weaned themselves off the freak shows and backstage hookers by then. Well, as much as one weans themselves from anything. More fiscal crop rotation than morality moves."

"I started with them in seventy-eight. Got kicked out of school for being bored. Well, not kicked out; I failed. They failed. My parents failed. Everyone…haha!" Jonah lowered his head to roll another smoke. Wyatt saw a little bald spot he hadn't noticed before. He got up to take a piss, twisting his way through the now packed bar. Jonah was leaning back in his seat when he returned, smiling inside the smoke.

"So… what have you been doing since we last did this?" He made a wide, Christ-on-the-Cross gesture with his arms. Wyatt dug in and told him about the train trip, Salt Spring Island and his west coast awakening, the lithium springs in Oregon ("Oh right, yeah, I was there once! Wouldn't get a fly high"....), the Moonies on the streets of San Francisco. His hitchhiking revelation, pulling cars over with his mind. Jonah kept nodding appreciatively.

"Oh, for sure; you can get into that zone when you're thumbing, where you feel like you're pulling them in, willing them to pick you up. That can come in handy..." Wyatt wound the tale down. "And got a ride here. Downtown is bleak. All the natives...fuck. I was hoping this thing you'd promised was real, not some fever dream! When you weren't on the lot this afternoon, I freaked a bit. I'm down to like fifty bucks now!"

It was quiet between them long enough for it to get a bit uncomfortable. The waitress came over to take their food order. Jonah ordered a large, loaded nachos, flew a disarming, charming smile up the flagpole and asked for "two straws with them, please." She laughed and carried on.

Wyatt spoke first. "So...How about you? It's safe to assume you left the Maritimes...?"

Jonah leaned in on his elbows, thick-knuckled fingers clasped.

"Yeah. I mean, I'm from Winnipeg and know enough about winter that I don't like it, but I hadn't been east before. It felt like the time to go east. I didn't stay much longer after we met. Maybe a couple of weeks. If you're gonna go east, though, you might as well go all the way, right? I took the ferry over to Newfoundland, saw the sun rise on Cape Spear. I've been half an hour late for everything since for some reason haha." He refilled their glasses from the pitcher.

"I was in Toronto for a bit. I know a guy with a studio there. He let me do some recording at night." Wyatt didn't know this about Jonah. It strangely and suddenly occurred to him he didn't know a goddamn thing about him. "You're a musician? What do you play? I play some guitar."

"I make music. Is that what a musician does? I don't really play anything. Not songs at least. Whatever a song is. What's a song? Lyrics? Melody? Whales make songs, right?" His hands were dancing through the smoke-filled air.

"You can get music out of anything. I like to go into a studio late at night and fire up the tape and see what comes out, you know? Find the moment in there and give it a feel. Make beds with keys and synths or build a groove that can go off on its own. Sound… I've got a bunch of recordings from the joints. We were in Mobile last year. I taped a couple of mics under the boards and recorded. Incredible what you can get! When I made it to Toronto, I finally got to use it. You hear the money land, the cheering, the soul-crushing groans of defeat haha. The back-and-forth side-conversations; stuff you never pick up on when you're working, you know? Then you just run with it."

Wyatt was rivetted. There was something about the measure of his cadence, the shine in his eyes, that resonated and pulled him in. He did his best to show Jonah he got it; show that he understood the subterranean truth of what he was up to, which was way beyond the three chords he knew on the guitar.

"Yeah, so I've got like twenty reel-to-reels of stuff from Toronto. I'll get it transferred later so you can hear it if you want. I wouldn't mind hearing it! I think I was there for a month, maybe. Everyone shits on Toronto, but I love it. There's all the great food and cafes in Little Italy and Kensington Market. I saw Laurie Anderson do a show!" Wyatt nodded, pretending he knew her music, when he'd only heard her name a few times in a Lou Reed context. And he only knew Lou Reed from a couple of tunes; Sweet Jane that the Cowboy Junkies, a Toronto band, had covered, and Walk on the Wild Side. He could namecheck the tune Heroin, was able to toss out little flares of credibility referencing Warhol and The Factory. But it was bullshit. He was faking it.

"I landed at a few galleries, local openings. There's a lot of art in Toronto. Lot of art everywhere!" He affected a posh British accent. "Oh, yes, art everywhere you look, but not a lot of good art!" and continued "Most of what I saw, I'd seen. I paint a bit when I can. That's harder to do. You need to be in one place for a while to paint."

He leaned back in his chair again.

"I wandered in on an opening on Queen Street West at a loft one night. The music coming out the window caught my attention. You expect shitty jazz at these things. This stuff was chunky and grating. You could feel stuff breaking inside it. I was just standing outside listening, then followed a few people up the stairs. The studio was sardined with critics, students and artists all dressed in black, wall to wall!"

Jonah rolled another smoke and filled their glasses with the rest of the beer. The sounds of the bar smashed around them.

"This art was different. Some of the paintings looked like sound would look, if you know what I mean. How do you paint music? I always wanted to do that. There were these huge canvases angled off the ceiling. Cones. Cylinders. It was mathematical in a way, with lines reconfiguring the way runes might, you know." His hands were doing their moves again.

"As if you had some old Viking seer tossing them onto a wolf hide. Shaking those bones around and they came up with a message from the other side. You could feel this intense energy coming off the paintings, right? It was feeding the whole scene. The loft was humming, wrapped up in the visuals and the soundscape this guy had created; the rhythm of the room.... I never saw anything like it. Turned out to be quite a night."

Wyatt laughed along with him. "Sounds amazing. When was this? I was probably passing through on my way out west when you were there. Shit!" He allowed himself an 'in the know' laugh. "What'd you do after Toronto?"

Jonah's hands were palms-out on the bar table. 'Well... what would Jesus do! I've got a kid, you know. Oh wait—you don't know! I've got a daughter out on the Gulf Islands. Gabriola—you know it?" Wyatt nodded.

"So... I was probably there when you were on Salt Spring. Her mother is a hippie. We split up last year. I think she got tired of me making fun of her friends and crystals and healing and all that horseshit. But Aleshia—that's my kid—is cool... she's six now. I see her as much as I can; summer and fall are tough...But kids, you know? They're usually fine. Better for her that her we split up. She's bright. She'll figure it out." Again, Wyatt nodded. It tended not to be his experience back home. Most break-ups he knew were nasty affairs involving battles for custody, fights over money, and messed-up kids.

"Anyway, I stayed there until it was time to fly to Florida. The Dade County Fair kicks it off. It's a big one. I have to be there to make sure I get good games. It's kind of like seniority, but it only works like that of you're there right out of the gate. And it's nice to get some sun to start the season. Tan lines instead of fault lines haha! So, I've got the Milk Can on Line A and the Birthday Game on Line B this year. Should be pretty good. It's different every year. You can almost use the Midway as a barometer of how the economy is doing, right? People don't mind coming out and blowing a few hundred bucks if things are going okay. Then again, it can be a welcome distraction when they aren't. Jury's out on my theory, maybe." He took a drag off his cigarette.

"Either way, I can pay you a hundred bucks a day while we're working. Nothing when we're travelling between cities, but at least we'll have each other then. Quality time, as they say."

A hundred bucks a day was okay with Wyatt. It was a hundred more than he was making now. Besides, he wasn't signing on to this for the dough. Whatever it was, it had nothing to do with money. Well, not nothing…

It got quiet, the space between them filling with the sound of sports from the TV on the wall and the free and easy laughter of the locals. Wyatt had forgotten what that felt like. To be a local. The wind had come out of the sail of their conversation. The long day felt like so much more, as though the last four months had funnelled down to now, to this spent conversation at a table in a bar with a stranger who was no stranger at all somehow. He was yawning as Jonah put forty bucks on the table and led them out the door.

4

Wyatt woke to clanging kitchen cups and the low drone of male conversation that slipped up the carpeted stairs to his room. He took in his surroundings. He had collapsed on his bed in the dark after the bar and came to surrounded by cardboard boxes full of books and magazines. It reminded him of his ex's mother, who was a chain-smoking hoarder, and that opened the door of the day to the familiar regrets. He wallowed in thoughts of the past for the first time in a long time, sitting on the side of the bed, waiting for his body to make a decision. A "Hey Wyatt, let's get it going!" from Scott prodded him into the day.

Jonah was up and gone by the time he came downstairs. Scott, slumped on the couch, tangled up in his hair with coffee and a smoke, grunted a greeting. Bruce was in the kitchen.

"Alrighty then! Mornin' Wyatt: I assume you need a coffee! I just concocted this fine Costa Rican Dark Roast from freshly ground beans left behind by Mr. and Mrs. Jensen. Not bad at all, if I do say so myself!"

He was way more chipper than anyone had a right to be at this time of the day. Wyatt took the baby blue cup from him, then turned to look out the window over the sink. It was a lovely back yard, the verdant green of early summer. Bruce nattered on behind him.

"Should be fun today, eh? I can't wait. I got here from Calgary a couple of days ago on the bus. Boy, that was a wild trip! I didn't even sleep. A couple of guys just out of jail were at the back and I ended up drinking with them. We got really high too, smoking hash in the can! It was crazy." Wyatt reluctantly turned around to acknowledge him, struck again with his Buddy Holly-esque appearance. He was skinnier than he had noticed yesterday. He had on a white short-sleeved t-shirt with a pack of smokes rolled up under, and rolled-up jeans with torn knees and red Chuck Taylors. He held his smoke at the tips of his fingers.

"Yeah. Sounds crazy." Wyatt couldn't bring himself to say anything more. He sensed a need for acknowledgement from Bruce that always resulted in the opposite result. Kind of like the Loonie Tunes Spike and Chester cartoon. "Hey Spike, wanna get some cats, Spike…?" Then he felt shitty for feeling that way and tossed him a "Good coffee" bone.

"Yeah, right? Really good beans. I always have the best coffee back home. How about you? Not coffee, I mean where did you come from? Come here from…"

"Back east. New Brunswick." He wouldn't roll out the whole carpet for Bruce. "I met Jonah in the Maritimes and thought this might be an interesting way to get through time."

Bruce was nodding and smiling.

"Oh yeah. I'd love to get there someday. My grandfather came to Calgary from Nova Scotia back in the fifties. I guess it sucks there now, huh? Everyone leaving for something better!"

Fuck off, Wyatt resisted saying. *It's a beautiful place with people who've been there for centuries who are connected by blood and tell stories and play music from the Scottish-Irish traditions and I'll take that over bullshit oil money any day!*" All that was rising within, but he just grinned.

Scott coughed out from the living room "Someone call a cab; we've got to get going!"

5

The three of them got out at the south end of the carnival grounds. The transformation from when they'd left was astounding. A skyline of rides had been erected, steel and iron gleaming under a forever blue sky that in the blazing morning sun looked as deep as the ocean. They walked past the Scrambler, the Tilt-a-Whirl, the Gravitron and the Zipper. The Ferris Wheel was the largest Wyatt had ever seen. There was a roller coaster, a double-looping behemoth that dominated the line; the Doppel Looper. They stopped and stared as two guys wandered around it, tightening things with large wrenches.

"Takes a dozen trucks to haul that fucker! We only use it for the really big fairs," said Scott as he lit a smoke. This was his second year working for Jonah, and Wyatt could see he wore the world-weary vet vibe well.

"Imagine hauling that thing all the way from Florida! Crazy…" He shook his head, spit and they carried on, shuffling past the now erect Fun House, House of Mirrors, Haunted House…. The joints were all set up in their lines, canvas siding pulled down tight, looking vaguely military in their symmetry. Wyatt thought of Civil War sepia photos.

The sides were up on the Milk Can game. Jonah was on his knees screwing a small platform together and didn't look up as the three of them gathered around.

"Morning. The plush got in a couple of hours ago. Let's get at it, okay? Scott, you know where the truck is. Let Greg know you're getting the prizes for Milk Can 'A' and Birthday 'B'. Make sure you get all big ones for here, okay? He fucked up in Dade and all the smaller ones were hung before I got there. I'd rather not hang 'em, take 'em down and hang more." He stood up and lit a smoke. "There's a couple more people coming in today, but I don't know when. No time to waste, though…"

They peeled away, with Scott in the lead. They went down the side of the trailers, walking until they came to an open one with wooden stairs in the back. The giant clown face oversaw the operation. About twenty people were milling around in a semblance of a line, smoking, laughing and swearing and greeting each other.

"Hey Scooter, you made it back for another run, eh? How's it hanging haha." An older woman in a hoodie, shorts and flip-flops gave a big hug to an even older guy in a sleeveless jean jacket, knocking the ember off his cigarette and making him exclaim:

"Jesus, Martha, watch it for fuck's sake! How are you!" There were little knots of familiar talk murmuring their way up and down the line while the three of them stood silent. They inched their way up while people lugged bags of colourful stuffed animals past them.

The animals for the Milk Can game were huge. Giant panda bears, cats and elephants about five feet high. They could only handle two at a time, so it took a few trips to get everything they needed for the joint. Scott and Bruce went to another trailer for the stock for the Birthday Game; smaller, shinier prizes for the most part, while Wyatt got the last load of giant plush. He stumbled back to the joint with the final two elephants, threw them down and looked up to see Jonah and two smiling women standing in front of him.

'This is Des," said Jonah. "She's gonna be working with us." Wyatt stood up and offered his hand, looking without staring. Beautiful. Dark hair and darker eyes, high cheekbones, short jean shorts and olive tan legs in leather cowboy boots. She reached out and shook his hand, holding it and his eyes in a firm grip.

"Hi, Wyatt. Really nice to meet you!" Her voice was low, single-malt smoky.

"Hi. Nice to meet you too." That was all he could come up with.

"And this is Trish." Trish, Wyatt saw, was shorter than Des, though striking as well. Her blond hair was pulled back in a ponytail with a few strands on her cheeks. She had wide, sky-blue eyes, and wore a tank top and the obligatory jean shorts. Like Des, she gave him a bright white smile.

"Good to meet you. We've heard a lot about you!" Wyatt thought he saw a wink. He wasn't sure what she could have heard, but laughed as if he knew and shook her hand. "Not much to hear! Nothing to see here folks, let's just move it along." They all laughed, which felt good. He'd spent a lot of time alone lately and forgot he had a sense of humour.

"You two go to the Birthday Game, okay?" Jonah pointed towards the B line. 'Scott's here on his own. I'm going to start getting the plush up here with Wyatt, and then I'll be over. Gates open at five o'clock. We've got time but there's a lot of shit to do. Wyatt, pass me that panda."

They spent the next hour hanging plush in the joint, using a pole to put them up on hooks, descending in three layers of stuffed symmetry. It was getting warm now, well past noon. By the time they had them all up, Wyatt was sweating hard. He took a break while Jonah went to the stores trailer, sat on the boards of the joint and looked around. Thick black electric cables snaked in and out of the joints and in under the side games. The flipped-up trailer fronts housing basketball games, water gun races and dart boards were already blinking coloured lights up and down the rows. The A line spoked off westward from the Himalayan ride, an enclosed circular track that undulated through wintry, mountain scenes under the watchful eyes of an Abominable Snowman. A couple of shirtless ride guys were suspending speakers below a giant mirrored disco ball, while another one checked the stanchions of the seats, opening and slamming them shut.

Jonah had left his cigarettes on the small platform he'd built in the middle of the joint. It was square, about two feet off the ground. There was about four feet between the boards on the outer edge and the riser. The sounds of the grounds—slamming, shouting, idling diesel and the cacophonous meld of music from the games and rides—felt far away. Wyatt hadn't smoked for a few years, since his undergrad days, but it felt right to reach over to Jonah's pack, pull one out and light it.

Head down, beat-up leather hiking boots beginning to burst at the side. It was many miles behind him, wasn't it? Slow down for a minute, open the window a crack and the shoulder shadow sneaks up again. He tried to talk himself through it. "If I stop moving, it's here again, wrapping 'round my head, a summer scarf that's hard to breathe through or see through. It's all in your head, remember. C'mon Wyatt…"

He felt the agonizing truth of himself in his roiling guts. Ran his fingers through his hair and counted the ones that stuck to his hand, as sure as could be that this too was a result of choices. The inner volume increased, haranguing. "Because this was the plan all along, wasn't it? Letting go but no no no you are lying to yourself. You didn't let go, you were released, stumbling through the gates not to the finish, but to serve your sentence. Sitting here in a fucking carnival game, broke with busted boots. That's how you can tell the street people, right? Shitty shoes. Look at these things."

Up and down the lines the lights were on, broad daylight, the rides whirring and banging through the practice runs, the Doppel Looper groaning as the cars crept to the top. He faux flirted with getting up and walking away, constructing a fantasy of hitching back to the islands and digging in there, ascending. He knew that was bullshit.

6

Jonah walked towards him with a large, silver-grey milk can hoisted on his right shoulder. It looked like he was carrying the Stanley Cup, and when he passed it to him inside the joint, Wyatt resisted the urge to lift it over his head and cheer.

"There you go, Wyatt! In case you were wondering where the centre of the universe is, now you know." Jonah climbed in and centered it on the platform in the middle, nudging it incrementally back and forth until he was satisfied. He stood up, spread his arms wide and smiled. "Ladies and gentlemen, may I present the Milk Can game!"

He emptied a bag of softballs onto the riser. "For the goal is simple, you see." He held a ball up on the tips of his fingers, rotating it for Wyatt to see. "It's just a game, easy as can be. One for two or three for five, it's as easy as sin. One in wins!"

He laughed and tossed the ball to Wyatt. "It fits. Check it." He grabbed another ball and dropped it onto the raised rim of the can. It bounced a couple of times, then slid down and into the hole, landing with a thud on the wood below.

"They all fit. Nothing here is rigged like the old days. No shaved spindles on the Crown and Anchor, nothing stuck to the shelf in the bottle toss. It's all odds. Everything is calibrated so there's a thirty percent win-ratio cost per unit. Like those bears–" Jonah pointed to the hanging plush above them.

"These are the big prize on the Midway. The Clown wants to have some schlepped around the grounds on shoulders of triumphant men. Winners. Evidence of success. Proof of upward mobility, right? You want to take in at least a hundred bucks for every thirty in unit cost. Retail Economics 101. People see a winner and think they can be a winner too."

He reached under the boards and pulled up a can of Lemon Pledge.

"No cheating, but there's a few things you can do to help with the odds." He sprayed the concave, three-inch metal rim of the can for about thirty seconds, grabbed a rag and polished hard, forearm muscles knotting. He motioned Wyatt outside the joint. "Try that."

Wyatt grabbed the tossed ball and leaned in. "Nope. Can't do that; no leaning past the edge of the boards. Hands back. Hands back. You're gonna be watching for that."

Wyatt had always considered himself a pretty good baseball player, but the first one he tossed missed completely. The second hit the rim and flew off and bounced on the pavement. The polish seemed to accelerate it. The third did the same. Jonah climbed out of the game with a couple of balls in his hand. He held the ball with his fingers over the top.

"Backspin helps. You're gonna have to get good at this so you can show the skeptics we're on the up and up." He gave the ball a high arc, just under the feet of the lowest bear. It hit the far edge of the rim, spun to the other, went up in the air and straight down the hole with a popping sound, like when you snap your finger inside your cheek. He made a pistol with his right hand and blew the smoke off his finger.

"See? One in wins!"

Wyatt tried a few shots while Jonah put the Pledge away in a box beneath the boards. "I'd say we're good to go here. Let's see how they're doing on the other line."

7

As they walked to the Birthday Game, Jonah gave a nod or wave to most of the people he passed, then stopped to talk to a dark-haired woman with mirrored sunglasses, Wyatt hovering behind him as they caught up on the latest. Snippets of their chat alluded to people and circumstances Wyatt knew nothing of, so he ignored it as best he could, pretending to be interested in the guy checking the water guns in the horse race joint across from them.

He heard Greg's name, who he figured must be the same guy from the day before, who'd been spray painting the Midway outline from the day before. Something about a "fucking suck-up" who had bumped Jean (her name) from the A line with her Crown and Anchor joint, costing her a lot of money. Jonah was nodding and shrugging, agreeing that something was off with it, and she should talk to Greg before they left Winnipeg.

"Oh, hey." Jonah turned to him. "This is Wyatt, all the way from the east coast. Working the Milk Can."

Jean offered a hand.

"Hey Wyatt. Good to meet you. First time, eh? Ha, this is year, what…fifteen for me? Is that right Jonah, did we start fifteen years ago? Fuuuck!" They laughed, then fake cried, which made Wyatt laugh.

He and Jonah continued to the Birthday Game.

Jonah talked while they walked.

"It's a way different game than the Milk Can. Luck, not skill. That's why I've got you in the Can; you need to …umm…guide the action a bit. You'll see what I mean. The Birthday is less of a straight-up hustle because all you do is pick a month, toss a ball and see where it lands. That's who wins. No skill."

The sound of a feedback-whining mic-check up ahead interrupted him. "Check. Check one two"..._squuueeelllll_... "Check one two."

Bruce was standing inside the game, messing with the mixer while Scott was finishing hanging the prizes: plush that was a lot smaller than the Milk Can's zoological inventory, Bart Simpson dolls, mirrors with weed leaves or liquor logos.... A lot of shiny, cheap shit. Trish and Des were leaning on the game with their backs to them. Wyatt noticed a couple of ride guys from the Zipper pointing towards them, laughing, making obvious sexual gestures. He'd always hated that shit.

Jonah climbed into the game. In the middle was a white table with six-inch-high plexiglass sides all around it. There were holes cut into the white plywood with each month of the year written underneath. Around the perimeter of the game, on varnished woodgrain, the months of the year were repeated on all four sides. A dollar to play. If you got the orange street-hockey ball to land in the month you picked, you'd win. A sign above the board indicated how far up you could trade your prize with each additional win, from odd little stuffed hotdogs to a rubberized Bart Simpson two feet tall.

Jonah gestured Bruce away from the PA, took the mic and gave it a little run. The feedback squelched. He tweaked a few knobs and tried again. "Check one two, check. Hey hey hey, today's the day! Come down, come on in, anyone can play, anyone can win. If you've got a bellybutton, you've got a birthday one two one two."

He looked around the joint, checked his watch and nodded, satisfied with the set up.

"Okay. Good to go here, I'd say. It's three o'clock and the gates open at five. I'm going to get your uniforms. The food tent is set up over behind the Funhouse. If you guys want to go get something to eat, I'll get you uniforms and meet you there. Looks like three large and three mediums."

He vaulted out of the joint with one hand on the boards and headed towards the stores trailer. They watched after him for a moment and then slowly snaked to the food hall.

8

The blazing sun was muted under the red and white canvas of the food tent. Long wooden tables with tubular frames were surrounded by dozens of orange plastic chairs. Across from the entrance, a sign with moveable letters advertised the offerings: burgers, pancakes, fries, pizza, western sandwiches, pop, milk, coffee, tea…. They grabbed trays and moved down the line. It was quiet around their table at the back as they ate. Without Jonah there, it was a little awkward. Wyatt was the first to speak.

"So…where ya from?" He said it in a faux creepy pick-up voice that got a chuckle from everyone. The ice cracked. He gestured widely with his hands. "All of this and a uniform too?" More chuckles. Des spoke up.

"Hahaha. Yes, exactly! How could you turn down an offer of long hours, low pay, sketchy living conditions and unlimited cotton candy?" She lit a smoke and continued.

"I met Jonah in Toronto." She nodded to Trish. "That's where we met too. We were both at U of T. I was just taking a couple of courses, still working my night job. We were at an art opening. I think he just wandered in off the street, I dunno. I got kind of wasted." Trish rolled her eyes, playing her bit in the scene, and climbed into the conversation. She spoke more softly than Des.

"I met him that night, too. An interesting guy, right? Something different about him…. It was a wild night. It was an opening for Petr, one of our friends. Things got a bit crazy"—Des, recalling it all, shook her head in disbelief—"and I met him after my friend here checked out early."

They looked to and then away from each other.

"We were up on the studio's roof, and we watched the sun come up. Then I guess he made me an offer I couldn't refuse."

Des chimed in." Yeah. Same. I kept working my other job for a while, but I got to the point that I just couldn't do it anymore, you know. Sick of it all. Sick of the sick. So, here I am." She smiled at Trish. "I mean, here we are. What about you guys?"

They went around the horn, sketching out their biographies. Bruce built his up, alluding to adventure, rebellion against his wealthy parents in Calgary, wanting to live on the edge. As he talked, he smoked with his cigarette at the tip of his fingers, which to Wyatt lessened the authenticity of his mutinous claims.

Scott adjusted his hat and pulled the hair back from his eyes. "I've been here before, man. I did the whole season last year. I wandered onto the lot looking for work last June. Jonah hired me. You don't need a resume to get a gig here, haha. It beats the fuck out of being chased around Canadian Tire by idiots who can't find the duct tape."

They all laughed. He lit another smoke and passed one to Wyatt's outstretched hand.

"Seriously. I mean, this is nuts and all, but the money isn't that bad when you think that you can go on EI for six months after. Not many job openings for 'Milk Can Expert' when they investigate whether you're looking for work in the off season."

Expectant eyes turned to Wyatt, who was saved from the ordeal when Jonah came into the tent and sat down at their table with an armful of green aprons and blue cotton shirts, short sleeved with an orange and black clown face patch on the left front above the pocket.

"Ha. Looks like *A Clockwork Orange!* Can I be Malcolm McDowell?" Bruce waited in vain for a laugh. "Ultra-silence," said Jonah as he lit a smoke. That got a chuckle from Wyatt.

"Okay. We've got an hour before the gates open. Scott, you're gonna be in the Milk Can with Wyatt and Bruce. It's all Pledged up. I'll go get your float and be over before five. Des and Trish, you'll be in the Birthday with me. Today's Wednesday, so it's not going to be too busy. Kids with ride bracelets and no cash. It'll give you a chance to get a feel for things, memorize the astrological signs of each month." He crushed out his smoke and pulled away from the table. They followed him into the Midway in single file.

9

The Midway had come alive while they were eating. Music pounded out of speakers in the rides up and down the lines. Lights were whirling and flashing the colours of the rainbow in broad, bright daylight. The Ferris Wheel spun through the sky, the roller coaster whined, groaned and whipped through the double loops. Creaking doors and screams of terror from the Haunted House mixed with maniacal laughter from the Fun House. Basketballs banged off rims beside the spinning, clicking wheels of the Crown and Anchor.

The Himalayan Express was the closest ride to the Milk Can and had the loudest sound system. Wyatt walked into a wall of AC/DC when he arrived at the game. He hadn't factored loud music from someone else's playlist into his calculations of how the days on the Midway would roll out. He shouted into the game.

"Hey Scott, I guess this is all day and night, eh?"

"Yeah, pretty much. Only while we're open. If you're sleeping under the boards at night, you can get some decent shuteye." Wyatt hoped he'd never end up doing that. Bruce stepped out of the game with a handful of softballs, passing him a couple.

"We better practice a bit. We need to be able to demonstrate our ninja-level skills to the unsuspecting."

They started tossing, mostly missing. Wyatt was using the backspin Jonah had shown him, and after a bunch of tries finally got one in.

"It's harder than it looks," said Scott as he lifted the can up and removed the ball. "Don't worry; you won't be doing the demo from out there. We just toss them from in here, from the corners. The people just want to see that the ball fits. You'll get good enough that it'll look easy. You can usually grab someone walking by with a well-timed throw, reel them in for a try. We're gonna be working this together. Two of us in the game all the time, and when it gets busy, like after supper, all three of us. One-hour breaks until then; then just piss runs."

He handed a smoke to Wyatt. Bruce was still trying to get a ball into the can.

"You might want to start buying your own! Man, you smoke a lot in this gig.... But yeah, it'll get really busy at times and we'll need all three of us in the joint. You have to be hustling all the time, trying to pull them in. Lotsa patter, you know—"Hey hey, give it a try" shit. Lame, but it works. Eye contact is key." He bent down, grabbed the can of Pledge and gave the top another polish.

Jonah climbed into the game with the float. They all tied their aprons on, opened them up and let him dump the change in.

"Twenty-five bucks each. Two bucks or three for five. Three for five is the one we want to hustle, okay? Keeps them at the joint longer and gives you a chance to build a good tip."

He turned to Wyatt and Bruce. "A tip is a crowd around the joint. That's what you want. Once you've got a few people locked in, people start getting curious and stop for a look. That brings in more because it looks like something is going on. The balls start flying and the money gets a mind of its own. You'll see. But you've got to be ready; locked in, like Speer in Spandau." He started juggling two balls with one hand.

"The thing is to be on, ya know. It's all energy, all about being ready for it when it happens. You're gonna be tired, you're gonna be bored, you're gonna be pissed off at them, us, me, but fuck that. Doesn't matter. You've got to be on."

10

Five o'clock arrived on a cloud of trumpets blowing out the giant clown mouth at the front gate. Heavy metal from the Himalayan kicked in at ridiculously high volume. Wyatt had anticipated a rush of humanity tearing through the Midway, a cross between *Planet of the Apes* and a zombie apocalypse flick. Nothing remotely resembling a rush happened. They dribbed and drabbed their way in twos and threes, with the odd family unit trying to contain the younger ones from running ahead in the acres of open asphalt.

He watched the first couple come closer, hand in hand, leaning into each other, laughing and looking up at the high rides. They were maybe fifty feet away when, a couple of softballs in his hands, he tried his first patter. "Hey there. Hey! Check it out! We've got the big ones, biggest animals on the Midway! Win one for your girlfriend!" The couple looked over for a second, the man whispered something in her ear and they both laughed and walked past.

Wyatt felt a small, slow burn.

Another couple, a family with a young, curly-headed kid who stopped to look up at the elephant staring down at him. Wyatt, smiling, held out the balls.

"Two bucks. Three for five. All it takes is one in the can!" The mother pulled the kid by the arm, and they walked away quickly. A couple of teenagers went by with smokes hanging out of their mouths, laughing and one giving him the finger when he held up the softballs. And on and on.

Bruce and Scott were having no better luck. "It's slow, man," Scott yawned. "No need for all three of us here right now. I'm going to get a coffee and take a break. I'll be back in an hour." He climbed over the boards and shuffled away.

Bruce got the first mark, which bugged Wyatt a little. An older couple, the man a beefy guy with sideburns and a button-busting belly. Three balls clanked off the rim and onto the ground. Bruce scurried to grab them while the wife laughed, but they were already walking away when he stood back up. Still, he was annoyingly upbeat. "Broke the cherry anyway, right? Gotta start somewhere! Yes, indeed!"

All Wyatt could conjure up by way of congratulations was a reluctant, "Yeah…" He then started scouting the asphalt with renewed purpose. An hour in and no money, but more people were arriving all the time. The Midway lights were beginning to rival the late-day sun.

The music from the Himalayan was loud and incessant, punctuated with the endless ride-guy invocation over the PA—"Do you wanna go faster?"– and the already predictable screams affirming their desire to, in fact, go faster.

Wyatt channelled his inner cynic. "What the fuck did he expect? No, this is just fine?" The music sucked.

Two couples walked up to the game. "Two bucks or three for…" The guys were already holding their five-dollar bills out. He gave one of them three balls and hustled to the table for three more, a little surprised at the rush of adrenaline kicking in. It had taken close to an hour, but he had his first mark! Bruce had another on the other side of the joint. Under the canvas-and plush-insulated top, the clang of the balls on the can could be heard above the racket of the rides and the barkers with mics further down the line.

Clang. Clang. Ting. Scott came back into the game as another couple came up an open side. It was something you had to watch out for, apparently, not just focus on directly in front of you. Head-on-a-pivot type of action…

It materialized quickly. All four sides had someone throwing. A burst of laughter and "Let's go, Kevin" and then a rise and fall of excited voices when a ball hit both sides of the rim and bounced away.

Wyatt caught Jonah out of the corner of his eye while gathering a couple of balls off the ground; Jonah leaned against the rail by the Himalayan, smoking and watching them. Just as Wyatt gave him a smile and a wink swollen as a tick with a sense of accomplishment, he heard the *pop* of a ball hitting the hole dead centre and dropping in, with accompanying screams of joy from the two women. Jonah looked down, shaking his head.

"The elephant. I want the elephant!" one of the women yelled. The two men laughed, high-fiving each other. The winning guy pointed to it—"Gimme that one"—while the other guy, clean white t-shirt and even whiter teeth, teased him about having to carry a stupid elephant around for the rest of the night and how they should have played later.

Wyatt pulled it down and passed it to him, but the woman grabbed it, hugging it like it was real. Wyatt was smiling as they walked away, about to turn to Scott and Bruce and talk about their first tip when Jonah appeared in front of him.

"That was alright, eh?" He held up four fives to show him. Jonah flicked his butt onto the ground.

"Not really. Remember, I told you we're running retail here.

Ratios…odds. He nodded to Bruce and Scott.

"We've got, what, sixty bucks for so in? Maybe eighty? These plush are sixty wholesale, so we need about two hundred per unit. Maybe even a bit more. You're not even covering costs. You've blown one out of the joint, so you're way behind already. Now you've got to work harder just to get to even."

His disappointment was thick, almost edible to Wyatt. Pin in the balloon, down on the guts. "Oh. Right. Okay. Got it." Bruce was nodding like an idiot beside him, while Scott sat on the boards smoking. Jonah spun away.

They didn't say anything. Wyatt got a smoke from Bruce and promised to pay him back when he got a pack. He scraped his sneaker back and forth on the ground to keep from spiralling away, skipping out of town on the highway in his head. He wrestled with the golden past and thoughts of escape under red and blue fuzzy animals. "Who am I kidding?" The sensory overload on the Midway threatened to overwhelm. He remembered how easy it had been to slip away, and how hard it had been to get back, during the endless dark of the previous winter. "Talk all the talk you want but you're not going anywhere but here, on a fucking Midway far away from…"

The voice inside had a mind of its own.

A mark walked up unbidden with a five in an outstretched hand. Wyatt boomeranged his brain back to the joint, snapped the cash with one hand and delivered three balls with the other. The guy leaned in. "No, you have to be back behind the boards." He held his arm out and moved it up and down. "Nothing past there or it won't count." No more easy ones, he vowed.

By 8 o'clock the Midway was packed. The three of them, working all four sides, started to get a good groove going. There hadn't been another winner, so the money they were grabbing was getting them back in the imaginary black. Wyatt was pacing back and forth on his side of the joint, working on pulling people to the game. The competition was stiff, as the hoots, and bells, lights and screams and smash of metal on metal kept the heads outside the boards turning this way and that. He dug in hard to his patter.

"Here we go! Biggest bears on the Midway. Elephants! Come on in and give it a try, you've got nothing to lose, three for a fin, one in, one in one in wins!" Over and over, incantational in repetition, and grabbing a few takers. The fives started to accumulate, with a few twenties at the back of the wad in his hand. Wyatt felt like he was getting a feel for it.

They burned through opening night. Only one more bear had been won, and all three of them had been steady in pulling people in. There hadn't been any big crowds or concentrated tips, but it had gone alright.

Jonah came back after closing, climbing into the joint as the stragglers made their way to the gates. He took the cash from each of them, minus the float, and did the math. His lips were pursed. Slow, barely perceptible nods were followed by glancing up to see the gaps in the animals above. He looked at Wyatt and gave him that grin of his, one that warmed and reassured, and he already knew he had invested way too much of himself. It was no longer theoretical, wasn't tied to nebulous, esoteric conversations about consciousness and energy. Thoughts into action and all that shit. He was here, doing it.

"This is good, guys. You covered it. Better crowd than last year on opening night. It was decent down in the Birthday too."

Bruce interjected, "Yeah, boss, we had a good night in here. Indeed! A well-oiled machine, eh guys?" Scott nodded and Wyatt gave him a sort of smile because it had been alright. Day one done. Jonah got up.

"I'm gonna go make sure the girls close it down right." He gestured widely. "Scott, you take care of the rest. You guys, pay attention. I'll meet you at the van in fifteen."

11

Back at the house, they crashed, legs over armrests, backs against the wall, all sprawled on the floor around the living room, devouring the pizzas Jonah picked up on the way home and washing it down with beer. Des and Trish sat side by side on the couch, with Jonah at the end next to Trish. Exhausted, giddy laugh-talk wrapped itself around them.

"And then the guy took his shots with a fucking ice cream cone hanging out of his mouth. Almost popped a ball into the can and dropped the cone onto the boards when he yelled."

"Kid tried to pass a fake twenty, but the Queen was crooked, right off a photocopier! I shouted 'Police!' and he ran like a rabbit!"

"I can't believe how busy that got; they were three deep around the joint trying muscle in on the month of July! Idiots!"

More beer and cigarettes, the buzz of the first day strong enough to keep them going way past midnight. Jonah smiled and nodded his head indulgently.

"This was a good day. You all did well. See what I mean about the tips? It just takes a couple of people to catalyze the joint, you know. The energy starts to build a bit, then a few more get pulled in. You get a vortex that feeds on itself. Kind of like an inverted tornado. More balls in the air, more money flying, more hopes and dreams…that's almost unique to the Milk Can on the Midway."

He looked at Wyatt and held his eyes. "See, they have to communicate with each other as well as focus on their shots; balls that hit each other are still attempts, so don't get a redo. If yours gets knocked off the top of the can as it's about to roll in, too bad. It's you against them, but it's also them against each other. The guy with the girl on his arm doesn't want the other guy to win. Emasculation ensues. Use that to your advantage."

Jonah's hands wove as he spoke. Scott was passed out with his head back in the Lazy Boy, Bruce was holding his head up off the floor, cupped in his hands, fighting sleep.

"And you guys, gals I mean, were great in the Birthday. Really." Des and Trish had tired grins.

"To be honest, I've never had many women working for me. Something about those good looks and smiles had 'em coming from miles! And the Birthday is so wholesome; no skill, no competition, just slide on up and bet on your birthday!"

"That was a total ball!" Des lit another cigarette and went on in her smoky, low voice.

"I…we"—a nod to Trish as she put her arm around her shoulders—"didn't know what to expect. I mean, hearing about it is one thing, but being on the other side? Not being the kid running around from ride to ride and game to game…totally different look at it all, isn't it?"

Trish, legs stretched out in front of her, head back, her eyes closed, murmured, "Yep. Different for sure." Wyatt liked her voice—it sounded sweet; pure.

"I think this beats the hell out of researching the provenance of old paintings at the McMichael this summer. That's what I was supposed to be doing."

"Or dancing," said Des. Wyatt wasn't sure what she meant by that, but nodded with the rest of them. The late-night quiet filled the space between them. Silence snuck in and took over, and the remains of the day evaporated.

12

Morning light sliced through the curtains, extricating Wyatt from another dream. It took some time to orient himself; half his head was somewhere in the mountains with her memory, laughing, hand in hand down a winding road. He was aware of his thumb moving up and down on her wrist as he woke, but he was caressing the cotton quilt. The longing to return dissipated as he opened his eyes, the pieces of the dream-puzzle falling away. There were voices coming up the stairs from the kitchen, and the smell of coffee, cigarettes and bacon. Cutlery clattered.

He was the last one up. Everyone was at the table while Jonah filled plates with scrambled eggs, bacon and toast. There were glasses with orange juice.

"Free-range oranges. Surveillance-free bacon. Embryonic eggs, haha. We gotta fill up on the good stuff while we can; this is the one town we're going to have a house to crash in."

They took their plates from him and dug in. All the chairs were occupied, so Wyatt sat on the floor, leaning against the fridge. It got quiet while everyone ate.

Trish pointed her fork at the plate and then at Jonah. "Mmm... this is so good!"

"So, our fearless leader is a great cook, too!" Trish continued. "Can't wait to see what other surprises are in store for us!" They all chuckled a bit in between chews. Wyatt noticed Des steal a quick glance at Trish.

Jonah smiled. "Oh...they're only surprises once. Then they're expectations. And expectations are bound to disappoint. I guarantee I won't be cooking once we're out of here. Food is only fuel when we're on the road."

Wyatt and Des cleaned up when they were done. Wyatt washed and Des dried as they performed their first conversation, nearly verbless biographical sketches meant to inform, but not expose.

"Yeah, I met Jonah back east," Wyatt said. "I blew off grad school and travelled for a few months before coming here. BC. California. You know, *On the Road* and all that shit. Kerouac without the writing. Anything to get away from where I was. Every level of where I was." Des's eyes were on his, her attention seemingly genuine. It was her turn.

"Kind of the same, I guess. But I left home a while ago, after school was done. Was working around… then ended up in Toronto. Took a few courses; that's where I met Trish. And Jonah, I guess." She was quiet for a second. He handed her a plate.

"School ended and I didn't want to stay in the city, so I worked for a while. I had Jonah's card from that night in Toronto. I got tired of the work, so Trish and I got hold of him. And here we are." She spread her arms out and smiled. The dishes were done.

Wyatt got Jonah to stop for smokes at a convenience store on the way. He'd been bumming a lot and knew himself enough to know the smoking wasn't going to abate. He was committed now, passing them around the back of the van. When they got to the fairgrounds, they all piled out and strode down the middle of the Midway, six across, Jonah in the middle. Wyatt thought of *Gunfight at the OK Corral*.

13

The gates opened at noon. It was Friday, another warm, sunny prairie-sky day. There were already more people on the Midway at noon than there had been at five o'clock the day before, but Jonah said most were walkers and gawkers and decided two people in the games early on would be enough. He left Des and Trish alone, and Bruce and Scott manned the Can once they had taken the canvas sides off. Wyatt and Jonah walked up and down the lines, Jonah doing most of the talking, Wyatt most of the listening.

They stood in front of the Whac-A-Mole and watched a couple of kids trying to beat the pop-up rat over the head with Styrofoam mallets.

"This one's a big one. Huge, actually. He didn't invent it, I think it's Japanese, but BillyBob—that's his real name, a good ol' boy—turned it into a carnival game, maybe ten years ago.

"That's him over there." He pointed to a short, fat guy on the other side of the line with a cowboy hat and shades, talking to a younger guy with blond hair and shades.

"That's Ethan, the heir apparent to the carnival empire. Well, him and his twin sister Eva. When Bob came up with the Whac-A-Mole, it blew up. Jammed, lined-up tips on every line. Three of them at every fair. That first summer, he'd be emptying bags of cash into the safe in his RV every night."

They continued walking down to where black cables coiled and snaked their way down a row of RVs and vans. The most opulent RVs were the furthest from the Midway.

"That one over there is BillyBob's." He pointed to a huge RV with a satellite dish on top and a golf cart parked in front. "BB's made millions, man. That's what he likes to be called, BB. He thinks he's up there with BB King. He's always flashing a big chunky Rolex hanging off his wrist like a Vegas hotel sign. He's loaded, and could stay in Florida, but he loves coming out on the road. A lifer. I think he grew up in North Carolina working games and rides. He gets the prime spots on all three lines. He owns the Moles, and a bunch of other joints. Makes a ton of money for the twins; those other two big RVs are theirs. They don't usually come for the whole run, but Bob does. His wife stays in Florida, so he gets to screw all the young ones who end up working his games up here. Liquor, blow and dough. It's a shitty movie." They circled past the trailers and went back onto the Midway.

Jonah opened his arms to encompass the surroundings. "It's a microcosm, you know? Everything that's out there, is in here. How it works, who makes it work, where the money goes, who is fucking who… it's all metaphor on the Midway. The inherited privilege, the big boss and his minions, the puppeteers. Levels of affluence and influence. Infidelity. Bribery. The whole thing, from Jupiter Island mansions to joint jumping and sleeping on top of stuffed animals in a stinking trailer behind the horse barns. Stratified. Trickle-down economics. Name it, it's here." They kept walking, Jonah nodding to a few people along the way.

"How it works for me is, I take a cut of the gross—fifteen points—in the games, and pay you guys out of that. Some of the humans running the joints pay a percentage to their workers, but I give a guarantee. It's not tons but at least you can count on something instead of hustling for twenty bucks on the slow days. That's fucking demoralizing. It balances out. If we have a crazy good run, I throw a few more bucks in the pot. Try and be fair. There's so much turnover…it helps keep people." They stopped by the roller coaster, around the corner from the Milk Can.

"So, what'd you think of yesterday? Did it live up to the hype I pitched in the bar back east? Maybe not as multidimensional, or…?"

It felt like a test to Wyatt. He waited for a minute, trying to compose his impressions and articulate an answer that would dovetail with the esoteric conversations they'd had about it.

"Well… Bruce is a bit needy, eh?"

Jonah threw his head back and laughed, a big smile affirming.

Wyatt continued. "It was a come down in the beginning, to be honest. I guess I expected there to be more…something. It started so slow, it looked like a bad zombie movie with the people making their way onto the Midway, stopping and gawking at everything like they've never seen a fucking Ferris Wheel. It was a long day in there after two hours. Different once it picked up, though. We had a couple of tips happening"—Wyatt was secretly proud he was using the official terminology now—"where I got a feel for it, you know? Balls in the air, eyes on the prize and that swollen moment before the ball hits. I definitely got that. And it's more of a blood sport than I thought."

They both laughed.

"After we blew that elephant out of the joint so early, I kind of realized what it was about. Control, right? I mean, not that you can control it all, but I got a feel for it, I think. Keep the patter up, keep the peripheral vision focussed…"

Jonah jumped in.

"Yeah, exactly. It's more about being ready than anything else… When it's just a shooter or two you home in on them, if you know what I mean. Subtle tricks to…not distract, but to…influence. If that makes sense." Wyatt was nodding as Jonah spoke.

"I'll mess with my apron," Jonah continued, "count some money, move a bit to the left or right. Not enough to be obvious; maybe just slide over a bit to the corner, reach onto the table for a few balls. Those are easy things. When it's a big tip happening—I don't think you've had one of those yet—you have to adapt to the energy that comes with it. You start to learn to identify the gamers, the real shooters. You'll see them here tonight and tomorrow; they like the weekends. It's bizarre, but there are guys, and it's always guys, who think they have a black belt in Milk Can. Like it's the entire focus of their trip to the show. You get a tip happening with a couple of these guys in on it, and you can blow out a lot of stock pretty fast. They'll try and throw you off your game too. But that's not that often. Usually, it's just people tossing balls, trying to win, getting swept up in the excitement of the moment. Balls in the air, close calls, oohs and awws, lights and music all around. Sensory, you know. You get that happening and you really lock into it, you can almost conduct the event."

His hands waved an invisible baton. "You'll see. Bruce doesn't get it and Scott doesn't give a shit, but there's more than meets the eye happening in there. The charge in the air, tunnelling into the moment. Kind of amazing. You'll see, I think."

Wyatt kept nodding. "I think I get it. When I was thumbing, I could feel something like that sometimes. Could make eye contact with the right driver and they'd pull over. People who never picked up hitchhikers would stop for me. Made no sense, but it happened. Fuck. I sound like a New Ager!"

Jonah laughed. "Right. The Harmonica Convergence. Blues for a lonely planet. Salt Spring sensibility." He tossed his cigarette and ground it out.

"Alright, Wyatt. That's it for the lecture slash pep talk. Look around—the marks are coming! The marks are coming! Time to make some money."

14

They were on a "two hours in, one hour out" schedule in the joint. Wyatt climbed in and grabbed his apron.

"Guess you take the first break, then, eh?" Scott sounded pissed off.

"Oh. Sorry. Jonah and I were talking."

"Whatever..." Scott spit some tobacco juice into a cup he kept under the boards and climbed out. He and Bruce looked at each other, shrugged and started pacing back and forth on either side of the joint, splitting it in half. The Himalayan setlist was well underway. Wyatt had been able to memorize the order of the songs by the end of the previous day. Not something he was proud of. He wondered if they'd be open to suggestions. He took a look at the crew in charge, the "Do you wanna go *faster*?" top dog in particular, and decided that a guy who thought a cut-off Levis jean jacket without a shirt was solid fashion might not be open to a conversation about alternative music for the ride. He turned his attention back to the Midway.

'Hey now, here it is! Come one, come all, come on in and you can win! One in wins. One in wins! We've got the big ones here!"

A couple of polite rejections, but many more complete ignorations, though he wondered if that was a word. He tried some eye contact techniques, thinking back to how he had pulled cars over. This wasn't that different. It was still mostly families going by. The big crowds would be there after supper, but he had some success. A few here and there.

Bruce was grabbing some from his side as well, even with his lame, stilted patter ("Hey y'all! Get down and get in. Yes indeed!") It felt like the night was going to be bumping; he already had eighty bucks and Bruce must have that too, given that he'd worked an extra hour. He was feeling good enough to initiate a conversation.

"Good day so far. Should be nuts tonight, eh? I'm kind of keen to see what full-on crowds feel like in here."

Bruce fingertip-lit a smoke, nodding eagerly. "Indeed. Barbarians at the gates. Us against them, right?"

Wyatt smiled. "True enough."

"So, what's with Scott? He seemed a little pissed at me. I wasn't gone more than an hour, for sure."

"No, not at you. Don't worry about that. He was talking about how long a year it feels already. He did Florida, too. That's a seventeen-day run, and he's still broke. I loaned him a few bucks for smokes, but he's gonna have to hit Jonah up for an advance. Not a happy camper…"

"Good. I mean, good that it's not me, I guess. Here's hoping. It would suck if we lost the one guy with experience in here. I wouldn't know where to start on the tear down next Sunday."

"Agreed. Lots of people hire locals to fill their roster, but I know Jonah doesn't like to. Can't trust them, he says. Which makes sense."

Wyatt saw Scott coming towards the joint and started his patter again. He climbed in without saying anything. Bruce left for his break, and they worked back-to-back, back and forth for the next half hour without speaking. It was getting busier, but still no big tips. No stock blown out either, though. It seemed like a pretty good groove to Wyatt, who was moving to the rhythm of the music from the Himalayan. Song 17 of the list: "The Emperor's New Clothes" by Sinead O'Connor. A good song.

He could feel the frustration emanating off Scott. During a lull, he tried to start up a conversation.

"How's this compared to last year's first Friday? Busier? I've got no point of reference. No idea if we're making the money we need to."

Scott spit onto the ground. "Nah, maybe about the same. Fucked if I know, man. Florida was supposed to be big money this year and it fucking sucked. I barely had enough to get back here. Greg had promised me a truck to drive north but it didn't happen. I ended up getting a flight to Minneapolis and thumbing from there. Took three days for fuck's sake. I dunno man… Last year I did the whole circuit and managed to put a few grand in the bank and had good unemployment stamps to boot. Four hundred bucks a week all winter for sitting on my ass. I've already worked almost a month and I've got sweet fuck all…"

They kept talking while they grabbed a few bills and handed out balls, speaking between marks.

"That sucks. I've been living off peanut butter and prayers for the last month. Hopefully things will pick up. Jonah said he pays out more if the money is good enough."

Scott snorted and spit again." Never happened once last year. Don't get me wrong. I don't blame him. He's a good guy and everything, and the only one that guarantees money here. But no...I'm thinking the money isn't going to be that good. I gotta do something..." Some players approached three sides of the game. The beginning of a good tip had started to form.

15

The rest of the night flew. An endless parade went past the joint, pointing, laughing, flirting, arguing, yawning. The three of them stayed in the Can until after ten, when the crowd started to thin. Two bears were won, one by a shooter who coughed up at least sixty bucks, and the other by a young girl who fluked one in on her first shot. The guys gathered round groaned. Seeing a kid win, a girl no less, had them doubling down, impatiently waving five-dollar bills for more balls.

The three of them had worked well together, keeping up the patter, constantly moving back and forth, subtly affecting the concentration of the gunners. Wyatt doubted that Bruce and Scott were attuned to the metaphysics he was employing, but that didn't matter much; everyone has their own way of making sense of things. He had a thick wad of bills folded in his left hand, plus an apron heavy with change. It was slow enough for him to take a break. He grabbed the paper money from Scott and Bruce and went to find Jonah.

Wyatt took the long way around to get to the Birthday Game on Line B. Even after a couple of days, he was surprised at how normal the Midway had become. The music and screams from the rides, the smashing, spraying, click-ticking and barking from the games, the low-end drone of all the voices woven into one; the fairgrounds had morphed into a heaving, humming entity. *It's alive! It's alive*, he thought, recalling the black-and-white Frankenstein film.

According to Jonah, the Birthday Game was the most popular on the Midway. The B-line location pulls in a lot more cash than the A-line Milk Can, even though the prizes are smaller and you have to work your way up from a small plush or a mirror to a 20-inch Latex Bart Simpson. A lot of families would play it because there was no skill; you didn't have to point the spray gun at a target, get the ball in the basket or land a plastic ring on top of a bottle. Wyatt hadn't seen it since he was a kid, so he stood against the side of a joint and watched Jonah and the women in action.

They had a good tip going, especially for this time of night. Jonah was on the mic. His patter was more conversational, not the strident, monotonous voicings he'd heard from other joints; lame-ass hustle that was more decorative than compelling. Jonah had a pace, rhythm and style that was consistent with who he was. There was a musicality to it. He'd address individuals around the game, connecting with them just for a moment in a completely strange setting. "Hi. Yeah, you! Hi! How's it going? Gonna play? It's only a dollar. If you've got a bellybutton, you've got a birthday! Come in and give it a try. Oh, March, eh? Pisces? Sensitive, emotional player I guess ha." Lots of laughs among the players.

It was after ten-thirty, so most of the families were gone by this point. The tip around the game was more male than female, and it wasn't hard to figure out why. Des and Trish looked amazing. Jonah definitely had the most beautiful women on the Midway working the joint. They both had cut-off jeans and the sleeves on their uniforms rolled up high. Even from fifty feet, Wyatt could see they both hand an extra button undone so a flash of cleavage could be seen as they bent down to scoop up the change along the length of the boards.

Des... there was something about the way she moved in the game. Trish was smiling, laughing with the marks and clearly enjoying herself, but Des had another thing going on. It wasn't sexy, necessarily, or flirty, but she moved with sinuous grace, like she was dancing. There was a sultry magnetism that you couldn't ignore. Wyatt remembered then that she had said she was a dancer while they were doing dishes. He could still surprise himself, despite his age and experience, at how naïve he could be. She'd said dancer and he'd immediately assumed theatrical. Images of Swan Lake, ballet and soft-seat venues. Seeing her now, the veil was pulled back, as it were. Salome. Ahhh, *that* kind of dancer…

"Alright everybody, this is the last one for the day. We've got to get up in the morning and go to work too, you know." Jonah laughed. "*Aaaannnd* it's October. Alright, lucky October for the last win of the day. There ya go, a shiny Jack Daniels mirror framed in genuine black walnut, patent pending. Th-th-th that's all folks, and remember, if you've got a belly button you've got a birthday."

Jonah was shutting down the lights and killing the PA. Wyatt reached over the boards to hand him the cash.

"Hey Wyatt!" and "Hi Wyatt!"—Des and Trish gave him a smile while they did the closing, putting the stock away and winding down the metal sides of the joint. Neither of them looked like they'd spent a long, hot day working in a confined space.

Up close, it was even more obvious why the birthday game had been such a pull for the men on the Midway. It wasn't like Wyatt was ogling or objectifying them. He had always prided himself on not being a guy who only saw women in terms of physical appearance. He was still so raw and vulnerable from his breakup that he felt little attraction or desire. He didn't trust such a thing anymore. But beautiful is beautiful, regardless of how cultural norms would have you arrive at the judgement, right? He'd noticed a few of the other carnies eyeing them while he'd been waiting for Jonah to wind it down, elbowing, leaning in, whispering lewd garbage to each other. He hated that shit;

considered himself high above it. Still, they were hot. It was what it was.

16

The ten-day run in Winnipeg fell into a predictable pattern. Long days in the heat, fine-tuning the intricacies of the Midway in his mind. He started to think of it as Zen and the Art of the Milk Can. When he told Jonah, he got a chuckle. It felt good to get a laugh out of him, or an approving nod during a tip. It was clear that everyone in the crew sought his approval in their own way. Bruce with his needy, lapdog demeanor; Trish and Des subtly seeking more one-on-one engagement with him on breaks, or during the afterglow hangs at the house at the end of the day. You could see subtle strains put on their own connection as they maneuvered to get attention. All spoken without words.

It was Thursday of week two and they were laid out in the living room, a couple slices of pizza left in a box and a nearly empty case of beer on the coffee table. Jonah was on the couch, with Des and Trish on either side of him, Bruce sprawled on the Lazy Boy and Wyatt and Scott sat on the floor. There was a black-and-white cowboy show on the TV, muted. The conversation had stalled, sitting at the lights, waiting for the green. Scott cleared his throat.

"So, how's it looking this week, Jonah? Feels like it's been pretty good in the Can. Dunno about the Birthday, but we've been pulling in some good cash. Better than last year for sure. You think we're gonna get a top-up at the end of this run?" Everyone stared at nothing. Wyatt felt the air tightening in the room. It was like the joint in the late-afternoon heat.

Jonah looked at him over the top of his John Lennon specs, grabbed a smoke off the table and lit it.

"Don't think so, Scott. I mean, not unless we have a monster weekend. It's a little early to be thinking about bonuses. Remember last year? It was Toronto when we had enough money to do such a thing."

"Yeah, but I did Florida, too. I've already been working for over a month. And I got fucked out of my ride, remember? Fucking Greg… I'm broke already. I had to send money back to my ex for the kid. She got a lawyer. Monthly payments while I'm out here or I lose access to him when I'm done. Not an option." Scott ran his hands through his shaggy, tangled hair.

"Right. I get it. Lynn's down at the bank on Salt Spring waiting for mine on the first of every month, in line with the other earth mothers. The Antelopes and Moon Bears travel in packs on welfare and child support days! Can't do it yet, though. Too early in the run. Maybe if the Stampede is better…"

The rest of them kept quiet, breathing shallow.

Scott lit a smoke and kept running his hands through his hair with his free hand.

"Yeah. I figured. I did. Umm… I have to be able to see my little girl, Jonah. She's…"

His voice thickened and tears glistened.

"She's beautiful, my little girl. I can't afford to not see her, you know. I've made a few calls. Back home. Buddy of mine has a courier company. He said I could go to work if I wanted. Twelve bucks an hour. Forty hours plus some overtime. I'm thinking of taking it. I talked to him this afternoon. He said if I could fly out Sunday, he'd pick me up. I can start Monday. Shit…I'm sorry, man. I know I said I'd do the whole run this year, but my daughter…" His words ran out of gas.

Jonah sat back on the couch and crossed his arms. "Okay. That's fine. You can do the rest of the fair here though, right? Help tear it down on Saturday night. I'm gonna have to find someone…Fuck." Wyatt watched Jonah calculating.

Trish sat up, took a drink of beer and turned to Jonah on the couch.

"I might know a guy, Jonah. You met him back in Toronto. I know for sure he's not working right now. Well, he's working but he's not getting paid for it." Scott snorted softly. Trish put her hand on Jonah's leg and looked at Des.

"Petr. He's just doing art all summer. Well, not *just* art. You know what I mean. The guy who had the show where we met, Jonah. All the cylinders and cones hanging off the wall, remember?"

Des nodded, then furrowed her brow. Trish continued.

"We got close over coffee and Camus. He was a perfectly consistent cynic. About everyone and everything. It was refreshing. He'd be perfect here, don't you think?"

Jonah leaned forward and took a drink as Trish set her hand on his bare arm. Wyatt noticed Des notice.

"Yeah, I remember him. We talked for a bit at the show. He needed a cape that night, maybe a high-collared cape and a cigarette holder. Old black-and-white thriller villain, right? I thought that at the time…." He pursed his lips and slowly nodded, a slow smile appearing.

"He might work out. Might be just what we need. You can see if he's…game?"

Trish turned fully towards him.

"For sure. I can get hold of him. What should I tell him? Like, when would he start? Where would he meet us? This might be a ball, getting us all together. I think he'd love the change of scenery. He hates the city; says he hates the pretense there. I'll tell him we're in Opposite Land. Life imitating art, right?" Trish and Jonah laughed. Des played with the frayed edges of her jean shorts.

"Scott, you're staying until Sunday? Why don't you tell Petr he can either meet us here on Sunday or meet us Tuesday in Calgary for the Stampede. Can you call him in the morning and find out?"

Trish nodded and smiled. "Great. Alright." Jonah crushed out his smoke. "Well, would you look at the time." He checked his watch-less wrist. "I'm crashing." He stood up, arched himself back into a cat-like stretch, stepped over Des's outstretched legs, and walked up the creaky stairs to bed.

There was a long moment of stasis. Wyatt felt like he was back in the joint, antennae fully up. He was aware of Scott's relief. Going to go back, going to live a normal life. Going to be with my girl. Going home. He was breathing it, slower, deeper. His eyes were looking in on himself. Bruce had nodded off with a smoke still burning on the tips of his fingers. Wyatt reached over and put it out. He watched Trish watch Jonah go up the stairs, her lips lifted slightly at the corners, tuned into the tomorrow of possibilities with the potential arrival of Petr.

But Des... the signal was coming off her as she rocked slowly back and forth on the couch, twisting the white strands on her shorts in and out of knots. She had a smile on her face, but different than Trish's. He couldn't quite identify it. Rueful? Resigned? It was like she had a window in front of her she was staring through. He couldn't explain this concurrent sense of the room and all the variables within it that enveloped him. It was as though the carnival had infiltrated. 'Off-Midway,' he thought. *This is becoming an Off-Midway production.* He hauled himself up the stairs.

17

They got through a busy last weekend. Busier than Jonah had predicted. Life in the joint was different now that Scott had decided to leave soon. He was a lot livelier, juggling balls and pulling in more marks than he had been. He was standing straighter and smiling a lot more. When they were tying the joint down the last two nights, he made time to show Wyatt how it was put together, so Wyatt would know what to do once he wasn't around. Even Bruce had a bit more lead in his pencil, weaving in and out of the energy in the joint with what Wyatt judged to be a suitable amount of awareness and competence. Wyatt felt his status had elevated.

It was the last night in the house before teardown. Trish had managed to reach Petr. She was sitting beside Jonah on the couch. Really close. Des was in the Lazy Boy. Petr had thought about it and decided it sounded like something worth trying.

"He's intense, as you know. This might be just what he needs. That's what he said… He's going to fly in tomorrow afternoon and go to Calgary with us. This is going to be wild!"

They were passing around a bottle of Glenfiddich that Jonah had brought out as a 'proper farewell' to Scott. He made a ceremony of opening the bottle.

"Scotch for Scott." It got passed around. Wyatt pretended to take larger drinks than he did; hard liquor had never been his thing, but Scott, Bruce and Des were slamming it. Scott was getting sentimental, telling them all how much he was going to miss them and the carnival. "Best people, man. Best fucking people." Des would hold the bottle up, a couple of bubbles glugging every time it came to her. Trish had a hand on Jonah's shoulder, watching Des with what Wyatt could see was some concern.

"Petr, Petr pumpkin eater, had a wife and couldn't keep her." Des giggled after she had taken another snap.

"That's good. The more the merrier, right Jonah! All of us one big, happy family." She stared at Trish's hand until it was lifted off.

Wyatt could feel the ions recharging in the room. He had always been sensitive to his surroundings, but he was sure that the ten days on the Midway had attuned him even more to things happening in his orbit. Bruce was laughing along with Des, clueless as to the underlying anger and possible jealousy that Wyatt felt her words were soaked in. Or so it seemed to him. Scott was just smiling, big-eyed and happy, content with the new direction his life was taking.

Jonah stood up. "Oh yeah. We're all in this together, Des… make no mistake about that. We're just getting started." He held her eyes while the rest of the room watched. "Don't worry about tomorrow. You'll know it when it comes. And there's a tomorrow coming soon enough, right? Short time on the tarmac and a long time on the teardown. There's not going to be much downtime for the next couple of days. Might want to get some sleep while you can." He went upstairs. Trish followed him.

18

The morning light burned into Wyatt's eyes. Dried lips stuck together and momentary disorientation made way for the harsh realization they'd stayed up way too late finishing the Scotch. Fragments of the night tried clumsily to reassemble themselves. Bruce and Scott passed out on the floor; he and Des talking and smoking. Something about running away.… That out-of-time pre-dawn sanctuary of thought and deed when you are wrapped up in a moment whose foul lines run off forever. They'd understood something together. He was sure of it. Connected, as they say. Shared secrets he couldn't quite recall. Had danced around the truth of their reason for arriving here. Speculated. Confessed. What had it been about? Which had been the dream, which the woken moment? The pieces of the puzzle disintegrated as the sounds of the house, the banging of words together downstairs, ushered in the day.

Jonah pulled the VW onto the far side of the grounds. They were all laid out on the seats and on top of their bags and backpacks, because they were leaving for Calgary right from the lot. Trish was riding shotgun. The corral of RVs and trailers already had a lot of action happening. People were winding down awnings, packing up lawn chairs. They were taking apart the hot tub by BillyBob's behemoth. Someone was on the roof tying down the satellite dish.

"Preparations for evacuation underway," said Jonah. He opened his arms wide as the six of them walked down the Midway.

"We keep the storefronts open all day, but everyone's getting ready to pack up behind the scenes. Like a Western town on a Hollywood set. Facades. The hammers and wrenches are ready by the rides, the trailers for the joints are being opened. They've cleared out the crack pipes and piss bottles of the guys who slept in them all week. Try and get some food into you before teardown so you're not dying of hunger. It's different every time. Sometimes it's hurry up and wait and the sun is coming up like you're in a Tom Waits tune. Tom Waits for no man haha. Thing is, stay 'on', right? Focussed. There's still cash to grab, so don't get distracted by all the action behind the flat-front saloons. I'll be around the Birthday Game all day; Trish and Des haven't torn it down before. "You guys'll be alright getting the Can packed away with Scott. The VW isn't built for a loaded-up prairie run, so I'm gonna find Greg and see if I can get us a truck to take to Calgary—there's enough attrition they usually need a few drivers to haul the shit. And hopefully Petr makes it before the train leaves the station."

They were a little late getting the sides up on the joint. People had already started wandering past, so the Lemon Pledge stayed in the box. Wyatt wasn't sure if that would make much of a difference, but he wished he'd had time to polish it up hard like they had every other morning.

Jonah was right. There was a smaller crowd out for the Sunday, but they were spending. They got a couple of good tips happening in the joint by one o'clock, and there were lots of one-offs to supplement it. The weather started to change by mid-afternoon, however. The everyday azure was giving way to swirling grey clouds and a northwest wind. French fry containers and cotton candy cones skipped by the joint. The music from the rides and the racket from the games undulated between gusts of wind. Families leaned into it, hanging on to hats and mirrors, making their way to the exits before the rain came. Kids cried; rides sat still, creaking, as the Midway waited.

Wyatt had eaten before the weather changed. Double burger, fries and a cranberry juice in the cafeteria. It was after four, and the Midway was nearly empty, so he sent Bruce and Scott out to get something to eat before teardown. He was sure he could handle what few marks might wander up. It was dead enough that he was able to polish the Can without being seen. He caught a flash of distant lightning and waited for the thunder, but it didn't happen, or couldn't be heard over the Himalayan.

A couple of marks came up to the game. Young couple, nice smiles. Innocent and in love. He did the patter, grabbed a five and gave them three balls. Another couple stopped on the other side, money in hand. Older. Pink painted nails and rings on fingers and thumbs, he with a massive belly and a pack of smokes in the front pocket of his shirt. Then a guy in a leather jacket and shades up on his head. A family on the fourth side, blond kid about five, whining about wanting the big elephant, "Bobby got a Bart Simpson and it's not fair I want an elephant" and the father pulling a five out of his worn-down wallet wishing his wife would take his side for once and they could just go the fuck home before the rain starts, but she's got her arms around the kid whispering that "Dad is going to try and win it for you but don't cry if he doesn't but he's going to try." A few more and a few more slipped in out of the wind and under the lights Wyatt had turned on because the sky was darkening. Things coalesced.

The balls started to fly, and the kids cried, women cheered, men moaned and groaned as the Can clinked and clonked with close attempts, balls bouncing off each other in midair, onto the table, onto the ground, back off the boards. Wyatt heard his voice saying "No, you can't keep that one after it's been thrown, three for five want more?"

Wyatt hit full throttle for the first time since he climbed aboard the Carny Express, pacing clockwise around the inside of the joint, in sync with planetary rotation he's thinking, amused, high above the barking he's got going in the game.

"That's it, oh close bring it in now, three more for you, come in on someone's got to take the big boys home we don't want to haul them all the way to Calgary!" Spinning, stopping, subtle twitches and fingers through the hair and quick switches to another corner to mess with the momentum and focus of the guy in leather who for sure is a shooter, then more misses as the ball orbits the hole in the Can, almost in until another one knocks it away and the guy in leather yells "fuck" and the father of the kids winces wishing they hadn't heard that, pulling another five out his wallet thinking "that's forty bucks now I'd might as well just bought a goddamn elephant and we'd be home" but Wyatt meets his eyes and tells him "oh you're so close, so close you can't quit now, setting three more balls in front of him, and the tip gets bigger, people on the periphery wondering what the fuck is going on with fifty people on a dead Midway gathered round a game, while Wyatt keeps the patter, winding it up and down, breathing with the crackle in the game, the wind popping up under the canvas.

It went around and around. Wyatt a dervish inside the joint, catching Jonah out of the corner of his eye, leaning on a garbage can with someone beside him, a guy in street clothes without the clown on his shirt, both pointing and gesticulating. The wad of cash in his hand grew as the balls flew and the fever pitched. The family on one side, leather guy on the other and hands shaking fives at him on all sides. He could feel the peak of the tip happening, a crescendo of comments, cross talk and "this is the one this is the one" bouncing off each other like the balls. Wyatt knew that he had it in him to decide the winner, Svengali kingmaker, all-powerful director of energy in the Can.

He whipped himself around the joint a couple more times and grabbed the last, hesitantly offereing fives because it was "getting too expensive and we can't afford this for a goddamn stuffed animal" which has come to be much more to everyone cloistered around the joint. It was them versus Wyatt, them versus each other, them versus the losing. The father of the kid leaned in a little more, over the imaginary line but Wyatt allowed it, having decided the kid, the little girl, ought to be the one to take it home, snuggling with it every night for years, secure in the knowledge that good things happen to those who wait.

19

Slow motion now. Five o'clock sharp. The music on the Himalayan choked off. The sluicing sounds on the Midway; the thin tinkle of a plate breaking in a game down the line, the sputtering of a spray gun, the last pop of pellets at the "Shoot out the Star"; all were amplified in their insignificance. The loudest thing in the joint was the snapping of the canvas in the wind. Even the marks were wrapped up in the denouement, all eyes on the dad as Wyatt pulled back, arms wide and palms offered to the plush above. As he made his blessing, he saw Bruce and Scott with Jonah and the other guy, saw Greg the Midway Czar, in his golf cart, watching. The wad of cash felt as thick as his wrist. He nodded his assent, and the father launched his ball, the last ball, up under the elephant's trunk with a perfect backspin. It didn't even hit the polished rim. The pop of the ball hitting dead centre expanded out from the joint, buoyed by the breath of the tip. There was nothing for a moment, then the game was engulfed by whoops and cheers from the family and those who'd become their supporters; raucous "Can you believe it?" laughter, and another "Fuck" from the leather-jacket guy.

The tip evaporated as though it had never been there. Wyatt pulled the elephant down and passed it to the laughing little girl, gave the dad a smile and omniscient wink, and turned back towards the Can. He was surprised at the adrenal comedown inhabiting his extremities. He felt weak, satisfied, high and dry. There was validation hidden in there as well, a buzz of contentment born out of knowing what had begun with his theoretical conversations over beer in a bar back east had come to fruition. It's true, he thought. *It's all energy, waiting.* All this before Jonah climbed into the joint.

Wyatt handed him the cash, which Jonah front-faced as he counted and talked. "Well, that was a pretty good one haha. You were right there, in the middle of it, under that cone! That's exactly it, precisely the thing, right? To be on like that…" He snapped the counted wad with his index finger. "Over four hundred bucks. In case you need a barometer to measure your Zen. Black belt, right there…" Jonah gave him a big smile and winked over the top of his Lennon specs. Wyatt basked in the praise, still thrumming from the post-coital afterglow of the tip, aware of the absurdity of being validated by a carnival game while concurrently loving it.

Bruce and Scott stepped into the joint and started pulling down the animals, stuffing them into plastic bags. Jonah beckoned Wyatt out and over to the guy in the street clothes he'd seen him talking to. "Wyatt, this is Petr. From Toronto. Petr, Wyatt, cone-channeler extraordinaire haha. Glad you got to see him in action. That's the embodiment of it, right? Going with it. Wyatt's been refining his technique."

They regarded each other for a moment. Wyatt's initial response to Petr's thin smile was to smile wide, bright and high. Opposite. There was something about him that immediately killed his buzz. He thought of a line about why someone would take an instant dislike to someone, the answer being it saved time. Typically, Wyatt never had that reaction to anyone; he'd let them reveal who they really were through their actions. Even then, he was not inclined to judge. He just wasn't wired that way, but there it was. Right out of the gate he knew Petr was not someone he would like.

Petr had black hair pulled back into a ponytail, a thin nose and thinner lips. Short sideburns, a cigarette tucked under his right ear. A black t-shirt and black Levis. His eyes… Wyatt couldn't make out their colour—maybe dark blue, even dark brown—but dark, with more pupil than you'd normally see if hallucinogens weren't involved. Wyatt was taller by at least six inches, but something about how Petr stood made it feel as though they were seeing eye to eye.

Wyatt held out his hand, forced a smile to his face. "Hey. Good to meet you. Heard you were coming." Petr looked down at his hand for a moment before offering his own with awkward reluctance.

"It's spelled how the Russians would spell it. No last 'e'." Wyatt smelled the condescending tone in his voice, thick as the cotton candy still hanging in the joint beside them.

"Okay. Doubt that I'll be needing to write it down anywhere, and it sounds about the same as my cousin Petr back home, so I'll go with that." He took his hand, surprised at the weak, nearly air-like grip. And it was so dry. Wyatt's hands were dirty with Pledge, coins, bills and sweat. He was happy to squeeze a little tighter than usual.

Jonah watched the two of them with bemused interest as they made their acquaintance. Wyatt let go of the handshake without letting go of Petr's eyes. He flashed him an insincere smile. 'Love to stay and talk, but we've got some work to do."

Jonah took over the moment. 'Right. I'm going back to the Birthday Game. I'll take your bag with me, Petr, and stash it in the van until we're done here. Still haven't sorted out the drives to Calgary yet. I'll be back and forth between Trish and Des and here for the next few hours. I'll let them know you're here. They'll be excited." He lit a smoke, hoisted the bag onto his shoulders and beelined to the Birthday.

20

The sounds of the teardown swirled in the wind. Clanging metal slammed like stanchions as rides were dissembled. Hydraulic brakes hissed, the metal frontings of the 'house' attractions wobbled to the ground, sounding of distant thunder, and yells and whoops and cursing wove around the rapidly flattening attractions. The movie set was coming down fast.

Scott took charge of the Milk Can teardown. They wrapped the plush in plastic bags and hauled them two at a time to the prize trailer. The balls went back into the wooden box along with the Pledge, lights, and nuts and bolts that Scott was taking off the corners that held the sides in place. They pulled the boards off and piled them to the side, then pulled the spikes out of the asphalt that the ropes were tied to secure the joint in case of a storm. A sledgehammer did the trick, Wyatt wielding it with enthusiasm. He checked to see if Petr was watching him swing it, loosening the spikes.

The wind was starting to die, the storm having slipped around the fair to the south side of town, where the grey sheets of falling rain were visible even as dusk started to devour the purple sky. Scott was tearing the joint apart with more energy than Wyatt had seen from him during the whole run. The three of them were kept running back and forth between the joint and the trailers, lugging armloads of flats, four-by-four and two-by-six boards and storage boxes. Bruce would wait for instructions after each trip to a trailer, making idiotic small talk that they all ignored. To Wyatt's surprise, Petr was working hard, apparently happy to haul stuffed animals and rolled up canvas without a complaint. He made a joke about the sides they were schlepping being a different kind of canvas than he was used to. Petr had just laughed and said "Yeah. Work is work. Not afraid of a little work." He had hopeful expectations that this type of trench action would be above an artist from Toronto, something he could look down on him for, but the opposite appeared to be true. Petr was all in.

They were done by ten. They'd been quite efficient with the teardown of the joint, but a lot of the time was eaten up waiting in line at the trailers to put stuff where it was supposed to go. Standing in line with carnies from the other joints, Wyatt did the small-talk thing as best he could, pretending to be part of the larger brotherhood. A skinny, tattooed guy beside him from 'Shoot the Star" did some bitching.

"Fucking ridiculous, eh? Hurry up and wait. You'd think they'd have their shit together by now, eh? Idiots…" Wyatt nodded in agreement, bonding over a smoke, secretly impressed with the whole teardown operation. It was bullshit, of course, for him to pretend to have any shared experience with this guy other than standing in line. The last tip had confirmed the metaphysical suspicions he had about the game and his role in it. He was well aware of the absurdity of feeling superior to the rest of them as he stood in line holding onto a giant elephant and bear in plastic bags, yet he did.

When the Milk Can was finally all packed away, the four of them went down the now wide-open line to see if they could help with the Birthday Game. The VW van was parked beside them. Jonah was putting a lock on the back of the trailer, Des and Trish behind him watching. When they saw Petr, they both laughed and wrapped him up in their arms, murmurs of delight, kisses, a flip of his ponytail with one of their hands. Jonah stood up and came over.

"Okay. That's about it. I was talking to Greg. He could only get us one vehicle to Calgary." He pointed across the lot to a white Ford pickup with the Clown on the doors. It wasn't even a crew cab.

"The options are to all go together, or for whoever isn't into riding in the back of a truck lying on top of cables, toolboxes and the dreams of unborn children through the night for fifteen hours, to find another way to the ol' Stampede. There might be someone with a crew cab and room, but…." Everyone was nodding. "Grab your stuff out of the van, then. Sooner we leave, sooner we arrive."

He turned to Scott.

"You can take this back to my folks' place before you go?" Scott, shaggy hair bird-nested under his Irish cap, gave Jonah a thumbs-up.

"Not a problem, man. I'll throw the keys in the engine compartment." He paused, kicked at a broken bit of asphalt.

"Look, thanks. I didn't want to let you down, you know, but I think this is what I'm supposed to be doing now. Kid and all. A real job." He tried to pull that out of the fire." Ha, no, don't get me wrong. This is a real job…"

"More like surreal," Bruce chimed, getting laughs from the circle. He was thrilled with that, you could tell.

"Right, surreal haha. It's been great though, really. Great to meet you all." Scott's eyes had a shine as he looked around at them. "Part of me wants to come… but it's the wrong part."

Jonah laughed. "It's all good, Scott. You were great. Big help in Florida, and you got these guys baptised! I think I can speak for the academy in wishing you all the best in your future endeavours. And, from what I hear, being with your kids matters! Know that you'll always have a place in the Milk Can should you fail at your attempt at a normal life!" More laughs, handshakes and hugs all around. They stood in a semi-circle and watched him climb into the van and sputter away.

21

James brought the truck over to the Birthday Game and hooked it up to the hitch. Everyone tossed their bags into the back. Wyatt took a quick look around. The trailers and RVs were already gone. Inky black silhouettes moved here and there, shouting and cursing amid the exoskeletal remains of torn-down rides being loaded into trailers and onto flatbeds. Cigarette tips moved like fireflies. The irregular heartbeat of idling diesel engines surrounded them. For the first time in a long time, Wyatt could see the stars and hear the city beyond the Midway.

Jonah broke through his reverie. "Anyone ever driven a truck and trailer?" Crickets. "Anyone ever wanted to drive a truck and trailer? It's a long run through the night. We've got to be on site by four tomorrow. Greg wants the trailer in the line by then."

Wyatt reluctantly stuck his hand up. "I can give it a go. I've driven lots of half tons back home. Just not with a trailer." Petr offered to take a shift as well; "Never driven a trailer or a truck, but I'm an artist, so…" The women chuckled. Everyone else kept quiet, eyes down.

"Okay, we can take turns. It's about fifteen hours. We can't go past a hundred hauling this thing or it gets swaying. It's easy to end up in a ditch if you go too fast. Just keep it at a hundred. I'll take the first turn at the wheel of fortune. You all might want to use the can before we go. I'll stop at somewhere on the way out of town, so you don't starve to death. It's gonna be a long night. And day."

They did their business in the remaining couple of Porta Potties and came back one by one. Trish had already taken shotgun. The rest loaded themselves into the back of the truck. Des and Petr piled their bags against the cab and stretched out, with Wyatt and Bruce sitting on either side of the cap, heads resting against the windows. Jonah started the truck and slid open the window separating them.

"I'm wide awake. Pretty sure I can get us to Regina, or close to it. That should get us through the night. I'd rather have you guys driving when it's light out, just in case." He turned to Trish. "You're gonna keep talking to me, right? Tell me stories, recite some poetry, maybe slap me if you see me nodding off? Can't be killing a truckload of this much potential, can I?"

Trish grinned, said, "Oh, I can keep you awake!"— and slid the window shut.

In the back, Des and Petr talked in low voices about Toronto, heads leaning on each other. Wyatt heard something about a gallery but lost interest in listening. Jonah pulled into a drive-thru and got everyone some burgers and fries, which Trish passed through the cab window. No talking while they inhaled the food, then lit smokes and settled in for the ride.

Wyatt stared out the window of the truck cap, watching Winnipeg thin out and finally disappear when they turned onto the Trans-Canada Highway. He spotted the place where he'd been let out hitch-hiking a lifetime ago. He was trying to remember how he'd felt stumbling into town. Eleven days… it seemed like another incarnation of him had done that. He couldn't conjure up the feeling of slogging his ass into town, of the fearful footsteps through the minefield of down-and-out humanity on the way to the fairgrounds. His sense of whatever time had passed since he had boarded the train back east collapsed in on itself, leaving him looking at his hands as they were intermittently lit up by the highway lights they were driving under. Same hands. Epidermis. The skin over the bones, but whose heartbeat underneath? How can you get so high and see it all then get so low you can barely crawl? Bruce started to snore, but Wyatt was too tired to sleep; he'd gone over that line.

It was loud in the back of the pickup. The tires whined once Jonah got it up to speed. The weight of the trailer caused the truck to sway a bit, rocking them in a tin-can cradle. It was comforting to Wyatt to watch the indigo world outside slide by, lulling to have the rumble and vibration of the road anchoring him. Everything he'd done for the past few months—hell, for the last year or more—had siphoned itself down to this moment, invisible and anonymous, sardined in the back of a truck with a clown face on it, heading West. He lit a smoke and offered the pack to Des and Petr, saw two pairs of wide eyes floating in the dark behind the flame of the Bic. Bruce was down for the count.

Wyatt opened the bidding. "What gets you out of Toronto and into the back of a clown car? I know TO can be hot and gross in the summer, but this seems a bit drastic. It can't be the money, that's for sure!" He and Des laughed but Petr did not. He took a long haul off his smoke.

"Well, you see, Wyatt." Something condescending there, Wyatt was sure of it. "It can get a little… tiresome, irksome even, to spend all your time surrounded by nothing but your ideas, canvases hanging limply from studio walls. Flaccid."

He spoke in measured, muted tones, small pauses between the words, skipping like rocks in the sentences.

"I, uh, I have ended up kind of wrapping myself up in myself there, if that makes any sense to you." More of it, the condescension.

"I moved there from somewhere small with the purest of intentions, seeking opportunity of expression, creation, compensation. Waded through the mire of theoretical course work, studied 'the greats'"—slightly venomous enunciations with the 'S'—"and had a grand finale with a major show in the spring." He angle-nodded to Des. "She was there. Trish too. Where I met Jonah."

Des exhaled a low-throated gush. "Oh, Wyatt. What a show! The paintings had this…energy…coming off them, swirling, magnetic… power that pulls you in. It was incredible. I went a little wild haha. Petr is amazing!" Her face lit up briefly as they passed by an exit ramp light. Petr carried on.

"Oh, it was wild alright. Didn't see you again for months, Des, did I? So, yeah, I'd bought in, purchased the soul mortgage, sold the farm, whatever. Don't get me wrong; I like the city, love the streets, and even the cafes if there aren't too many posers sipping lattes through their perfect teeth. You meet all the right people if you stay in one place long enough, even in a city that size. I come from tiny town. Elliot fucking Lake. The first couple of years were great, but after a while, moths started to gather in the drawers, you know? Webs on the walls, in the corners. The classic conundrum; study it or do it. I did alright, Dean's List and all of that, but…"

Wyatt jumped in.

"Yeah, I know what you mean. I bailed on grad school, but it was a bit different for me. I am not 'finger quotes' an *artist*, but I wasn't able to reconcile another two or three years in the tusk tower, knowing there was more going on out there. Here. Like riding in the back of a clown car." They all laughed a little. Bruce stirred in his sleep and rolled onto his side.

"Right." Petr picked up again. "So, you do what you need to do. Next thing you know you've got your degree. The show I put on... It was the culmination and abandonment of the whole thing. Of all the history of art texts, of all the theoretical, heretical post-modern bile I'd been swallowing, without realizing it, for so long."

His voice was rising, the stones skipping quicker, spit spattering off this thin, lit-smoke lips. "I'd done my own research, you see. All the good ones, the best ones, steal, copy, channel or access dreamtime to come up with something new and true. But what's really going on is manipulation. Grabbing the energy, atomic energy in the hands, energy of atoms, you see, and reconfiguring it into a variation of the world, understand? Of their world, which is the world. That's what the show was. Lines into implied forms into shapes that can call down the thunder. Like water-witch sticks pulling this way or that." He paused, lit another smoke, and seemed to be waiting for a response from Wyatt that didn't come. "Maybe you had to be there."

Even in the dark of the cab, Wyatt could make out the up-and-down nodding movement of Des's eyes. Like a puppet show. Her voice slid through the night.

"No. I mean, yes. I was there. Absolutely could feel it, Petr. I never understood all the things you talked about when we were hanging out on campus, but when I saw what you'd hung in the loft that night.... One painting—they were more like tapestries—after another around the room. It was like the stations of the Cross, going from one to the next. There was a circular logic to it, walking around. I remember that even the sound of the room was insinuating itself into the work, or maybe the other way around. I'd never felt anything like that before, Petr. I mean, I've lost myself in a painting or to a song when I'm dancing, but this is different. Was different. New and familiar at the same time. Make any sense?"

Wyatt thought back to the last tip in the Can, how he'd locked into the thing that Des was alluding to. Well, maybe not the same thing, but certainly similar. It had been a verification of the oblique references Jonah had made in their conversations. The abandonment of self, of the idea of control as way of keeping things together. Like pulling a car over when you're thumbing but magnified, in Technicolor.

"I think so. I think I know what you're getting at... even today.... I mean, yesterday, in the Can. I had a tip going that was ridiculous. End of the day on the last day. It had a life of its own; I was just the conduit."

"Exactly!" Petr leaned closer, voice higher. "The Fibonacci sequence. Sunflowers, seashells, spiderwebs. Waves, galaxies. The human body. The body of any kind of dancer. It's everywhere in us and around us. The equation! That's the thing I was doing. Was trying to do, but they weren't getting it at all. I think they passed that final project—my exhibition—just to move me on down the line. I can be a pain in the ass, you'll be surprised to hear. But until Des showed up, it was all wine and cheese at a hip art happening in the cool part of town. Clueless fuckers. She got it...a little too much, huh?" Des nodded in the dark. "And then Jonah came in and knew immediately. He wove his way around the loft after having wandered in off the street. As if such a thing just happens. So, there it was, the only two people to understand, were those that weren't part of the program. Long answer to a short question. It was easy to come to the carnival and leave the circus."

Wyatt had a vague memory of a spiral staircase from a textbook in the past but had to pretend he was more attuned to what Petr was saying than he was. Fibonacci might as well have been an Italian Renaissance artist. What Petr was saying made sense in a vague way he couldn't put his finger on. He tried to hang on to the thread that was unravelling between them in the cab, but was pulled through the gates of the moment backwards, to the cold, cruel night in December when his tenuous hold on the trajectory of his life was revealed for what it was. The barely dormant knowing that sat under the surface of most of his days bubbled to the surface, roiling his guts with doubt and certainty. It couldn't be destiny if you had a choice. He'd made choices, all the way back, one leading to another to another. Whatever it was that pulled things apart and brought them together had no good or bad aligned with it. Joy and pain coexisted on their own terms within the equation. Was that it? He sank deeper into the coiled cables, resting his head on his backpack. The fumes of the conversation thinned out as he went under to the hum of the highway.

22

The truck lurched to a stop. They woke to bright rest-stop lights jabbing through the windows, yanking them from whatever sleepscape they'd been lolling in, to this cold, disorienting moment. Their dreams disintegrated as they reluctantly came to. The back of the cab snapped open and a grinning Jonah welcomed all to the world again. A sliver of dawn light stretched along the horizon behind him.

"Good morning! Ride and shine! Time to switch it up. Welcome to Regina…"

Bruce was the first to jackknife himself up and out the back, with the rest of them slowly birthing themselves onto the black pavement of the gas station/rest area/restaurant. Des wrapped her arms around herself, rubbing them up and down as she shuffled toward the red and white lights of the station. A ragged line of the rest of them followed, stretching and yawning, shoulders hunched in cold, dawn prairie air.

They grabbed what they needed before returning to the truck: coffee, Snickers bars and smokes. Wyatt watched the ball-capped truckers watch the women. Even at whatever time of the day this was, he thought, there are always guys staring without staring, sneaking glances, checking out tits and asses. Des and Trish seemed oblivious. Or maybe just impervious, he thought. Perv...

Jonah pulled the truck up to the pumps while the rest of them ate, smoked and drank. The roaring whine of a transport tore through the slow rise of the eastern sun. Wyatt wondered if there was a lonelier place than a highway gas station in the early hours of the day. He started singing Tom Waits' "Ol '55". Des joined in with the chorus.

"And now the sun's coming up, and I'm riding with lady luck, freeway cars and trucks..." She had a lovely voice, he thought. They ran through it a few times, louder and louder. Petr clapped in time, Trish did a slow dance spin and Bruce played air saxophone as they kept it going. A couple of truckers came out of the restaurant and stood staring. Jonah pulled around with the truck and got out, waving an invisible conductor's baton. They finished high and loud, laughter ringing up and around them, clapping and hooting for themselves. Morning had broken.

Jonah pierced the moment. "Well, that's it for me. Made good time, didn't we? Anyone other than Trish get any sleep haha?" He gave her a hug. "It's another seven or eight hours to Calgary. That gets us there around three. We should probably split it up. Petr, you want to take the first chunk?" Petr shook his head, blew out frosty morning smoke.

"Can't do it. Never got my license. I have trouble...concentrating on certain things, you understand. Didn't mean to mislead you before; I must have been swept up in the moment." Jonah shrugged, looked eyebrows-raised from Bruce to Wyatt to Des.

Bruce's voice cracked out an awkwardly enthusiastic "I'll do it" just ahead of Wyatt's half-raising his hand. "Okay, Bruce. Do three or four hours. Take your time, for fuck's sake. It's not like driving a pickup when there's a trailer this heavy behind. Keep it at a hundred." Bruce was nodding like a kid getting candy. 'Wyatt, you take shotgun. Stay awake and keep him focussed. I'm gonna crawl in the back and die now. Let's get going."

They pulled onto the empty highway and continued west with the sun sliding up into the pale pink sky behind them. Wyatt sipped his giant coffee and lit a smoke. Bruce held the wheel with one old-looking hand, held a smoke with the other. Wyatt let him talk.

"This is cool, eh? I love the open road, man. You just don't get this sense of freedom anywhere else. That's what my folks don't get. Dad had me a job at his golf club for the summer. Mowing, weed trimming. *Caddyshack* and all that. You've seen *Caddyshack*, right? Bill Murray is the bomb, man. My dad's an accountant. I'm the only kid. You the only kid?" Wyatt shook his head.

"I'm supposed to go to university in the fall and do a BBA, then become an accountant. I haven't been out of Calgary in my whole life for Christ sakes. Except skiing in the mountains. Once we went to Hawaii for Christmas. Love Hawaii. The chicks on the beaches? Man... I had a girlfriend but broke up with her before I left. My friend Brian knew someone who works at the Stampede who told him about the Midway. That they always needed workers. I called the Brantford office. Did you know they were in Brantford, Gretzky's hometown? I'm from Calgary but still liked the Great One. Not the most popular opinion. Anyway, they told me if I came to Winnipeg, I could likely get work. I flew on my mother's points. She doesn't know I did, but I know her password. Tilly—the name of her dog when she was a kid. When I got there, I went straight to the lot, and the first person I ran into was Jonah! Can you believe that? It was like he was waiting for me! I haven't even talked to Mom and Dad since the day I got there. They must be freaking out! I had a girlfriend, but she broke up with me before I left." Wyatt didn't acknowledge his rant, letting the silence swell until Bruce jack-in-the-boxed back into his monologue.

Bruce was getting more excited with himself and his story as he went on, looking at Wyatt rather than the road. The truck swerved to the right, Wyatt's coffee splashed onto the window; muffled shouts erupted from the back of the truck as Wyatt grabbed the wheel with his left hand and tried to right the vehicle. It jerked hard to the left, over the centre line, then slowly shimmied itself straight. Jonah slid the window open between the front and back and stuck his head through.

"Jesus, can't leave you two alone for a minute…Got it under control now? Can I maybe get a little sleep? Goddamn, Bruce. You could have fucking killed us if something had been in the other lane. What the fuck…?" Bruce's face was red, his ears redder. His wrinkled hands were shaking. "Oh. Indeed. My bad there. Won't happen again." He took a deep breath.

"What's going on, Wyatt?" Jonah's voice was calm, the words served on a cold slab of marble. "Get it under control, okay? You need to have control." Speaking to Bruce but staring into Wyatt's eyes.

"You don't let go of the situation for a minute. I thought you understood that." He snapped the cab window shut. The words sat heavy in Wyatt's guts, bringing forth sweat on the palms and stinging in the armpits. An admonition which threatened his connection to Jonah, his status as being one who 'got it', like when the shooters had gotten a big bear in the Milk Can back on Day One. The physical reaction to rejection that had owned his brain and body for months in the winter wasn't far away should the occasion arise. Familiarity and contempt.

"Pull over, Bruce. Right up here. None of us wants to die because you can't keep your shit together. You slept for six hours and you're nodding off now?" Bruce was deflating quickly as he pulled it over, still red-faced, running his free hand through his curly, Holly hair. Seeing this, Wyatt was infused with self-righteousness and stuck the knife in a little deeper.

"C'mon. This isn't some little game. It's not a movie. You've been half-assing it for most of the week. I probably grabbed twice as much cash as you yesterday. I might as well drive the rest of the way to Calgary too. Who needs sleep anyway?" The truck jerked to a geared-down stop, and Wyatt got out and walked around, switching places. It was quiet in the back, though he noticed Jonah's blue eyes watching them through the window.

23

He'd never driven a truck with a trailer before, but Wyatt felt it was important to act as though he had. He lit a smoke, tossed the pack on the dash and put in the clutch. Bruce, he didn't care so much about, but he knew that the others in the back would feel any mistakes. He eased the clutch out and pulled it smoothly onto the highway, shifting up to cruising speed with merciful fluidity. He did a silent humble brag, glancing at Bruce with arched eyebrows.

They drove in silence for the first twenty minutes or so. Wyatt remembered his head rattling against the window of the train months ago, in another life. The before times. The flatland stretched out in every direction, just as it had before, but it wasn't the same. He'd gazed in rapturous wonder back then at the endless fields of stubble-wheat, the aching blue sky beyond. Felt the sinew stretch of the past become thinner and thinner the further away he got, slicing through space and time, quick rail-clonking past grain silos, frozen-monument farm equipment, nameless, dreamless towns and lonely wind-punched houses on the outskirts. Lifetimes. It wasn't new now; nothing could be new once you've done it. You can't go back, but you can sure as hell drag it along with you. He felt his heart start to beat again, close to the throat. He changed the mental subject before it got to racing…

Bruce was sprawled in the shotgun seat, one foot on the dash. He was still chagrined, sulking and staring out the passenger window, right hand absently stroking his chin. A teen in a man's body. Wyatt was down for anything at all to change the trajectory of his own thoughts, so he threw him a conversational milk bone.

"Hey Bruce." Softer voice, a tightrope across the great divide. He felt bad/sad for him. "You must be looking forward to getting home though, eh? Any of your friends know you're a carny? Maybe they'll come and see you in the Can! You can tell them you get college course credits in marketing haha!" Bruce pulled his foot off the dash and sat up.

"Oh, ha. No no no! That's the thing. No one knew I did this; I'm still amazed at myself, Wyatt!" He looked at Wyatt gratefully, hungrily. "None of them had a clue. I told my folks I was going to a friend's place in Canmore for the weekend and told my buddies my family was going to Jasper. Imagine them calling each other to find out where I was on the Monday, huh?"

He was full frontal on Wyatt now, lighting a smoke for each of them. "No one thinks I can do things on my own. Never have. Mom even did all the applications for schools, programs and everything. I didn't have an option. Jesus, Wyatt, I don't want to do that. Look at you; you've got a degree and here you are magnificently driving the Birthday Game down the Trans-Canada highway!"

Wyatt couldn't help himself and didn't try to.

"Ha. Yeah, that's me alright. BA in History, MA in Milk Can. I'm hoping for a PhD in what the fuck am doing with my life…"

Bruce laughed and continued. "Indeed! Maybe BillyBob will need a philosophy consultant, right? I dunno…. This is the craziest thing I've ever done. Almost feels like the only thing. A few days ago, when I had a pretty good tip going—you weren't there for that one, but it was hopping, man! It felt like such an accomplishment. Jonah saw it. I don't know how I'm supposed to tell my folks about that. 'Hey, Dad, I rocked the Milk Can.' I've never known anyone who was un-adopted." A laugh tried to escape.

Wyatt kept his eyes on the ribbon of road in front of him. Traffic was steady and thickening as the sun hit noon. He knew Bruce was still staring at him with that stupid half smile, waiting for validation. He didn't want to, but he'd opened the door, hadn't he?

"Well, I think it's a big deal, Bruce. It's not exactly a career move, but you're not even twenty. It's not like there's a hurry…" That's all he was willing to offer in terms of solace or encouragement.

"Indeed. No hurry. Unless you're in one, eh?" They rolled by a sign for Medicine Hat. "We're making pretty good time. We'll be in Cowtown in three hours, give or take. By three, I bet." He yawned, leaned back, exhaled dramatically and closed his eyes. Wyatt was thankful for the break, glad he'd offered an outstretched hand to him, and happier it was done.

It had been a long time without sleep for him. He'd nodded off a couple of times in the back through the night, but not enough to slide into REM territory where real rest hunted and gathered. What remained of his giant coffee was cold. The wide, tired yawns of exhaustion were coming more frequently. He turned the radio on, sliding in and out of staticky stations. The only clear signal he could find was contemporary country, which he clicked off, willing to take his chances with an accident rather than listen to that cliché-ridden crap. Winding the window down every few minutes helped, the roaring blast of air buffeting him back into focus. He kept up with the alternative oxygen enhancement for a couple of hours until he saw the Calgary skyline slowly rising out of the prairie, the blue Canadian Rockies carved into the horizon sky.

24

He geared down, pulling the truck and trailer to a gravel-popping stop on the side of the highway. Bruce stretched himself awake while the human cargo in the back shifted upright. The window of the cab slid open.

"What's up? Where are we?" Jonah peered through the opening, adjusting his glasses.

"Edge of town, Jonah. Darkness on the edge of town." It was a little too early for any response to his Springsteen reference, apparently. He drummed his fingers on the dash while the others continued their slow emergence into the land of the living. Maybe the lack of sleep was catching up to him… He heard the tailgate crash down, so he pushed open the cab door and got out to meet them by the side of the truck. His back ached, his neck was knotted up, his knees felt like they were stuck at 45 degrees. All six of them stretched, groaned and cracked by the side of the road like a Department of Highways yoga class.

"Alright. That's good. You did well with the driving, Wyatt. Really well. Kept us out of the rhubarb." He shot Bruce a mildly withering glance. "Two o'clock. That's good time. We've got a couple of hours before we need to have this thing on site. I can take the wheel from here. There's a place near the grounds that's got a great all-day breakfast.

We can get some grub and a beer if we want."

Bruce piped up in his faux baritone "Oh, we want. We want..." Silence but for the mosquito scream of a passing transport. The rest of them nodded their heads.

They climbed back in, Jonah at the wheel and Trish back to riding shotgun. Wyatt watched the city tighten the noose around them through the side window in the back while they drove into the downtown core. The Saddledome was off to the left. Shiny steel and glass office towers butted against the crowded sidewalks. The four of them shared the windows on either side of the cab, Petr commenting on the appearances of the people they drove past.

"Oh, look, it's a real, live businessman in his natural habitat. Notice the unique tie choice, the paper folded under the right arm, the confident, purposeful stride. And over there, just beyond the intersection, a couple of young 'mating age' junior partners, looking for young, ovulating cowgirls to further the superior, capitalist bloodline."

They were all laughing at Petr's running documentary voice. Wyatt felt their bond of being separate from the rest of the world strengthening. Inside looking out.

Jonah parked the truck. It was mid-afternoon, so the restaurant wasn't too busy. They collapsed into a high-backed booth. A Stetson-lidded, cleavage-flashing waitress brought them a couple pitchers of beer and took their orders; steak and eggs all the way around. Jonah raised his glass.

"To the Stampede!" They clinked their glasses together, their eyes flashing into each other. Jonah took the podium. "This one is the second biggest money grab of the circuit. Next to the CNE. All that bubblin' crude makes its way into every hand you see, greases the wheels in the chuckwagon races, the roulette wheels on the casinos. The ham-fisted, Rolex-wristed, Wrangler sportin' good ol' boys will be following their manhole-cover-sized belt buckles down the Midway." Jonah had their undivided attention.

"It's a different crowd than Winnipeg. They're more, uh, self-assured. Confident. They've got God on their side, right? You won't see this ignorance and arrogance in such a delightful combination anywhere else, not even Edmonton, until we cross the border into the States, but not really until we get way south. This is war. As the man once said, 'Knowing others is intelligence'; great line. Especially in the Milk Can. They're gonna be looking down on you because you're carnies, obviously a lower form of life. They won't even really be looking at you, any more than they would a homeless person. The only difference is you have something they want."

Wyatt's attention began fading in and out of the tutorial. The lights in the pub were oscillating, the country music overhead sounded staticky, like the radio in the truck. He was sure he could make out the conversation from a booth at the other end of the room, endowed with a new exhaustion-fueled ability to read lips and pick up on the body language. "I'm not sure, Albert. I don't think I trust him. That's a lot of money. What if it doesn't …" He could see she wasn't happy, didn't want to be there. Hated him. Hated herself for having to pretend. Obvious. Petr's voice brought his attention back to the table.

"Hmm, the enemy. I like that a lot." He had his hands above the table, palms open, spinning slow circles.

"So, we're invisible. So much easier to harness the energy if you're not encumbered with being observed. Hiding in broad daylight, as it were, right?" Jonah was watching him over the top of his glasses.

"It's like we're a fifth column, isn't it? Destroy from within…" Petr's thin lips split into a smile. Wyatt noticed brown stains on his teeth. Jonah continued.

"I don't know about destroy. We're here to make money, not add to the murder or suicide rate. But yeah, Petr, you missed Winnipeg, but I know you get it in terms of energy. These paintings of yours…"

He turned to Wyatt, holding his hands high and wide. "He has these paintings, what are they, six-by-eight or something, and when I saw them back in Toronto the first thing I thought of was the Midway, the games. The Milk Can, specifically. Everything swirling from a circular base up into a vortex point, the peak of the cone. Same thing. It's right there for the taking, if you can manage it."

Wyatt knew he was nodding but felt like he was doing it from the other side of the room. He yawned and gave his head a shake. Jonah laughed. "Don't mean to bore you! No, I know you're tired. We're all beat, and about to get beater."

Petr took his wallet out and produced several white business cards, passing them around the table.

"Exclusive membership. Don't stampede, haha. And keep it among us, okay. A little…secret."

The cards were white stock, printed on one side. The word "Syndicated" stood out in bold, black font. Three thick lines formed a triangle underneath, the point sitting under the 'I'.

"Even the cowboys have business cards out here. This'll be ours. If someone asks you where you're from or what you do haha!" Wyatt noticed Jonah holding his in the palm of his right hand, nodding approvingly. Des and Trish regarded their cards and set them on the table in front of them. Bruce held his card between his index finger and thumb, smiling, like he'd made the high school basketball team.

"Oh wow. This is cool! I get it, man. Like a club for people who don't like clubs… Exclusive offers available on Line B haha. Free extra ball in the Milk Can!"

Jonah leaned over his elbows on the table. "Not exactly a membership, Bruce, but there are dues to be paid, of course. How can you earn the …uh…respect of your peers if you haven't paid your dues?" He took a drag off his smoke and continued, blue eyes locked on Bruce. "For example, this is your town, right? Born and raised?" Bruce nodded, basking in the attention. "Where are you planning on living while we're here for the Stampede? With us, or…?"

A quizzical, dog-like expression crept onto his face, brow furrowed, head tilted. "I was planning on staying at my house… my folks' house. We… they live about fifteen minutes from the grounds. I figured I could take a taxi, or maybe borrow their car. They're away, gone to Vancouver for a couple of weeks. I called Mom yesterday, or I guess it was the day before, from Winnipeg. On a break. I just wanted to let them know things were fine and I'd be in town for a bit. So, I was going to stay at my house. Kinda looking forward to sleeping in my own bed for a change, you know?"

Their silence drove the pitch of his voice higher.

Jonah had the look of a teacher not believing a student's "dog ate my homework" excuse. "I would have thought you'd have taken the rest of us into consideration." He looked around the table.

"How was your room in Winnipeg? Bed comfy? Coffee and breakfast okay? What do they say in the old country, your Scottish family vault? In for a penny, in for a pound? To be clear, I've been waiting for you to step up with an accommodations offer here. I didn't bother booking a motel yet, so they're probably all gone. Looks like we'll have to sleep in the joint, or one of the trailers, I guess… But for sure, enjoy your bed. The one you made…"

Bruce stuttered and sputtered his way into the conversation. "Oh, no. I mean, yes. Yes! I forgot about what I was going to ask you! If you"—he gestured to everyone around the table—"if you all wanted to crash at my place, I mean my parents' place, while were here. I can't believe I didn't mention it. Lots of room. We even have a pool.

Absolutely. Please. Please stay at my place. Save some money." Jonah stared at him over his glasses.

"Well, since you put it that way haha—I think I can speak for all of us in accepting your kind offer, Bruce. Most generous. It won't go unnoticed by the…Syndicate." Everyone chuckled and Petr smirked. Jonah checked his watch, leaned in and lowered his voice.

"It's past four. We need to move. Let's leave a little at a time, okay? Ever done the dine and dash?" He didn't wait for a response." Your town, Bruce, so you'll be the last man standing. He passed the truck keys to Wyatt. "You go out with Trish and Des and get it started. Petr and I'll come, then Bruce. Good, clean fun."

Bruce's smile froze beneath his glasses. "Oh. Me. Okay. Sure, yeah. Used to do this all the time. No problem. Stick it to the man, right?" The vibrato in his voice belied his claim. Wyatt and the women pushed away from the table and went head-down out the door. A couple of minutes later, Petr and Jonah joined them in the idling truck, climbing in the back. Wyatt sat in the driver's seat, watching the door for Bruce. He felt the noose of the collective tightening. Thought about the waitress who'd served them. Over thirty, maybe even forty. She'd smiled and laughed at the little jokes they'd made while ordering ("Over easy? No one easy at this table haha!") and brought extra napkins to them. Probably had a family, might have been separated. Single mom with a couple of asshole teenagers at home, doing her best getting no support or payments from her ex who used to slap her around. Could have gone to college, could have made something of herself. Could have been a contender. Who was going to pay, her or the owner? Sticking it to the man by screwing one of the common people.

He was aware his utter exhaustion was responsible for this sentimental, internal diatribe but felt powerless to rein it in. His mother, for fuck's sake. It could have been his mother, who'd worked so hard to keep it together after his father had died. She was someone's mother. She might have to pay for the sparkling sky arrogance of this table of entitled twats out of her own pocket. Not right. Not right at all. He was about to kill the engine and go back in to settle the bill when Bruce pushed open the faux Western swinging saloon door with his bony shoulder and speed-walked to the truck. He dove into the passenger side. "Hit it" he yelled. Wyatt slammed the truck into gear and pulled away.

Hoots and hollers and hands pounding on the sides of the fiberglass cap buffeted the inside of the cab as Wyatt gunned it down the road away from the restaurant. Bruce was laughing hysterically, his giddy voice cracking high with adrenal glee.

"Oh yeah! Free for the taking! Y'all come back now, ya hear!" He was over the moon with himself. Had proven his worth, his courage, his rebelliousness. Wyatt felt like slapping him and knocking those fucking Buddy Holly glasses off his face. He drove on as Jonah started calling directions from the back. 'Left up here, then right. Then another left at the next lights. Got it?" Silence. "Got it, Wyatt?" Wyatt saw himself in the rear-view as he made the turn. No smile to be seen. "Yeah, I got it…."

25

They pulled through the chain-link gates of the Stampede grounds and drove slowly past the permanent buildings on to what was becoming the Midway. Rides were spread out in every direction in various stages of erection. Wyatt thought of *The War of the Worlds* and the giant, metallic aliens that had been on the cover of a copy of his book way back when. Ride guys and local hires were pulling pipes and boxes out of possum bellies, shirtless, jean-jacket sleeveless, tattooed arms greasy as their hair. He wove the vehicle through until Jonah told him to stop.

Wyatt hadn't even shut the engine off when he heard the yelling to his left. "Hey, you're late! You're two fucking hours late!" He saw Greg chewing up the space between them, striding across the asphalt. His sunglasses were bouncing off his pink Lacoste shirt. Wyatt felt the adrenalin in his guts and started to climb out of the cab as Greg put his hand on the door and held it.

"And who the fuck are you. Is that beer I smell? Have you been drinking and driving? Do you know who I am?" Paralysis. The best he could do was shake his head back and forth, hating the fact he was so intimidated by Greg. Dark scenarios of being fired, being broke, having nowhere to go sped through his core. Wyatt was speechless as the rest of them clambered out of the back. Bruce stared at the floor.

Jonah slid up beside Greg. "He's one of mine. He was working the Milk Can in Winnipeg. I drove most of the way, just hit the wall a couple of hours outta town. It's not his fault. He was driving slow and careful. We stopped for a bite and a beer before we got here. Not drinking. Not a problem, Greg."

Greg held up a spray can in his right hand and gestured to the left. "I've got the marks all down and we've been waiting. Whatever. You get behind the wheel, okay, and get the Birthday Game down. And don't let anyone else drive." He spun on the heels of his leather and disappeared down the line.

It was a torturous set up, far more than the hurry-up-and-wait scenario that Jonah had alluded to in Winnipeg, because they didn't have the luxury of a few days to get it all together. The Stampede, the self-proclaimed "Greatest Show on Earth," was due to open at noon the next day, but vehicles, RVs and people were still straggling in. There were impatient lineups at the trailers for the joint materials. Once he had backed the Birthday Game into place and taken the truck to the rear of the lot, Jonah left Bruce, Trish and Des to set it up while the rest of them got the Milk Can materials. Petr and Wyatt lugged the boards, beams, boxes and canvas from the trailer in the late-day light. Even at six, there was still enough heat to stick their shirts to their skin. The evening air was infused with metal crashing, wood slamming, yelling, cursing and the distant lowing of cattle in the exhibition buildings.

Jonah oversaw the assembly of the joint. Nobody was talking too much, exhausted as they were. Wyatt and Petr followed curt, clipped orders to lift, move and tighten the composite, painted parts. His impatience with their inexperience was palpable, each trying to outperform the other in the knot-tying, spike-pounding and canvas-hanging categories. After a few hours they had it up and wired, ready for the hanging of the animals. Jonah left them to go help with the Birthday Game. Wyatt thought he'd invoke his seniority.

"Why don't you go the trailer and get the plush. I can hang them. I did it in Winnipeg. It's gotta be done just right so there's room for the balls to fly, but not so much they can get too much height and get a direct line into the hole. It's a huge skill, you know, assembling all the pieces of the puzzle." He thought his voice sounded as though it were coming from somewhere else.

More than twenty-four hours without sleep, he thought. *How the fuck am I gonna make it through to midnight?*

Petr stood outside the joint, looking at him quizzically.

"Well? What? You want to hang them? You haven't done it—you don't know how?" Petr gave him the tight-lipped smile. "You didn't say anything. How am I supposed to know what I'm supposed to do here if you don't say anything?" His mouth was moving, but Petr's words were ringing around the joint, hollow-echoed and muddled. How was it he wasn't being heard when he could hear his words? He sat down on the sideboards. The Milk Can lay on its side under a counter.

He gave his head a shake. Exhaustion. He hadn't gone this long without sleep since the cold, hopeless winter days back east. He gripped the corner post with his right hand, grounded, re-entering.

"Sorry. Fuck. Really sorry. I'm right out of it. What I thought I said was would you go get the animals and I'll hang them. Jesus, I haven't been this beat in a good long time. It's the trailer over behind the Funhouse, or House of Mirrors. One of 'em…" Petr was still sliver-smiling, looking amused.

"Sure. I can do that. You want anything else? You look like you could use something else…"

"No, I'm good. Let's just get this done and get the fuck out of here." Wyatt lit a smoke and vised his head in his hands, elbows on knees, and watched Petr walk quickly away. He swatted at little mosquito thoughts of doubt and regret, content to silently diminish Bruce and his attempts to drive tie-down spikes into the asphalt. The sound of Petr pulling the animals out of their protective plastic bags brought him back to where he was.

"Some interesting characters over by the stock trailer. Met a guy named Scooter. I didn't bother asking him where he got that moniker. Sometimes it's better not to know. He works the plate-smash on Line C. I said "Line C" and laughed when I said I could use a line of C right now. Turns out, lo and behold, Scooter knows where we can get some blow if we need to. And speedier stuff. Not sure it won't have the quality and consistency of Cotton Candy crystals, but I determine it to be good information to have. Just in case, right?"

Wyatt was on the table, hook held high, hanging a giraffe. "Sure, I guess. I dunno. I just want to get this shit done so I can go die somewhere, wherever that'll be. Bruce's place, I guess. Keep 'em coming, Petr. Sooner we're done, the sooner we're done."

They finished getting the joint hung around ten o'clock. Wyatt couldn't be bothered to go check on the Birthday Game. He lay down and out on the sideboards and picked little pieces of animal faux fur off this hoodie while Petr, who had a lot more gas in the tank, went to check on their progress. He brought them all back with him.

Jonah looked down on him, extending a hand. "Good job on the joint. Your aesthetic is shining through." A genuine smile as he pulled him vertical. "Must be Petr's artistic experience. All those gallery shows finally manifesting themselves in a commercial context haha."

They gathered around him, a slumping, stinking, yawning excuse of a team.

"So, I talked to Greg. I explained Bruce's generous offer to host us at his house while we're here for the"—radio announcer voice—*Greatest Show on Earth!* He's offered to let us use the truck for the duration. That'll save us a ton of time; taxis are kind of at a premium here during the Stampede."

They tied down the sides of the joint and shadowed down the Midway. The Ferris Wheel creaked in the evening breeze; the slamming of seat stanchions from the Scrambler sent sonic waves out onto the grounds. Someone yelled "Fuck!" All the joints were tied down, though there were whisper-voices slipping out from under the canvas.

"Settling in for the night," Jonah explained in a soft, low voice. "If you don't have a trailer, and can't afford a motel, you can sleep there. A lot of people do. You can stretch full out in a sleeping bag underneath. There are usually free showers on most grounds." He pointed to the bandstand in the distance. "In the morning it's a mix of cowboys, clowns and carnies. Sometimes you don't know which is which. They keep their uniforms hung far apart from each other in the showers. A clown or a cowboy would be able to fit in on the Midway. Not so sure about a carny in the chuckwagon races."

The RVs at the far end of the Midway were a colourful little village unto themselves. Patio lanterns were strung out in green, red and yellow gumdrops of light, strung over little decks with lawn chairs and barbecues, from Airstream to Winnebago. Jonah pointed to the four largest RVs: BillyBob's, Greg's, and the twins'. "That's the high-rent district. We're more the red-light district…" They all laughed a little as they passed, low enough to not be heard.

26

It took about twenty minutes to get to Bruce's parents' place. The now officially named 'Clown Car' wound away from the chunks of steel and glass downtown into ever denser suburban sameness. Jonah was driving, dutifully following Bruce's "Left. Right here. Left again" directions in the cab while the rest of them lay collapsed on each other in the back. They pulled onto a steep driveway and piled out with their backpacks and bags.

Bruce was giddy. "Right around here. Follow me. Dad leaves the key under the garbage can in the back. Watch your step! Still got the cover on the pool. We can go for a swim in the morning if you want; it's heated. Here it is. Come on in, just toss your stuff downstairs in the den. Excellent! Indeed!"

They snaked their way past family portraits hung on the papered walls. Bruce undimmed the light and spread his skinny arms wide. "Help yourself! Ma casa et ta casa! My room is down here—plus the couch—it's a pullout couch if anyone wants that, and two upstairs. A bathroom here and one upstairs."

Their collective exhaustion collapsed in on them. Wyatt fell forward onto the couch. "This is mine. Good fucking night, day or whatever." He could feel himself slipping away immediately. The voices of the others muffled into a diminished buzz as they sorted out their sleeping arrangements on their way upstairs. The last thing he heard was a toilet flush and pipes reacting in the walls.

27

Gotta be a dream. Wyatt was aware of a voice...his voice...reverberating under a dome up above. He was somewhere in the old country, a European or English town with cobbled streets and low, overhanging eaves. Cats skittered into dark places. He held his hand up in front of his face, opening and closing it until his index finger picked a direction for him, down an alley that led into a mountain valley, verdant, speckled with wildflowers, cradling an impossibly blue lake. The air was fragrant and warm. On the other side of the lake, he watched a woman in a white dress walking along the edge of the water. She spun underneath an umbrella, stopping occasionally to pick a bluebell and toss it onto the frozen surface of the lake. Birds shot by and fat, striped bees bent the fragile stems of Van Gogh buttercups as they gathered gold pollen.

The same voice, deeper and slower, called out to the woman on the far side. "It's me! Wait for me there. I'm coming!" He started running through the tall, lakeside grass towards her, timothy and thistles scraping his bare legs. Frogs and snakes jumped or slid under his feet. He could see her directly across from him, strolling, smiling and waving to him, but no matter how fast he ran, the distance remained the same. She was exactly opposite him. "Stop! Wait for me to get there! Just wait for me!"

The voice was his but wasn't coming from him. She looked up and smiled under her twirling umbrella, her face suddenly close though she remained on the other side of the frozen blue lake. It was her… the one he had too late found out he loved. "Dreaming Wyatt" was euphoric, enveloped in a sense of joy and relief. He was coming home, back where he belonged, watched his hand reaching out to her, felt her beautiful smile light up the under-dome. But she kept walking, a slow dance stroll along the lake, still on the edge but pulling farther away from him bit by bit. The lake began to lose its circular symmetry and elongate, something he felt inside. Panic slowly set in as he realized she was getting smaller. He opened his mouth to call her name, but a clot of butterflies flew out and fell into the long grass. A Tinker Bell fairy flitted over them. He bent his legs and leaped high, so high, in the rare thin air, landing with crunchy crack on the cold blue ice. Tried to Bambi-run towards her as the ice creaked and started to fissure. She was waving, beckoning with her open hand to join her. The laughter. The laughter left her mouth, smoke-ringed towards him as he slipped and stumbled his way, now with bare feet starting to get numb. A loud 'pop' split the sky open, the blue beyond as dark as the water starting to swallow his legs. He tried to hook his arm through a smoke-ring circle as he went under, howling her name in bubbles. Blue went black.

"Hey… Hey…" Wyatt could hear Jonah's voice from far away. "C'mon, you've gotta snap out of it." A higher pitched "We are here. We are here haha" from *Horton Hears a Who*. He slowly extricated himself from the dream, cracking open his sleep-crusted eyes to see Jonah standing over him with an amused smile squeezing the smoke in his mouth. Wyatt's shirt had sweat-soaked through.

"Sounded like quite the dream there, Wyatt. Everything okay at home? I had a cat once that sounded like that at certain times of the year. The *wah-wah-wah* haha. Hopefully there's not a lot of toms lined up outside…"

Wyatt crawled away from the shards of the dream and pulled himself upright on the couch.

"Fuck... that was crazy...." He shook his head. The sense of loss remained, so palpable and profound he had to fight back tears. He turned away from Jonah.

"What time is it?" Bruce emerged from his room, looking more Muppet than man to Wyatt, with his disheveled hair perched atop a too-small head. His annoying voice kicked in. "Nine bells! Is all well? C'mon cowboys and gals! Coffee first, then the Greatest Show on Earth!"

They sat at the round table in the aptly named sunroom. Mid-morning rays layered themselves in bands of cigarette smoke and dust particles. At the end of the table, Des shielded her eyes with a flattened palm salute, gently blowing the steam as it rose from her cup. They all sat staring into their coffees. The radio played low in the adjoining kitchen. "Today's the big day! Make sure you get over to the Stampede and visit the C103 booth for a chance to win some big prizes!"

"Really big show! Really big show!" Petr was mimicking the radio in a decent Ed Sullivan impersonation, pulling a chuckle out of the introspective collective. Jonah spoke up.

"This one's a lot different than Winnipeg. A lot different than any of the other spots, to be honest. We must be honest! Got some true believers here in Calgary. The strong, self-reliant makers of their own myth. Stetsons, belt buckles and Wranglers tight on top of genuine Corinthian leather cowboy boots. Again, not such a big deal in the Birthday Game, but good information to keep in your back pocket in the Can. Personal destiny, personal responsibility... Marlboro men." He lit another smoke and continued.

"There's an arrogance without the American naivete you see south of the order. Not so likeable in a way. These fuckers expect to win, think it's a foregone conclusion. They see us as…less than…. Well, most places see us that way, but this is different, just because of that sense of self-made man bullshit. You'll see once they jump in and commit. Being so underestimated can be used to your advantage. Those etched leather Zane Grey wallets at the end of the chains are stuffed with oil money. But it's our money waiting to come home. Think of it as our money. Your money."

Petr had his elbows on the table, hands a tented prayer under his angular chin.

"Us against them. Good guys? Bad guys? Which one are we? Anyone?" His eyes did a slow scan around the table. "Doesn't matter much, does it? We're not the cavalry coming to the rescue, though it's generally considered a good thing when they come riding over the hill. Or is it? Coming to the rescue of who, settlers who stole the land? Killing for Christ? Homage to Catalonia? Or Machiavelli? I mean, it's all relative, right? I'm no Einstein, mind you…"

He was talking a mile a minute. Despite his slow creep back to consciousness and the land of the living, Wyatt noticed circles under Petr's eyes that seemed darker than the day before. He watched Jonah regard the speed of Petr's speech with raised eyebrows, noticed Des gently knock his leg with her knee underneath the table. Silence joined the sunroom gathering.

Jonah checked his watch. "Nine-thirty. We should be out of here soon. The traffic's going to be heavy, especially when we get closer, and the gates open at eleven. Get your showers and shit together. We leave at ten."

28

Jonah was right. They'd barely been able to get the top of the can Pledged before the first people started wandering down the Midway. The rides were up and running, laughter and screams of terror, the song loop of the Himalayan punctuated with the ringing bell from the 'test-your-strength' sledgehammer, the rat-a-tat of the 'Shoot Out The Star' and calls of the carnies.

"Right here now. C'mon and give it a try. Right here now!" After only one ten-day run in Winnipeg he already regarded the workers in the other joints with disdain. Such a lack of imagination in the hustle, so oblivious to the deeper metaphor of what was happening around them.

He had to give it to Petr, though. Right out of the gate, there was an ease with which he settled into the game. His patter was unpredictable, something which Wyatt reluctantly admired.

"Hey there. Excuse me—yes, you! Here it is, the answer to your stampede dream. Look at these rare and wonderful animals. Be the belle of the ball, the king of the corral, the chuck of the wagon yessir! Three for five and staying alive. Hahahaha stayin' alive!"

A couple of hours in, and he managed to keep it fresh, which was no small accomplishment compared to the other carnies, or even to Bruce, who tried but mostly failed with any attempts at originality. It was slow enough in the beginning that they decided one person could handle the first hour, that one person being Bruce. He and Petr went to the canteen for a coffee and a break from standing. Wyatt went to get their Styrofoam cups of shitty coffee, magnanimously offering to pay for it while Petr grabbed a table. He had barely settled into his rickety, tube-metal chair before Petr went off.

"Thanks for the uh…stimulant haha. Need more more more more to get through this day, don't we just?" He affected a high-pitched "more more more" to the Andrea True lyric. "Yeah, can't get enough of that Sugar Crisp!"

Wyatt opened his mouth to chime in something…anything, but Petr squeezed him out of the monologue. "Amazing! Can't believe we're here on a goddamn Midway. Never saw this train leaving the station. Loved it when I was a kid, way back. Did you have 'em in the Maritimes?" Wyatt again started to speak, and again Petr kept his words running through that small opening. He decided to sit back and listen, lighting a smoke, leaning his head on his hands, acting interested.

"It suddenly occurs to me we hardly know anything at all about each other. Well, not entirely true. I've heard a thing or two about you, heard it through the grapevine. Don't get me wrong, I'm fine if you're not mine! Loved Marvin Gaye…the songs, the voice…even the name for fuck's sake!" He took a breath from his cigarette and continued.

"I had a few on and off-site chats about you—all of you—before I got here, you know. Nothing too serious, or too nasty—you know how rumours can sink their teeth. Heartbreak got you out the door, right? Had you running away and running toward. I'm gonna take a wild guess and say you're a Pisces, yeah?" Wyatt nodded, suddenly a bit more interested in the staccato words spitting out between Petr's tobacco-stained teeth.

"Yeah… sensitive type, eh? I can see it for sure. Oh, don't look like that. It's fine. Seriously—everyone's gotta be something right? Me? I'm an on-the-cusp kind of guy. Always been that way—not astrologically, haha. Temperament-wise. Never here or there. Or so they used to say, way back when it mattered to me what they said. I think we're both country boys, aren't we?" Wyatt nodded again; he felt like this possibly chemically induced flight of rhetoric was just beginning to taxi down the runway.

"Thought so. Actually, I knew that too haha! I grew up, as much as anyone grows up—I mean, don't we just slowly fill the pre-ordained skin we inhabit?—in the country. Umm, not so much the country as in a small town surrounded by stone and root and wood. Way up there on the Canadian Shield. Elliot Lake. Heard of it?" A shake-of-the-head 'no'. Petr affected a high, faux gay voice.

"Oh my god, you simply HAVE to go—it's to die for!" His voice dropped back down to its lower, smoke-infused range.

"The main claim to fame is as a uranium mine. My family moved there in the fifties. Made the great escape from a furniture factory in Montreal to the glowing promise of Elliot Lake. Thank God! Imagine having to grow up on the Plateau, with all the attendant cultural distractions, when you could have an endless boreal forest out your back door, a Legion and a hockey rink for your aesthetic distractions. A company store. Maybe an Eaton's catalogue. The whole world at my fingertips, my mother used to say. I remember sitting with her on that horrific green couch, flipping the shiny pages." He paused, lit a smoke, his eyes fixed on some far-away horizon beyond Wyatt.

"Dad worked in the mine. Just me and mom and home, alone, most of the time. That's how I remember it. Him gone working the night shift, working overtime, working weekends. He wasn't so much a father to me as a concept; the idea of what a father did. Work, and work some more. There wasn't any time for what they call 'bonding'. Don't get me wrong. It wasn't as though he was mean or didn't try to do things. He showed me how to run a trap line; a way for me to make some pocket money so I could order what I wanted from the Eaton's catalogue. That's what he told me. We'd take some snare wire into the bush behind the house and set them where the tracks in the snow led. It'd make me manly, too. Don't think he used the word 'manly', but it was somehow implied, alluded to in whatever way my mostly non-verbal father alluded to anything. Must have been after I flamed out in hockey. I'm sure he did his best to get me to play, but I disappointed early and often in his dream of me playing for the Montreal Canadiens. Can you imagine? Jesus Christ…By the time I was ten that had been abandoned. Horrible on the ice but did well in school. I was a reader. Couldn't get enough of books. Any books, whatever I could get my hands on up there. You too?"

Again, Wyatt nodded without speaking. He noticed for the first time the chewed, ragged nails on Petr's smoking hand.

"Yeah. You can travel far from where you are with a book. I did a lot of travelling. But he was right about the trapline. I used to call it a trapline, though it wasn't far or long. Some of the men up there, the ones that weren't working the mine, had traplines that took them away for weeks at a time, far into the bush. Jack London, *Call of the Wild*, *White Fang* level, you know? Ever read *In a Far Country*?" Wyatt shook his head. Petr's staccato spiel had rendered him speechless. He felt like one of those old Christmas toys his mother used to have, nodding, up and down.

"Oh"—again with the lame gay—"you simply must!" And again, back to his normal vocal range. "It's my favourite of his. Always was. Seems to have some relevance to our current…. circumstance. If you get a chance…" He lit another cigarette.

"Those snares got me through the winters, at least. It got dark at four in the afternoon for what seemed like eight months a year. Felt like eight years a month. I did like going off on my own to check them. Dad thought it was good for me. There was something gratifying about stomping up the steps of the house with a pack full of frozen carcasses that felt…good. Sometimes, you'd get there before they were dead or frozen. It's a sound you don't forget, you know, the squeal of an animal struggling to escape a garrot noose under a darkening, winter-grey sky.

It makes its way through the undergrowth, around the trees and rocks across frozen streams and lakes into your ears, down to your bones. Into your blood. It's what death sounds like, and I used to think it must be what childbirth sounds like. My mother said I never cried as a baby, but I don't know.... Surely the slap on the ass got a reaction. I mean, it usually does, right? Dad always said I needed a kick in the ass. One time I found a fox that had nearly chewed off its leg trying to escape. It was hanging by a marbled red-white tendon, the crying high-pitched enough it got into my spine. Exquisite, don't you think, the way an animal can sound like a human sometimes?" He sighed a dramatic, dreamy sigh and continued.

"I made enough money to order things that I wanted. All that time alone.... I'm the only child, the golden child...the Stolen Child... Yeats there, right? Likely a little spoiled but it's hard to be objective. If you're not playing hockey you must fill up that void with something. I'd trade the furs in for books, mostly. Until I was thirteen or fourteen; then I got into art. Painting. It was a revelation that I could make the world colourful, not just the black-and-white world my body was surrounded by. Ironic, isn't it? Now I see the world as black and white, even out there..." He motioned with the tip of his cigarette to the Midway. "It is what it is. There is no nuance." Another pause as he harvested his thoughts beneath his furrowed brow.

"I gave up the killing of innocent life not long after I started painting haha. It became obvious quickly that I could take that skill I learned in the bush—objectively gather the dead or finish off the living—and do it on a canvas. Create worlds, lives, people. Then put them in any situation imaginable and have it be forever. Or paint over it as though they never existed. *This is real power,* I remember thinking—the ability to create and destroy. That's about when I changed the spelling of my name, too. Hard sell at sixteen in Elliot Lake, insisting on any kind of change, let alone one so large and small as the removal of a letter. Another by-product of being a reader in an illiterate town. As in Russia, as in Great. Maybe a bit pretentious, but I think I've grown into it haha, if I do say so... got me into U of T on a full scholarship.

"That was after the 'incident', mind you. Small towns, right? I assume you know what I'm taking about; the East Coast always struck me as something like the Shire in Lord of the Rings. " Wyatt didn't want to but had to laugh at this.

"A collection of contented hamlets untroubled by the troubled world beyond its borders. People Tolkien it for granted, hah, as it were, but we both know better, right? Every little house with chimney smoke curlicuing up like a Currier and Ives Christmas card is full as a tick of secrets, disappointments...the underbelly. The never-talked-about. Turns out even in Elliot Lake there were some things that crawled out from under the sawdust insulating the foundations and made their way in the public...discourse." He paused, checked his watch.

"It's not as though we weren't of the legal age of consent. There were a lot of empty upper floors in town. I managed to convince my parents I needed a studio. I didn't really need permission; I was paying for it myself with my fur fund. That's what I called it. It was a revelation, to have space away from the little people. Away from prying, inquiring eyes. I had canvases spread out everywhere. Oh, to be there then with what I know now, right? Still life, abstract, realism, surrealism, cubism—any 'ism' became a chasm I dove deep into. Wasn't it Wilde who said talent borrows, genius steals? I was born to be Wilde ha! But that was all fine, you know. I could keep up a veneer of normal for the good folks of Elliot Lake and get into the real stuff in my studio. I so loved being able to say I had a studio at sixteen! I started wearing a beret—a beret in Elliot fucking Lake!"

"The human body. That's the thing, right? The ultimate artistic challenge. David and all that shit. Figured I needed a model, which wasn't something you advertised back there back then. Can you imagine? But I found someone. That was the first time my antennae were up for that sort of thing. A male model—had to be a man—I had David on the brain, delusions of Michaelangelo. Angel is in that name. There are many kinds of angels, aren't there? This…boy…was one. Kevin. Sweet Kevin. He was fourteen. We were both in the art club at school. I promised to pay him to pose. With clothes, then slowly, with fewer. And fewer." Petr had a horizon smile splitting his thin lips. There was a long pause, food trays crashing in the background.

He gave his head a small shake. "Things followed their…natural…. course, shall we say. He was perfect. Smooth. Like Italian marble. Translucent. I filled my frames with variations of him. I truly believed I'd perfected the techniques, and then some. I'm sure there was some …talk. Even my father eventually asked what I was doing spending so much time in the studio with the principal's son. 'It's art', I'd say, as aloof and pretentious as you'd imagine.

"When the landlord went in to fix a broken water pipe, our…my… cover was blown. It was quite the scandal. The paintings—there must have been a fifty—had gotten progressively more…intimate, shall we say. Far more than the town could handle. It's a bit of a blur now, of course. So much water under my bridge, you see. But suffice to say, it was decided my"—Petr made quotation marks with his fingers—"*artistic pursuits* were not welcome in tiny town. My folks arranged for me to live in Toronto with my mother's sister and finish high school there. Never looked back. Never went back."

He looked at his watch again, shook his head and pushed himself up and back from the table. "Whew, that hour flew, huh? Your turn next time! Time for a quick trip to the bathroom before we spell Brucey off, right? Wyatt, still running the frames of the verbal movie he'd just watched, nodded and followed him back out to the Midway.

29

It was the confirmation of the stereotype that took some time for Wyatt to get used to. The Midway was steadily filling up. By early afternoon it was nearly as choked as some of the peak times in Winnipeg, and the assortment of black Stetsons, boots and bandannas was bizarre and impressive. The cowboys walked with legs wide, chewing up the asphalt with a sense of purpose. The fauxboys (as Petr labelled them) with their "I'm a visitor from out of town" white Stetsons, less so. Women with mountainous breasts and silicon valleys clung two-handed to thick biceps, pursing their painted, Botoxed lips underneath wide sunglasses as their men tossed balls, rang bells, shot stars and acted out their Midway version of *How the West was Won*.

He and Petr paced the joint, side to side, like a couple of big cats in a zoo, eyeing the marks and pulling them in. Bruce worked the front side, facing the Himalayan, where it was loudest. Nothing was said, but Wyatt was compelled to step up his game to keep up with the cash that Petr was pulling in. He wasn't normally competitive, but this was day one and he wanted his experience to show. By the time the first animal made its way out onto the Midway—a couple with a kid who picked an elephant because "she loves elephants and oh great, I'm going to have to carry this around all day now can I leave it here and come back and get it later haha"—they were well ahead of the odds. Both had a good fold of bills in the bands, which Petr constantly faced and unfaced as he worked the crowd. No major tips; just a good steady flow.

The action slowed down mid-afternoon. Wyatt hadn't recovered from the overnight from Winnipeg and was fighting back yawns. Jonah stopped by the game.

"This is a good time to take your breaks. Grab an hour each now, and hopefully you can get a meal into you a little later as well. It's a bit of a calm before the opening night storm. Who's first?" Petr and Wyatt looked at each other. Petr nodded, "You go ahead. You look like you need it more than me. I'll take mine after, if I take one. Feeling pretty good right now."

Wyatt slid through the crowd, upstream and sideways, ducked around the back of the Funhouse and went into the cafeteria. The tarp-filtered light cast an orange hue over the groups of two and three sitting at the wooden tables. He grabbed a cheeseburger special (special had an exclamation mark tacked on after it on the menu board) and went to an empty corner table, sitting back to the canvas wall. Even fifty metres away, the sounds of the Midway were muted. He kept his head down and leaned into the meal.

"Hey, mind if I join you?" Des slid her tray onto the table and sat across from him. "Oh, yeah for sure." She had a Styrofoam plate loaded with one of the more congealed piles of poutine he'd ever seen, a dozen packets of salt and pepper piled beside it.

"Welcome to Chez Midway, purveyors of haute cuisine since 1923. Try the veal…"

Des laughed her throaty, low laugh. "High life for sure. How are you doing? Honestly, you look fucking exhausted."

"Only cause I am. It wasn't much of a sleep last night. Eight hours felt like half that. I wandered the wilderness of lucid dreamland for fuck's sake. Through the looking glass. It's hard to get rest when you're awake in your sleep."

"I hear you. I mean, I don't get…haven't ever had a lucid dream. I know a bunch of people who do. Don't get me wrong, Wyatt. I had a lot more sleep than you on the way here. Great job on the driving, by the way. Jonah was impressed, that's for sure. He sang your praises in the back of the truck."

Wyatt was surprised again at how good Jonah's approval felt.

"But I bet I got about as much sleep as you did last night. Petr and I shared the room upstairs... No, it wasn't that. Trust me, it wasn't that for sure. He was wired for sound, though. We spent a lot of time together in Toronto when we were in class together. I love how his mind works. He finds...connections. But this was so different. Talking in circles, riddles... a lot of stuff about the business cards and cone configurations. So bizarre. About how this carnival is like a physical manifestation of the paintings he was hanging at his show. I finally dozed off at dawn to the drone of his voice, but I don't think he slept at all. And he was the first one up, before Jonah and"—small but perceptible hesitation—"Trish." The clatter of plates and sizzle of the grill filled the space left empty between them.

Wyatt dipped a fry into a paper cup full of ketchup, twirled it, tossed and caught it in his mouth. "One in wins. How's it going in the Birthday Game, Des? I haven't had a chance to see you on the mic yet.... Got your patter down by now, I imagine."

"Yeah, I guess. That's one of the hardest things for me, to be honest. I've never worked with a mic. I'm still having a hard time with talking without being heard. No, that's not it. They hear, but only as a part of the carnival cacophony. When I'm dancing, I'm the centre of attention. People think they're seeing me, but I'm not even there; it's just my body, or a fantasized version of me. A projection. It's odd to be on the mic and not command any attention. Not control the situation. You can, if you isolate one person to focus the patter on, but that's not how it usually works. It's normally noise."

Wyatt rejoined the conversation, back from drifting off to the sound of her voice, the tent, the Midway beyond. "Dancing...right. Almost forgot. What kind of dancing, again? Uh, classical? Or...?" Des looked over the top of her Coke, finished sucking it up through the plastic straw. Loud ice bubbles slurped, pulling a few bored looks from the other tables. Her long-lashed, dark oval eyes, framed by arched, thin eyebrows and high, full cheeks, smiled sadly. He'd forgotten she was beautiful. Travelling in such circumstances as they were, he now realized, you forget about these things.

"No, definitely not Swan Lake. Wyatt, I was…I am a stripper, Wyatt. No, was… it's definitely a 'was' on that. That's how I made my way for the last few years, but I'm done with it. It's not… It's kind of complicated. I'll tell you all about it sometime. Or not. I have to say, the money on the Midway is about a tenth of what I'd normally make, but I'm happy doing this. It's ironic, I realize, but being a carny seems more honest than being a stripper to me. I'm not selling anything other than a ball bouncing around a box. The hustling of the erotic fantasy was something I got good at. It came kind of… natural to me. I got a little too good…" She looked up at the clock above the menu board. Wyatt waited. "Gotta get back. Nice to chat. See you later tonight."

He watched her walk away, high-cut jean shorts, cowboy boots and tight white t-shirt. The ride guys at the table in the corner gave an elbow and a nod to each other as she slid past. Objectively, he knew she was sexy, attractive, hot…all that shit, but truly felt no sexual attraction to her. That had always been a thing for him, being able to have female friends. He sat up high on his holier-than-thou "I'm not a sexist" horse, looking way down his nose at the lecherous lowlifes. He watched them until they looked away, acting like he was her boyfriend, or husband, or lover.

30

Walking between the trailers back out into the fray, he was struck again with how normal the carnival noise had become for him. The sonic cellophane wrapped itself around him. A foundation of rumbling wheels on metal tracks, bells, haunted house tin-thin cackles, music pumping from a dozen rides mixing itself up in the middle into an unrecognizable conflagration of bass, feral wailed melody amid pockets of singalong by the rides. Then, on top, the human din; laughter, finger-pointing conversations about what game or ride to try next; low, close-to-the-ear admonitions from parents to kids threatening to "leave right now if you don't start behaving" and screaming preteens careening from joint to joint. Objectively, it was overwhelming until it became the norm, easily ignored if he so chose. For the bulk of the days spent under the baffle of the stuffed animals, he hardly noticed it.

He wove his way through the people knot to where the A, B and C lines met in front of the Himalayan. Not invisible with his clown shirt uniform on, but completely anonymous. No one talks to a carny unless they're looking for Guest Relations ("the idiot at the Shoot Out the Star said there was a little bit of red left but that's bullshit, and I've got it in my hand going to show them and get the prize upgrade. Fucking rip-off") or the bathrooms. He still had a few minutes before he was due back in the joint. The three of them had maintained a punctual schedule in terms of breaks in Winnipeg, and so far, with Petr replacing Scott, it was working out here. Two hours in, one hour out until it got busy enough for all three.

He leaned against the Himalayan speaker, just out of sight of Bruce and Petr, and watched the Milk Can action. It was steady, with a few players who'd obviously been there for a while; previous wins of small prizes set down beside them, a girlfriend checking a watch looking bored as fuck.... Bruce was doing his thing with a goofy, imploring smile on his face, cigarette at the tip of his fingers.

Petr had something else happening. It was the first time Wyatt had watched him.

He paced more than walked the inside of the joint. A continuous back and forth; step step step, pivot step step step. Mechanical, sliding over the asphalt underneath his leather-soled shoes. Shoes that he'd thought looked funny with shorts and white socks but had refrained from ridiculing. Petr hadn't shown himself to have much of a sense of humour, unless the barb was at someone else's expense; when that was the case, he'd make a caustic comment and spit out a dry chuckle (At the scene of the dine and dash: "Look at that waitress's legs—a roadmap of misery written in varicose veins").

There was a rhythm to his movements that Wyatt recognized from his own time in Can; a subtle, circular sweeping over the table, back over the boards and the open palms beckoning out to the Midway towards the players and potential marks. Part 'come hither' and part 'Jesus on the Cross' on display. Constant, calculated movement that alluded to the dynamic of the art exhibition they'd talked about in the back of the truck on the trip from Winnipeg. He had the bills folded tight in his left hand, had his shoulders back and head tilted forward, ponytail twisted tight. Bony shoulders. It looked more challenge than enticement, a subtle non-verbal dare to play and try to beat him and get the prize. After having only done the run in Winnipeg, Wyatt had come to recognize his own strategies, which involved more eye contact, more disingenuous smiling, more of that Springsteen 'human touch." Exactly the opposite of what he could see from Petr's approach, which he could not deny was working; the billfold was impressive, even from fifty feet away.

There was something else though, an underlying freneticism that looked to be fueling his movement. Wyatt carried the snowballing exhaustion of the past couple of weeks like a heavy blanket, could feel it in his knees, his eyes, his neck, but Petr maintained a fluidity that belied the sleep deprivation that was apparently going to be the norm from here on in. All of them drank litres of coffee and smoked at least a pack of cigarettes a day. He was younger than Petr by five years, but felt far less energetic than the swift, efficient entity he was watching from afar.

They burned through the rest of the night without taking a break. The tips were big and steady, turning over like tables in a busy restaurant. Belt buckles the size of manhole covers, beefy paws passing oil money over the boards as though it were a Monopoly game, big guffawing laughs slowly turning to strained, weather-beaten cheek smiles as they failed to bag the big prize. The three of them got a great groove going, Bruce working one side while Petr and Wyatt shared the other three. Seamless flow, back and forth, pacing, three-way patter. "Here it is folks, bigger than a chuckwagon and better than an oilpatch! Stampede on up here, one in wins!" Unspoken eye contact between them forged a commitment to not let any of 'these redneck motherfuckers' take a prize out of the joint. Petr met Wyatt bending over the table picking up softballs and hissed through tight teeth "Fuck this. These assholes don't win." His eyes coal-burned, pupils huge, reflecting the neon of the Himalayan. Wyatt knew better, knew that there had to be some winners to keep the system functional. He knew Bruce would be less attuned to keeping the cowboys out of the winner circle, so he kept a close third eye on who he was hustling. If it was one of 'them', he slid over behind him and subtly moved him along to the side he'd just vacated.

31

Miss Stampede led a parade past the joint at one point, after the calf roping and bronco busting were done for the night, a coterie of cowboys, cowgirls and elected officials parting the Midway throngs, who appeared to revel in their great, good luck at being so close to royalty. They clapped, cheered and posed for pictures. A little girl broke away from her parents and rushed towards Miss Stampede, possibly sensing a kinship in their shared blonde bouffant. Wyatt thought of the photo of soldiers marching off to World War Two and the kid who ran out of the crowd to hug his father one last time, then shook his head and smiled at the absurdity.

Somehow, the twins, Greg and BillyBob, had been infused into the retinue. "Here come the Romanovs." Petr tilted his head towards them. "Where's the fucking firing squad when you want it?" Wyatt laughed out loud. It was the first time Petr had said anything he'd found funny and seized upon the opportunity to upgrade the absurdity of the situation. At the top of his lungs, even over the AC/DC pumping out of the Himalayan, Wyatt called out to her.

"Hey! Hello! Miss Stampede! One in wins. Right here. Free shot for you!" He shot a disarming smile at her escort. "Take home a real prize," which got quite a few laughs around the horseshoe she was enveloped by. The Clown contingent—the twins, Greg and BillyBob—didn't laugh. She smiled an ivory smile, straightened the 'Miss Stampede' ribbon across the front of her gown and glided over to the joint.

"Your majesty, an unparalleled joy to have you grace the game with your presence!" He used his best fake British accent, did half a bow. More laughter as the crowd gathered, three deep on all four sides. All the shooting had stopped.

"It's a simple prospect. Take this ball"—he held it up on the tips of his fingers—"and toss it into that can. No broken wheels, busted broncos or skewered clowns. Just a ball and a hole, and the biggest fuzzy prize at the greatest show on earth!" She was playing along and laughing. "Oh really? How much did you say?" "Oh, my queen, free for you, free forever!" Suddenly, they had their own show happening.

"How am I supposed to trust you? I heard all these games are rigged." Wyatt feigned shocked. "How could you say such a thing? Just look at me and my compatriots, loyal subjects all. We wouldn't dream of misrepresenting the empire." More laughter. The crowd tightened up around the joint. Petr was smoking, watching him intently. He could see Greg with his lips pursed and chin in the palm of his hand.

"If you'll allow me to demonstrate. Perish those thoughts of doubt and distrust." He took a ball over to the can and dropped it on the rim, so it hit one side, the other and fell through the hole. Clunk on the wood. "See? Honest as the day is long, m'lady!"

She laughed an easy, beautiful laugh. Wyatt decided she had a nice smile and a sense of humour. She was actually alright.

"Easy for you to say, my good man, but throwing it in looks much harder. Especially from over on this side. You could give me a thousand free balls and I bet I still wouldn't win. It looks impossible." Wyatt held up the ball again. "Never know if you don't play, right? Looks like you already won a crown tonight; maybe Lady Luck is still in the house?" A rush of surety rose from the asphalt into Wyatt's extremities, filling him like a balloon at the helium tank; the same sense of channeled knowing that he'd used to pull cars over with in the before-times; that he'd held that huge tip on an empty, closing time on the Midway in Winnipeg with. He stepped over the boards and stood beside her.

"I'll tell you what. I wouldn't normally feel compelled to prove myself and the integrity of my trade to anyone, but this"—he gestured around the crowd—"is different. The common people must be able to trust their institutions, am I right?" The tip was taking up the challenge, several of them yelling "Yeah! Do it!"

"There's no artifice, no gimmick, no sleight of hand. It's a matter of focus! Of believing! One in wins. Simple as that. One in wins. I can't hear you, Calgary!" He exhorted on, pumping his arms wide. The crowd started the chant slow, picking up in volume and intensity. "One in wins! One in wins." Wyatt was lifted by the choir, held the ball up for all to see, and leaned his knees against the boards.

He'd practiced the shot hundreds of times in the past couple of weeks, outside the game before the gates opened in the morning, inside during downtime. Wyatt had always been athletic and knew the value of practice, repetition; in being ready for when you had your chance in the game, be it hockey, baseball or Milk Can. Muscle memory. Do anything enough and you transcend the mechanics of it, which allows the natural rhythm of the task to happen, unencumbered by thought. "Zen and the Art of the Milk Can" he'd christened it, co-opting the famous Pirsig book. I was all about feel, romantic rather than classical processes.

He spun the ball until the seams were running along the tips of his four fingers and under his thumb on the bottom. Held it over the counter with his arm extended. Pulled back slow and snapped his wrist as he straightened his forearm and released it, arcing the ball up over the table, just under the trunk of an elephant and down to the Can. He saw Jonah on the other side of the joint at the back of the throng, gleaming a smile behind the smoke clenched in his teeth. Petr and Bruce stood in each of the far corners, arms crossed. The sound and fury of the Midway retreated and wrapped itself around the outside of the joint, so the only thing that could be heard by the three-deep tip was the clonk of the ball on the outer rim, the back spun clink on the other lip and the plop-thunk of the ball going through the hole and hitting the bottom. A moment of disbelief was quickly rent asunder by belt-buckled seal clapping.

As soon as he released it, Wyatt knew the ball would go in. It had the right feel off the tips of his fingers. He had already turned towards Miss Stampede before the ball's second hit off the rim, smiling disarmingly, arms open as it fell through. "See what I mean? Piece of cake. It's all in the wrist action, you know." She laughed, her polished teeth tinkling Midway lights. Wyatt climbed back into the joint.

"That's amazing! How did you do that? I can't do that!" Wyatt lifted the edge of the can and pulled the ball out from under. "Lucky ball," he said to her, pressing it into her cool, dry hand. He took her by the wrist and turned her hand over, arranged the threads on the ball so they sat under her fingers. "Just hold it like that. Don't grip it too hard. The main thing is to get it up in the air high enough with a good backspin." He made a backspin gesture with his hand. "It's all about letting go, if you know what I mean." He pivoted his gaze around the periphery of the joint, skimming over expectant eyes.

"Okay everyone, let's lean in on this together. She's got this, right? Can't quite hear you. Do you believe, ladies and gentlemen, do you believe?" Titters and chuckles and whispered "yeah" and "no way!" Wyatt channeled the latent southern Baptist preacher snake oil tent revivalist ghosts of carnivals past, exhorting the tip to chant once again.

"One in wins, one in wins, one in wins…" Tribal, guttural, absurd. Miss Calgary's blue eyes sparkled like the fake diamonds in her tiara. She did as she had been told, pulling her arm back and letting go with a perfect backspin off the tips of her manicured, blood-red nails. The ball spun up and over the table, popping like a finger in a cheek as it landed perfectly in the hole. There was a sliver of time between the end of the chant and the start of the explosion of cheers when Wyatt stole a look at Petr on the far side of the joint. He was already moving towards the table to retrieve the ball. "One in wins! One in wins" buried the AC/DC cranking from the Himalayan. A star was born.

Miss Stampede genuflected towards Wyatt, shared a delightful laugh and set her smooth, white hand on his forearm.

"That was more fun than the chuckwagon race! I can't believe I did that…that's an impressive parlour trick you've got happening here. Don't know how you did it. Amazing! Don't worry about the prize—I've got enough baggage already." She laughed, then addressed the crowd.

"You can put your hands together for this guy! Get some balls and see if anyone can top that!" There was some chuckling and a collective shuffling away from the joint by the assembled crowd. A few took her up on the suggestion, but it didn't result in much. Greg walked past with a quizzical, suspicious sideways stare at Wyatt before falling in stride with BillyBob and the twins.

Jonah stepped up to the boards and did a slow clap, which Petr and Bruce joined. "That was…Seriously, Wyatt, I've never seen anything quite like it. You had the entire kingdom in the palm of your hand—the queen, the praetorian guard, the nobles and the plebs. Incredible." He pulled a pack of smokes from his front pocket and passed them around.

"How did you know it would go in? How'd you do that twice?" Bruce was giddy, rocking back and forth in his beat-up Chuck Taylors, looking from Wyatt to Petr to Jonah as though they were able to provide an answer. Cartoonish. Petr took a long, thought-filled haul on his smoke.

"You know what that was, don't you? Inspired. Vulnerable. Confident. Only some of the best performance art you'll see off-Broadway. That's the thing, isn't it, to believe in what you're doing enough that everyone else buys into it. That's how you transcend. Couldn't you smell the confusion? The hoping for failure from your fellow man in the gathered mob. The reluctant and finally triumphant acquiescence to the power of the Can, so far beyond any individual's ability to control or comprehend. A syndicated scene if you know what I mean." He tittered a bit, grabbed a cloth from the box, soaked it in

Pledge out of sight of the marks and worked on the rim.

Jonah flicked his smoke away, gave his knuckles a couple of cracks. "Big night, gentlemen. Big night in the Can. There's the greatest show on earth, and there's the Greatest Show on Earth. That was pretty special." He clapped his hands twice. "Let's take it home, an hour to close. Meet you at the truck." He walked down the A line to the birthday game, bobbing in and out of the thinning knots of people.

32

The clock hands crawled to 11. The adrenal rush of the Miss Stampede moment had receded, leaving Wyatt slumped on the edge of the game with his head in his hands, drained. There was a rule about sitting down in the game, but he didn't care much about that at this point. All he could manage was to stand and get out of the way while Petr and Bruce pulled down the sides and tied the joint up for the night. Out of body in his head, aching back and knees descended upon him. He yawned a yawn that swallowed the Midway lights. He flashed back to his bleak winter days of desperation in the east, muscle memory meandering through his pores, reminding him that what was, still is. He shook his head, hoping to avoid acknowledging the truth of "you can run, but you can't hide." He could almost see the hope briefly engendered by what had happened now running away like a dog on a prairie quarter-section. All he wanted was everything he didn't have.

Petr tied the last knot and told Bruce and Wyatt to go ahead; he'd catch up to them. He veered off, quick-stepping towards the stock trailers. Exhausted anger bubbled out of Wyatt.

"Fuck sakes. He'd better not keep us waiting. I'm beat as a drum." Bruce nodded, tossed a smoke ahead and ground it out with his heel.

"Indeed. I don't think he'll be long. He's got a guy he's meeting—some weird nickname—sounds like a ride guy. He was talking about it earlier while you were on break. You've no doubt noticed how chipper he's been…More than coffee at work in the joint, methinks!"

They rounded the corner. Des and Trish were cranking down the sides of the Birthday Game. Bruce handed all the cash from the Can to Jonah, who did a quick count of the bills, sifting, sorting, facing, opening his apron up so the change could cascade in from Bruce's.

"Good night, good night. I'll run this over the trailer. Where's Petr?" Clipped cadence.

"Had to make a pit stop on the way. Won't be long." It was clear Bruce loved being the communicator of essential information, feeling closer to the centre when he was able to.

Wyatt leaned against the game with his eyes closed, unconcerned with the prospect of falling asleep on his feet. The voices of the other three distanced themselves from him, as though he was listening to a television show from the fifties, or radio static. Trish was tired, she said she was tired, Des was wondering why Petr was taking so long, Bruce was gushy happy to be one-on-one with the women. Doors slammed, the hydraulics hissed from one of the big rides shutting down, a couple of stragglers late to leave the grounds were laughing, bouncing a ball back and forth. He could feel himself start to fall and jerked awake with a start, poked by a memory shard that the reason we do that is an evolutionary memory of trying not to fall out of trees. Petr was standing in front of him, smug inside his thin-lipped smile.

"Easy there, big boy. Can't have you falling down on the job…" He had grabbed Wyatt by the right biceps to hold him up, which Wyatt tightened instinctively. Petr gave it an odd, hard little squeeze and let go as Jonah returned to the group, breezing past them with a nod and heading towards the trailers and trucks. They fell in line beside him, wordless but for whispers coming from Des and Petr bringing up the rear.

33

Morning came in cruelly through the curtains. Wyatt didn't bother to fight the crawl back to consciousness. There were feet on the floor upstairs, creaking the joists like bones, back and forth, back and forth. Bruce's bedroom door was open. Everyone was up before him. If he was going to get a shower and a coffee before they left for the grounds, he'd have to hustle. He swung his legs over the edge of the hide-a-bed, shed the skin of his sleeping bag and went to get wet.

Bruce and Des were clearing the table when he came upstairs. Bruce handed him a cup of coffee and pointed to a pile of toast on the table. "Dig in. There's some raspberry jam. Mom always makes sure my favourite jam is well stocked haha. Milk is in the fridge." Wyatt grunted a thanks.

Petr was stretched out at the table, legs extended, hands clasped behind his head, eyes closed in repose. Smoke curled up from the ashtray in front of him, defiling and defining the golden morning light. He spoke without opening his eyes.

"Finally! I thought you'd never make it. The toast is cold, the coffee is almost gone. It's a helluva way to treat a Midway hero. You'd think someone who rubbed those royal elbows would get breakfast in bed." The drapes on his eyes opened. "All you had to do was ask." He tilted his head and gave Wyatt a wink.

Wyatt ignored him, fell into a chair and knuckled his fingers around the handle of a warmish cup of coffee.

Des spat a reprimand—"Oh, fuck off, Petr. Surely to God a coffee in peace isn't too much to ask at the start of the day. Not everyone's as chipper as you..." and continued putting the dishes in the washer. The wall clock ticked the rest of their time in the kitchen away until Jonah stuck his fresh scrubbed face around the corner. "Five minutes!" He and Trish went out to wait in the truck.

Day what of the run was this? He'd been trying to keep track, all the way back to Winnipeg, but the linear accounting of time was beginning to lose its relevance. Wyatt wasn't even sure what day of the week it was. He was somewhere between here and there; 'here' being sneakered feet scuffling back and forth back and forth in the joint, moving of their own volition the way the mouths of the marks slipping past opened and closed, part of his splintered consciousness marvelling at the muscle memory of walking, talking, breathing, wondering how it was possible for people to float along in their lives without just stopping; 'there' being the ever-present dreamscape that he woke up from each morning, before it started slipping away from the cloying, outstretched lifeline on his palms. The fence that separates the two was buckling, becoming easier to jump.

The Stampede was crowded every day, heaving with humans in the peak hours. It was barely noon of whatever day this was, and his eyes burned with cumulative grit. He splashed ice water from a cup onto his hands and rubbed it on his face, but no amount of cold, wake-up water worked. A voice he vaguely recognized as his own spewed half-hearted hustle at the marks as they meandered by, game-gawking like idiots. It sounded robotic even to him, reminding him of the first day in Winnipeg when he'd lost all focus. He had yet to grab any cash while Petr, fresh as a Goldwater daisy, seemed serene, strolling the sides of the inside, pulling in a slow but steady amount of dough.

Jonah's voice from the side surprised him, snuck up as it had from the blind side. "Hey, Wyatt. How's it going? You here, or ... somewhere else? You look like you're really dragging your ass. You're missing a lot of money." He had his mouth next to Wyatt's ear, close enough that Wyatt could smell his sour, coffee-tobacco breath. Petr stayed on the other side of the joint, absently spinning a ball in his hands.

"Don't take this the wrong way, but last night was last night. Long gone. You're not lighting it on fire today. You need to pick it up; I give you a guarantee here. No one else does that, remember. It's a leap of faith, you know, to do that rather than just give you fifteen points on your take. You'd starve if you kept up with this entropic hustle you've got going on now, and we can't have a refugee crisis in the Can, right? This is a big day. Step up and get the money from these fuckers." He slipped back into the crowd down the A line.

Petr sidled over, tossing the ball from one hand to the other.

"What's up? Trouble in paradise? A lot different under the unforgiving glare of the sun, isn't it? There's only room for one star in the sky in the daytime. I knew a guy that used to love taking a magnifying glass out on the hot days. Looked around his neighbourhood for anthills in abandoned, owners-at-work lawns. He'd spend hours sending up little puffs of smoke, signals of his sickness no doubt. Knew him well. Jesus, you look like shit. The boss giving you some grief?" The way he said 'boss' sounded derisive to Wyatt's still-burning ears.

"Yeah. No. It's okay, just a little pep talk. It's easy to forget we're in a fishbowl here. We spend so much time looking out it's easy to forget people are looking in. Not gonna lie, Petr, I'm hitting the fucking wall today. I've been at it a couple of weeks longer than you. I had the same zip as you during the first run, but I can't seem to catch up to what I lost in sleep on the overnight from Winnipeg. It is what it is. Wish it were something else…"

Petr absently tossed a ball into the Can. "Hey, we're all tired. Don't let this clean-shaven baby face fool you, I'm feeling the metaphorical

Hoover sucking the life out of me already. I looked in the mirror this morning and I swear I saw Nosferatu staring back at me. Had to check the ends of my arms to make sure my hands hadn't sprouted long, hideous nails. Remember the nails on Miss Stampede? How the hell do people get anything done with claws like that? That was a bizarre bit of carnivalizing going on last night. Epic. Syndicated channelling, triumph of the will! You were Superman. Not the one with the tights, more the Nietzschean type. Even more impressive given the lack of proper…stimulants in the mix. Coffee and cigarettes will only get you so far, until you find yourself empty as a tank, waiting for the Midway to happen to you."

He skipped over to the other side of the game and took five bucks from a couple of kids, smooth and slick and quick, three misses in under thirty seconds. He turned back to Wyatt.

"I met a guy at the stock trailer the other night. Works the Shoot Out the Star on the A line. Tall, balding. Lots of ink." Wyatt knew who he meant. He wore a bandanna and had the short sleeves of his Clown shirt rolled up, so his tattoos were exposed.

"Nice guy. He's from Thunder Bay. He's been with the show for ten years. He knows people in every town. The right people." Petr peered over the top of his sunglasses and kept eye contact. "I'm surprised, honestly, but he's got access to good blow and speed. He set me up the first night we got here. I wasn't expecting much quality." He elongated 'quality', a habit Wyatt had begun to be aware of with Petr; his stretching out of words when he was keen to make a point.

"I figured it'd be a combination of cotton candy and candy apple lacquer. Good for a little lift before the jangling sets in. Ever been on a speed rip? No? You start off fine. When I was first working on the last exhibition, the one where I met Jonah, I was smoking it. It was perfect for the project, the ideas were cascading, careening, coalescing. It was all I could do to keep up. There's a grace period, once you start with it, that allows you… access." The word was reluctant to leave his mouth.

"I was on such a roll with the art that I couldn't imagine abandoning it for any amount of time. You should have seen it, Wyatt. These huge tapestries spread out on the floor of my studio. I was dancing from one to the other into the wee small hours for weeks. Like a massive tip, but one you give a fuck about haha. Thought of that when I was watching you whip around the joint in Winnipeg on the last night there. My first exhibition. Yeah, I needed to keep the skin in the game and smoking speed was perfect for it. I could see the whole thing in front of me. Just needed the energy and focus to bring it to completion." He kept casually pulling in the occasional mark as he talked, multi-tasking, barely breaking the content of his thesis with the hustle-patter. 'Yeah, three for five, there you go thanks, oh no close one, here it is damn one last tr… aww' then back to the previously scheduled programming.

"The speed helped me carry the installation across the finish line. It got me noticed, so credit where it's due. It's perfect in finite, limited quantities. Kind of like …love, that way. Just great until it starts to wind itself up inside you. That's what happens. It starts to become the means rather than the ends and goes full Machiavelli on you. The centrifugal force got harder and harder to hold onto. It was taking more and more to lift off, and more again to maintain acceleration so I could bust through the limitations of gravity, of my atmosphere. By the time I finished with it, I was looking at another person in the mirror—a gaunt, sunken-cheeked poster boy for AA; Artists Anonymous. There was nothing to guide this 'other me' towards, nothing that he could point to as his own. The centre cannot hold. It outruns you."

Wyatt was taken aback by Petr's diatribe and his acknowledgement of vulnerability, albeit drug induced. They'd spent a lot of time inhabiting the same space; the week seemed forever longer than possible; circling, pacing, smoking, eating sleeping talking, jousting.... Of course, the blow had fueled it, but somewhere amidst the careening chaos of his raving, Wyatt got a peek, a Polaroid exposing in reverse, of Petr. He could almost name it, then it went away. He watched him pacing back and forth; one two three turn one two three turn, light a smoke, toss a ball, face a bill. There was a manic precision to every movement.

34

Of course, Wyatt knew what cocaine was. And speed. Everybody did. He was no stranger to drugs; mushrooms, acid and weed for the most part, usually in the context of an event or outing or a Grateful Dead concert where "too much of everything is just enough!" All things in moderation, including moderation. He'd tried coke a couple of times in the past but had found it to be an underwhelming disappointment. A bit of numb gums and sniffly nostrils but no buzz, no high that could justify the hundred bucks a gram the people he knew were paying for it.

He felt like a fly on a sticky strip the rest of the afternoon. He couldn't shake the exhausting fog in his head that had him feeling like everything was in slow motion. *Exhausting*, he thought. Exhaust. Coming out of the pipe, coming down the pipe, filling the game like a garage with a car left running. Left it running, they left it running but there's nowhere to run. He gave his head a shake, pulling himself back from the edge, back into the game. His feet scuffed back and forth inside the square, grabbing whatever sporadic cash there was. The crowd was steady but manageable, so they continued spelling each other off. He'd spent his break with his head pillowed on his folded arms on a rickety wooden table in the cafeteria. Lulled, carried slowly away to the hissing of the hydraulics, the peels of joyous horror from the Haunted House, the cloistered conversation of some ride guys a couple of seats away.

"You should have seen her. Man! Huge tits, just massive. And she wanted it for sure. I kept letting her and her friend stay on, just so I could see those hooters coming 'round the bend! She said she's coming back at the end of the night. Gonna be hoppin' behind the Himalayan tonight, boys haha!" and guttural agreement all around. Wyatt grunted derisively, slowly slipping away.

He woke to "Hey. Hey. Wake up!" and Jonah's bemused face staring at him from across the table. "You're a little late answering the bell, big boy. Everyone's dying to see you at the party." Wyatt made a futile attempt at ignoring the intrusion before crawling back to consciousness. 'Ugh…sorry, man. I must have drifted away when I put my head down for a minute." He started to get up but sat down when Jonah lit a smoke and leaned back in his chair. "It's okay. They'll be alright for a few minutes." He gestured to a coffee. "Thought you might need another one of those…"

"So whaddya think? We haven't had much quality time together ha. Is the carnival living up to the hype I hustled? You certainly had it rockin' in the Can last night. It was all the rage when I saw Bob and Greg this morning. They said they'd never seen anything like it. 'Better than the freak shows of days gone by', I think was the expressed sentiment. Pretty impressive…"

It felt good to be acknowledged. He was grateful as well as aware of how ludicrous accolades in this setting were. The idea of having done a good job while giant stuffed animals surrounded him wasn't something he was going to write home about. Still, he was more comforted by a little one-on-one time with Jonah than he would have expected.

"Yeah, definitely. You didn't oversell it. There's a lot more going on…as much as you want to see. That's the thing I like, or get, or want.

Like might be a strong word. But for sure, there's a metaphor around every bend, isn't there? You never know what's gonna happen, even with the most mundane exchange. It's what we talked about way back. Being ready for the moment. So, yeah. I guess I hadn't factored in the toll that's taken physically. Still getting my sea legs, I think. You saw me earlier. I was aware of not being there at the time, but fuck, there was nothing I could do about it. I felt like I was in my own movie…"

Jonah smiled. 'It's a crazy way to make a living. But maybe no crazier than shoe-horning your suited self onto a subway to get to a tower and slave under fluorescent lighting. Imagine how tired you'd be after thirty years of that. Pales in comparison—and you're so pale at the end of it…. This thing's a marathon, though, not a sprint. Remember that. It's not those manic, twisting tips that are going to get you over the finish line every day, it's the slow and steady. The long march. If you're there for the ones and twos through the day, you'll be ready when the vortex descends. You have to pace yourself. One mark at a time." He pushed himself back and up from the table, an ironic smile filling his eyes. "Alright kid, let's go get 'em!"

Wyatt followed him out of the food tent, elevated, adrenalized.

35

He stepped back into the game, giving no weight to the pointed 'I'll look at my watch and back at you' passive aggression from Petr. There were the beginnings of a tip happening. The three of them locked into it, pulling in some decent cash for the next hour, blowing a couple of animals out of the joint. Judging by the cash they all had in their hands, Wyatt figured they were well within the profit margin. A well-oiled machine….

The buzz from the coffee and the conversation with Jonah faded fast and furiously, the gravity comedown pulling the asphalt up to his knees. There was nothing left in the tank, and they still had a couple of hours before close. Petr slid along the boards next to him, popped a smoke out of his pack and stared at the passing people while he spoke. Bruce huddled in.

"I'm not sure if you're interested…" he performed a little snort… "but to be honest, I feel like I'm carrying the two of you today. You're dragging your asses. I think I might have a solution to this… dilemma. A way to ratchet up your game, as it were." He pulled a small, folded square of paper out of his pack.

"A little bit of blow, if you're interested. It's surprisingly good, given where we are. I was expecting Borax and sucrose…"

Bruce was practically gushing with anticipation. "Pick me, pick me!" His wrinkled fingers gently took the square from Petr. "This is just what the doctor ordered. Indeed!"

Petr rolled his eyes.

"Just a line, Bruce. Just do a line and bring it back. And be careful with it, for fuck's sake. Break it and you buy it, right?"

Bruce jumped out and headed towards the bathrooms in the bandstand.

"You trust him with that? I'd take odds on him spilling it or sneezing it into the toilet."

Petr shook his head. "He'll be alright. He wouldn't dare…"

Bruce was back in ten minutes, jumping the boards of the game with exaggerated enthusiasm, putting on a show. He passed the packet back to Petr, hauling a couple of large sniffs through his nostrils, making the point.

"Oh yeah, feel the love baby, feel the love!" He grabbed a couple of balls off the table and juggled them with one hand, barking, "Here we go folks, we're on the home stretch. Get the big ones here! One in wins!" A beefy cowboy and his wife lumbered toward the Can.

Petr smirked, nodding his head towards Bruce. 'Exhibit A. Whaddya, say? Game?" He mimicked a talk-show host: "This offer won't last long, folks. Act now and get a free Ginsu knife to cut the lines with. That's right—free!" He had the packet in his palm, hidden from the eyes of the passers by.

Wyatt remembered something then, took a quick synaptic trip back to his twelve-year-old self, sitting on a log in the woods by the school, staring at the cigarette he'd stolen from his mother. He'd been aware at the time that he was making a consequential decision, one that would take him down certain paths and negate others. He knew it was true, even at twelve. To light it was to commit to…something else. An underworld that was more in sync with the booze and beatings that were happening at home than the top-of-the-class marks he was getting in school. He'd held the cigarette between his fingers for a long, lonely moment before lighting it, sealing the deal. He took the packet from Petr.

The bathroom under the bandstand reverberated with the low-end sounds from the Midway. Bass booming from speakers by the big rides he could feel in his feet as he sat backwards on the shitter, facing the tank, the thudding thump of the crowd leaving the bandstand, cascading down the stairs. The walls of the stall shook. The door to the bathroom sprung open and smashed closed, mouthing the carnival sounds underneath boisterous man-voices, telling the world to wait while "I take a fucking piss." Self-assured words echoed off the yellow cinder blocks, side by side at the urinals, eyes straight ahead, "look ma, no hands" as they evicted the ten-dollar beer. "Good show, eh?" "Oh yeah, they fucking rocked it for sure, man. For sure!" He had forgotten about the country concert happening.

Wyatt had his knees tight together, with a pack of smokes balanced on top. He carefully cracked the cardboard square open, lifting the top two flaps up and over as though it were an origami that he'd need to remember how to return to its original form. Inside, the white, crystalline powder had settled. He carefully let some of it slide from the crimped corner of the cardboard onto the smooth surface of the smokes. Just a little bit, enough for two small white lines, parallel, like a highway, then gently set the smokes on top of the tank and folded the packet back up, relieved at not having sneezed or spilled it. He stood up, but kept his head bowed so he couldn't be seen above the stall as people came and went with the slamming door.

He'd left his apron in the joint—you weren't allowed to walk around the grounds with it—but pulled a twenty that he'd borrowed from it out of the front pocket of his shorts. He wound it up tight and bent over the blow, stared at the two benign lines, feeling twelve years old and twenty-five at the same time. As soon as he heard the door shut and the room go quiet, he dove in, snorting line up each nostril. He remembered seeing people rubbing their gums with the residue in movies, and so, did.

Wyatt felt the change almost immediately. The exhaustion dust was broomed from behind his widened eyes, electric air flew through his nose down into his expanding lungs. He ran his tongue over his numbing gums, marvelling. The air was cleaner; even under the buzzing fluorescent lights in the bathroom, the air seemed clearer, the edges of things in sharper relief. He clenched and unclenched his jaws, teeth clicking. It was so different from the time he had tried it before. So, this was what all the fuss was about…. He hauled the stall door open, secret packet safe in his front pocket, and strode out of the bandstand back onto the Midway.

The crackling carnival world of screams, lights and laughter was wound around cotton candy and deep-fried mini-donut smells. There was power and purpose in his legs as he high-stepped down the game line, slickly weaving in and out of the overflowing tips, around hand-in-hand meanderers, ducking underneath ropes that tethered the joints to the blacktop. He skipped over the heavy, rubber mats covering the myriad power cables, thrilled with the surge of purpose that now inhabited his head. Wyatt had been a runner for a while during his university days and was familiar with the second wind. It was amazing to him that he could feel this rush of energy so quickly and palpably. It carried him back to the Milk Can with a smile.

Bruce and Petr had a decent tip happening. He made a beeline for the Milk Can, 'scuse me and pardon me'ing through the throng, deftly jump-stepping over the boards and into the game. Balls were flying from all four sides, clanking off the rim of the can to oohs and aaahs, bouncing onto the table and ground. He grabbed his apron, scooped up three balls, staking his place, pacing quickly back and forth, beckoning the marks to try a little harder, to make it happen, to get one in. His voice was clear and loud, cutting off Bruce's ineffectual ramblings with what he was sure was superior patter.

"Who's gonna be the lucky one, folks? Bears in the air waiting for a new home away from home far from the Midway! Who wants a forever friend? Three for five, keep it in the air keep that hope alive. That's it right there, oh no so close and yet so far, three more for you, of course!"

He was locked into the spin and swirl of grabbing cash, picking up balls, keeping the third eye on the shooters who were leaning in a little too far, bringing the arm gate down in front of them. "Gotta back off a bit there, sir, okay? Perfect, thank you very much and thank you for shopping at the Milk Can this fine evening. You wouldn't want to win with an unfair advantage doubt if you'd be able to sleep at night haha! Three more?" picking up on the rhythm pumping out of the Himalayan speakers, bobbing to Sinead O'Connor's "Emperor's New Clothes." He could see the colour of every eye, sense the release points as the balls were tossed in the air, calculate his manipulative movements with subtle, effective accuracy. The rim of the Can rang and rippled.

They worked the tip together, what really felt tight and together, for the first time. Eye contact from the corners of the joint, quick smiles and a wink towards a live one that could be milked for more cash. A nod down below when they were picking up the balls of failed attempts. Bruce's smile was carved into his face, his child-like joy at being on, and in on it with the two of them palpable, innocent, and in truth he was doing a great job of keeping his side of the game engaged but under control. He was focussed enough to not blow a bear out too soon, animated and goofy in the way that he was goofy, 'awww shucks'ing his way through the vibrations in the joint.

Petr was a portrait of grim efficiency, a cigarette stuck in the corner of his mouth while he monosyllabically urged the players on. "Good. Close one. Too bad, jeez. One more?" His movements were less cartoonish than Bruce's, not as flowing and circular as Wyatt's. Controlled, refacing the bills in his left hand as he grabbed them, swiftly setting balls on the counter in front of the marks in a way they wouldn't roll off. Arms bent at 90 degrees, rod-straight back and neck supporting his nearly motionless head. His shifting eyes kept track of the essentials, wary and ready.

Wyatt had come to recognize the point in a tip when it had peaked. It was a subtle transition, from group dynamic, osmotic enthusiasm and intensely focussed competitive spirit, to an entropic waning of commitment to the glory of winning the big prize. You had to be ready when things started to turn and try and find a way to keep it going if it seemed like the potential was there. A good, two-deep tip might last for up to fifteen minutes, money and balls flying like they were inside a bingo ball dispenser.

During a good one, there would be core players who'd stick with it the entire time, more methodical if they were experienced, likely less disciplined and easier to manipulate if not. Wyatt sensed that if they timed it properly, they could extend the life of this tip. The wads of cash all three had accumulated meant they were in the black. AC/DC blew out of the sound system on cue.

The three of them made eye contact as one of the shooters decided to pack it in, turning away with a reluctance that smelled of disappointment and resignation. A young guy with an innocent look about him, and Wyatt just knew he was a nice young guy, could see it as plain as the Pledge on the can, had been in the tip from the beginning, trying to win a bear for his girlfriend who wore an impossibly white t-shirt. She was patient, beautiful in that wholesome way he'd never been able to resist; high cheeks, blond hair pulled through the back of her ballcap, bright green eyes. He looked to Petr and subtly tilted his head towards them. He nodded and passed it on over to Bruce on the other side who, to Wyatt's surprise, got it.

He slid over beside them, could smell her fresh-as-a-summer rain, and set a ball on the counter in front of him. Spoke in low tones.

"A freebie. You've been at it for a while, man, coming so close." He gave the girl a wink. "Let's get one for the dreamers out there, okay? Stick and stay and make it pay..." The young guy's wide-eyed surprise and genuine joy was sad and beautiful to Wyatt. The idea that a free softball in a carnival joint would elicit gratitude was ridiculous, as well as an affirmation that no matter where or what, the moment is the substance of what matters. Give. Get. He retreated to a corner. Bruce and Petr did the same, timing their retreat with the forward lean and backspin-launched shot from the young guy.

Wyatt had been practicing what Jonah had called "the dark arts of the Midway" for the best part of a month by now. He'd developed an affinity for what was happening beneath the shiny, smiling surface of those gathered around the joint. Time on the inside had convinced him they were deluding themselves into thinking it was just a game, as though the wins and losses that happened were a result of random chance, or luck, or could explained away as a product of experience or skill, or the lack thereof. The blow in his bloodstream had widened his eyes to the potential of going beyond the subtle tricks of physical manipulation; a timely scratch of the nose, bending down to get a ball as someone is shooting, a volume increase in the patter or walking to the other side of the game to distract, and expanded the foul lines of what was possible. The summer night air felt molasses-thick with it.

They were a lovely couple, wholesome and holy, flashing perfect smiles and holding hands on the Ferris Wheel, doing no harm, standing on the edge of a life together, performing good deeds as they raised a family. Wyatt wanted them to win and swore to make it happen, entering and embracing another level of control in the joint.

As the ball floated through the air, the carnival slowed to a crawl, the Midway sounds elongating. The young guy's hand hovered after the release, fingers extended, his girlfriend's tongue setting softly on the lower lip of her perfectly parted mouth as she watched. An errant shot from a Stetsoned denizen on the other side missed the can entirely, bounced off the table, rolled to a stop by his foot. The low hanging lights hummed under an elephant trunk. The Milk Can collective inhaled when the chosen ball rang off the far side of the rim and popped straight up, recharging the remaining air in the joint with anticipation. Wyatt had neither inhaled nor exhaled; aware he was in the middle of the moment. There was the sixth sense inhabiting him; a knowing, without it being logically possible. It was almost as though his eyes were crossed behind his forehead, focussed on the ball, gently forcing it up and over as it clanked off the other side of the rim and began a slow drain swirl towards the waiting hole.

The temperature of the volume in the game grew, all joining in with the rising chorus of *ooooooaaaaahhhh* that was sutured to the fate of the softball. Wyatt scanned the perimeter as it became clear to him that the third-eye bending of the laws had been successful. A pair of manicured hands with a chunk of compressed carbon on the ring finger clasped in prayer before Botoxed lips. The redneck family of four beside Petr leaned forward as one, all eyes on deck, wide between blinks. Bruce blew a lungful of smoke that slowly shrouded the table. To already know.... The ball went around the contours of the rim, then around lower, stopped for a moment as it snugged into the hole before disappearing.

A roar flew up the flagpole that buried the bang of the ball as it hit the boards at the bottom of the Can. Bruce was clapping, knocking sparks off his cigarette. Petr had the smug smile of a mouse eating a cat.

"He did it, Daddy, he did it" from the smallest of the redneck family kids while Stetson man turned away in resigned disgust, having been there for the whole tip, had had his ball knocked away as it began its descent to what he had been sure was a moment of glory, not concerned about the money because he had lots of money from his job supplying oil rigs with valves and gaskets but for fuck's sake a hundred bucks and still couldn't win a goddamn bear for the wife?

The couple, though…Wyatt felt like a master of ceremonies, a presider over the nuptials, and granter of wishes. The young guy had a smile a mile wide, blushing bright as she wrapped her arms around his neck, knocking her ball cap askew with so much spontaneous joy and beauty that Wyatt wanted to do the same to her, flashing briefly back to when it might have been a possibility. All things at once. He allowed himself the indulgence before settling into the role of benevolent provider. He caught her eye and gave another little wink.

"Well how about that everyone? See how easy it is if you stick and stay and make it pay. We've got a winner!" Petr ceremoniously lifted the can off the table and retrieved the ball like he was pulling a rabbit out of a hat, holding it high while the tip continued to cheer and clap. Wyatt looked at the girl. He spoke right through her.

"Alright, you get your pick of the litter, the best for the best! What's your pleasure?" She smiled at him innocently, perfectly. A couple of the kids were yelling "Elephant! Bear, blue bear! Giraffe!" She arched her eyebrows into a question mark to the young man and said in a sweet, low voice, 'Elephant? Do we want the elephant?" "Sure. Yeah, whatever you want. I can't believe it! I've never won anything in my life!"

Wyatt couldn't help himself." Well, you've got her, haven't you? She's a prize for sure…" He flashed her his award-winning smile before realizing he was sliding a little too far over the line, retreating and refocussing on the task at hand.

"You've got more luck than most of us haha! So, the elephant? The elephant it is!" He nodded to Bruce, who stepped up onto the table with the long, hanging hook, pulling the elephant down from the plush-packed roof. He gave it to Wyatt. The tip had paused to witness the moment of redemption.

"Thank you very much, Vanna. Now, sir, if you'd just step away from the game a little bit. A bit more. A bit more… there! Alright everybody…on three!"

The people joined into the 1, 2, 3 with enthusiasm, cheering as the elephant flew to the waiting arms of the couple. They laughed, hugged each other and walked away with the elephant astride the young man's shoulders. Wyatt watched them melt into the throng, following the bobbing of the white elephant on the guy's shoulders for as long as he could.

He turned back to the game and dug in, well infused with a new sense of the possible. There was no denying what he'd just experienced. A manifestation of esoteric theory he'd flirted, flaunted and waltzed with for what felt like forever. But here? How was it possible to affect the course of things, the physical world, with your will…? The same thing he'd often maligned among the Tarot, crystal-chakra set was there, wasn't it? The self-help, consciousness-precedes-form mantra worked as well, maybe even better, with empiric measurability of cash and prizes in this asphalt emporium that was the antithesis of incensed air and windchimes above the runes.

The three of them worked well-oiled for the rest of the night, their nostrils flaring as they roamed the 64-foot perimeter inside the joint. Flared nostrils, he thought. Horses. Horse. Heroin. Ha! Wyatt was aware of the waning buzz of the cocaine (blow back, Petr called it when he mentioned it), but it wasn't the come down you'd get with, say, a psychedelic. More like coming in for a landing than a crash. Exacerbated, he was certain, by the revelations of the evening. Of course, he was aware of nightmare stories of cocaine addiction; the rattling, twitching, thieving abandonment of the tether. This wasn't that. They'd had a wicked night in the can, by far the most money he'd pulled in up to this point, and he'd also verified suspicions they were onto something big. They were warmed with congenial afterglow as they tied down the joint for the night. Even Bruce was in on the joke.

36

Jonah's eyebrows rose appreciably when they handed in the cash at the Birthday Game. He did a quick count.

"Well… that's a pretty good night. I snuck over there for a peek around nine-thirty. Looked like you tapped into the cone in the Can.

A lot more zip in the line than earlier today." He looked at Petr, then Wyatt, lips pursed, and head tilted. "The trick is to maintain it." He left to make the deposit.

Des and Trish still looked fresh despite the twelve-hour day. Hair back, smiles sparkling, it was something that Wyatt hadn't been able to understand. He always felt there was a complicated layer of life covering him by closing time. A combination of sweat, soot, dust and diesel. Even thick throat sticky smells of cotton candy, apples and deep-fried mini donuts coated his exposed skin and infiltrated the clothes he wore. His hair curled up, sticky grease gross. He surprised himself with his words.

"Look at the two of you! How the hell do you manage it? Is there a room in the game somewhere you go to reinvigorate?" A warm laugh made its way around the circle.

"We've got more of a portal. Or is it a Porta Potty? Which is it, Trish? Where do we go to stay so shiny?" The two of them laughed in unison. In key, even.

There was a flicker of eye contact between them and Petr, a little nod. The mirror, mirror on the mental wall spun like a disco ball as things quickly came clear to Wyatt. He'd been beating himself up for being so beat. The last one to drag his ass out of bed. The hitting of walls in the middle of the day on the Midway while everyone else seemed to be on their game. He had attributed his lethargy to not having recovered from the overnighter from Winnipeg, but it had been days since they'd dug in in Calgary. The familiar feeling of hindsight clairvoyance descended.

Des and Petr up awake all night, but it 'wasn't like that'? What was it like, then? There wasn't a 'thing' between them, though they were sleeping together. In the same bed. But not sleeping. Keeping the pipes clean, the passageways unblocked, air flowing, thoughts flying, connecting on that other level. The real one. Not sleeping together, instead zip-a-dee-doo-dahing through the night, talking talking talking. And Jonah… with all the years, expert in pacing, timing. Of course, he and Trish had their own folded packets sitting on the bedstand. He'd heard their springs bouncing from his bed in the basement. When all that should have been consummated, consumed, sleep welcoming, they were accelerating.

37

The remaining Calgary mornings of the Greatest Show on Earth slid into a collective routine now that the cat was out of the bag. Coffee, cigarettes and a couple of lines off a mirror or some speed slid into a half-emptied cigarette before hitting the Midway for the eleven-o'clock opening. The final weekend was busy all the way through, but they got away with two in the games for the afternoons, which allowed time for the person on break to tune up with a toot and spend some rare one-on-one time with each other in the canteen.

The talking came a lot quicker without the blanket weight of weariness on Wyatt. A couple of hours in the joint, a walk around the grounds, a line in the bathroom. He'd swing by the Birthday Game to go on break with whoever was tapping out for an hour. Quality time, elbows on wobbly tables with a shared ashtray in the middle, shining eyes with marble-wide black-hole pupils, taking it all in.

Trish was beautiful. As often as Wyatt had played the "I'm above ogling the eyes, lips, legs, breasts of women, I'm an enlightened feminist, not a fantasizing fetishist" card, he couldn't not bask in her blond beauty as she sat across from him. Gorgeous green eyes that didn't seem to blink. An hour was much more as his mind wandered in and out of conversation.

"My family has refused to believe I'm doing this! It's not exactly what they pictured their little girl would be up to for the summer before grad school; I don't think it's come up much in conversation at the golf club. Dad's a lawyer, a successful one. He's a partner in a big firm, and Mom's heavily involved with the Liberal Party. Good Catholics, so I've got four siblings. None of us are quite what they expected. Two of us are gay, one is super right wing, my oldest brother still lives at home, literally in the basement. Then there's me, the artist. Apple of my daddy's eye. We've got enough money that I get indulged. We have a summer place up in the Muskokas on Skeleton Lake, and the big house in Etobicoke.

"I started in engineering. Bizarre, right? For a very brief time we all did what was expected of us. Dad came from a poor background. Being rural Catholic meant you were on the losing team most of the time. He worked his ass off to get where he is. Sawmill in the summers, part-time job while he did his BA and law degree in the winters. Him and Mom assumed the trajectory would continue; doctors, lawyers... engineers. It skipped a generation with us! I bought in for a little bit, did that first year in Electrical, but being away from home for the first time.... I went a little wild. That's all it took to realize there was more going on, more options than anyone had led me to believe; just the getting away."

Wyatt was nodding at all the right times. She had a lilting, soothing voice that he nestled into.

"Being here feels like a natural progression. I got into art history first before I switched to a BFA. The transition from studying to doing. Them that can't, teach, and all that. That's where Petr and I connected." She gave her head a little shake and chuckled "Petr" before continuing.

"I had been focussed on painting before I met him. Pretty basic stuff, faux Group of Seven impressionist bullshit for the most part. I got to be pretty good at faking it, but even if no one else notices, you know you are, right?"

Wyatt nodded.

"What I loved about Petr was that he was trying to do something different than the rest of us. He was inserting himself into his art. You should have seen some of his assignments, Wyatt. Truly… confrontational. Being around him changed things for me; got me going in a different artistic direction. Or at least in some sort of artistic direction. I could never be moved by most of the art I saw because I couldn't feel any movement in it. Just static, stolid strokes. Not all of it, of course. The greats are the greats, but there aren't a great many of them, are there?"

Wyatt name-checked a few he knew, eager to impress. "Oh, for sure. Van Gogh; his stuffs fluid, dripping in those brilliant colours. Dark and dirty Rembrandt. I love the big skies of Turner, ya know? So much happening you can hear it!" He almost convinced himself he knew what he was talking about. Trish smiled and carried on.

"Right. I was a lot more comfortable working with things than painting them. Objects, material. A bird's beak, a piece of wire and some wood, bent and bowed to new purpose. It didn't really matter what it was. The idea of molecular motion, where nothing was permanent. Things are inherently alive whether they were breathing or not. Art should be like that. The old saying, art imitates life. I see it differently. Art is life. God, that sounds pretentious. Does this make any sense?" More nodding from Wyatt.

"Petr…he was actualizing that in and out of class. The last thing he did…. You weren't there, I keep forgetting. He did this last huge installation as his thesis, it was incredible. The place was packed, these massive canvases hanging precariously over the room, stations of the cross, really. He was that audacious and perfectly arrogant, thinking he could lead the sheep to salvation or slaughter or something; everyone wandering underneath, dressed in black, a black cape—honest to God! Blood red lips from the merlot.... To have constant circular movement within the art and beneath it? It was special. One of those rare nights when the world gets compressed. And expanded."

Wyatt was leaning hard on his elbows, nodding, holding her eyes, at the same time corkscrewing back to the devastating winter night when the house of cards he'd tried to keep together had collapsed. A flutter of familiar butterflies threatened to lift off, down deep. How was it things like this happened, the coalescence of circumstance into concrete consequence? Maybe it was inescapable, the result of ignoring the signs. He started slipping down the rabbit hole of introspection, hearing but not processing anything Trish was saying, watching her mouth move. With a conscious effort, he brought her back into focus.

"It turned out to be an insane night. Des was drinking; we went out for a couple before the show, but she went from zero to sixty in like ten seconds. Whipped out some coke in the bathroom. I'd never been around it before, well, before now, but it was obvious something was going south as soon as we got there. She knew Petr from a class they were taking together. They're just friends, obviously. We went to the show to support, you know. Solidarity with the artists and all of that. Can you imagine trying to organize a rally with artists? Herding cats. Anyway, it was bizarre. The two of them were tight together, going from panel to panel. Standing under each one with their heads bent back, Petr moving his hands this way, and that. Almost conjuring. I swear, it was like watching a couple of estranged members of Russian aristocracy, strolling through their personal palace. Rasputin and Anastasia. The party was rocking all around them. At some point I stopped paying attention to them, but when I heard the window smash,

I knew who it was without even looking. Crazy." She shook her head, lit another cigarette and continued.

"That's the night I met Jonah." Wistful, warm tone. "To be honest, most of the party and beyond is a blur. Des and I had a pretty good buzz on by the time we arrived, and there were gallons of free wine at the opening. I think Petr might have gotten a sponsorship from some guy he knew. I remember Des laughing…manically laughing…when I went over to see what was happening. I'd never been around anyone in that state before. It was really fucked up. Petr was more amused than upset, standing with his arms folded across his chest, like he'd won a prize or gotten a good mark. I'll never forget that. It looked like he was taking credit for it. People were grabbing their shit and rushing down the stairs as though a fire alarm had been pulled, when I saw this blond guy—Jonah—slip through them coming up the stairs. It made me think of a salmon jumping upstream through rushing water. He looked like he was ten feet tall. It was mayhem. Jonah made a beeline for Des. I remember he had his arm around her, talking to her, but once the dust had settled, she was gone."

Wyatt shook his head in authentic awe. How was it Jonah… Somehow, they'd ended up in this lab experiment together, pulled into the centre from all over the country. It didn't make any sense, at least not from the outside. Trish crushed her smoke out and rose. "Wow. That hour flew! Gotta get back to the joint. Still not used to calling it that haha!" She brightened him up with a smile, and he walked out to the Midway with her.

38

They fell into a predictable routine in the Milk Can for the last few days in Calgary. Coffee at the house in the morning, and a line to get going in the game in the early afternoon. Petr had gotten each of them a gram from his contact. A couple more lines to ride the peak waves of action in the Can. A hundred bucks a gram, which Wyatt figured he easily could make last for the rest of the run and beyond; maybe six lines a day to keep the energy level up, but only on days when he felt it was truly necessary. Maybe a bit of speed smoked. He was sleeping better, rested enough to not need a blast just to function. It didn't feel like a drug. Just a method for the madness.

They tore down on the second Sunday and headed north to Edmonton. They didn't get the same truck from Greg this time, so they had to split up. Jonah drove one of the Clown-faced quarter tons with Trish riding shotgun. The rest of them decided to take the bus. The consensus was three hours on the Hound was manageable; maybe get a nap and wake up in the City of Champions.

Wyatt was again surprised that the same sense of separation that bound them on the carnival grounds applied out here in the other world, though with the roles reversed. They wandered in the bus station like it was still the Midway. Staff taking tickets at the counter, staff in uniforms. People in lines. Shitty food in the canteen. Petr had donned the mantle of tour guide, pointing out all the perceived absurdities as they walked around the terminal, arms wide and barker voice loud enough to draw timid glances from the people in the rows of seats.

"What you see over here, ladies and gents, is the infamous Greyhound Bus, long regarded as an indispensable facilitator of escape, freedom and fantasy! Gotta get out of town in a hurry? Luck running a little low? Happiness is waiting for you, and you know it is! It's the journey, not the destination! Well, don't hesitate a minute more, folks. Climb on in and you can win! Just imagine being your very own blues song, roaming down a weary, fevered white-line highway to make it to your own personal crossroads at midnight! It's the stuff of the American dream! He who hesitates is…. lost!" He took a bow and the three of them slow-clapped appreciatively.

They tumbled into the back of the bus like high school kids. Once they'd pulled away from the terminal, the bus banked its way around the city, left-right-left, until it crawled onto the on-ramp and headed north. After a few minutes of chatter, the talk Petred out. They'd been up for over twenty-four hours straight, through the last day of Stampede and the tear down. Wyatt's head had a mind of its own, falling onto the seatback. The horizon opened as the suburbs dwindled. A couple of oil pumps pistoned beyond a herd of brown beef cattle. The blue Rocky Mountains rose out of the land, far away to the west. Every cliché in the book, he thought, as his eyes fell shut.

He was woken by the decelerating bus. It geared down and wound around the streets of Edmonton. Wyatt's eyes reluctantly cracked open. Bruce was still out for the count beside him. Des and Petr were murmuring in the back seat. He turned around and they stopped talking, breaking their eye-lock to regard him in tandem. Petr's eyebrows had that aggressive arch to them that Wyatt had come to dislike as well as distrust. Des had a thin, hidden-teeth smile happening. He opened his mouth to ask what they were talking about, thought better of it and cuffed Bruce in the side of the head to wake him up. Bruce's glasses fell in between the cracks in the seats when he stood up, so he had to lie down halfway on the aisle to retrieve them. Petr and Des snickered, which made Wyatt want to defend him, for reasons he didn't understand. The sense of collective they'd been giddy with when they'd gotten on had evaporated. He leaned down, cracked heads with him, whispered a "for fuck's sake, Bruce" before grabbing the glasses off the floor and handing them to him. The bus jerked to a stop in front of the station. They rose as one and staggered off.

Bruce crawled into the belly of the bus and tossed their bags out while the driver berated him. "Get the hell out of there!" He had to skitter across the parking lot to catch up to the others, who were already squeezed into the backseat of the taxi. Des gave the driver the address of the motel they'd be staying at for the duration of Klondike Days. Wyatt watched the world of his new temporary home pass by, block by block. He thought of the repetitive panels in the backgrounds of old cartoons. Des and Petr were exaggerating their sniffing on either side of him, in on their own little "we didn't sleep, we just did lines in the can at the back of the bus" joke.

The taxi made one last rounding turn and pulled into the parking lot of the motel. Bruce paid the twenty-dollar fair, which they all promised to get back to him. It was a functional, low-budget, two-storey motel, the Dew Drop Inn, with kitchenettes! according to the sign. It had an entropic sixties/seventies feel that reminded Wyatt of the picture where Martin Luther King had been shot in Memphis. It felt like it was in black and white. Des and Petr came back from the office with the keys. The four of them hauled their bags to the unit that was farthest from the road. A few carnies had already arrived. Wyatt recognized a couple of people from the games, and a few from the rides were sitting out front of their wide windowed rooms, manspreading in aluminum lawn chairs, having a noon beer break…

All four of them crashed in the suite for a few hours. There were two small rooms to the left of the kitchenette that Petr and Des retreated to while Wyatt and Bruce took the hide-a-bed and couch, respectively. They drew the brown/orange curtains shut, drifting off to their own silos for a few hours.

39

Triplet knocking on the door hauled Wyatt slowly back to the land of the living, the late afternoon light cramming itself into his reluctant eyeballs when he opened the door for Jonah.

"Room service! Rise and shine everybody haha. We're supposed to be at the grounds in half an hour. Hope you all some rest. It's a long one tonight and an early one tomorrow." Jonah stepped in past Wyatt, grabbed a pillow off the couch and whacked Bruce in the head with it.

"Let's go, old man." Des and Petr's voices rounded the corner from the other room. Des's rose a bit in pitch and volume. Wyatt heard something about "we're almost out" and "what the fuck…" and indecipherable mutterings from Petr that sounded defensive. Jonah stood in the kitchenette, head tilted, looking amused. "Hey you guys, we've gotta get going." The beds and bones creaked into action.

The novelty of setting up in a new, asphalted flatland had lost its appeal for Wyatt, though Bruce seemed as enthusiastic as ever. The three of them in the Milk Can had the drill down by now, taking turns running to the trailers for the joint material and stock, often working silently while they put it together. They were up, stock hung and tied down by nine o'clock, then wandered down the line towards the Birthday Game. The rides were in various states of construction. Wyatt thought of Meccano kits he'd gotten for Christmas as a kid. They sidled up to the game just as Jonah was lowering the sides for the night. "Oh, excellent! In sync, wouldn't you say? Timing is the key to comedy… Good work."

They stood in a ragged circle, batting around some ideas on what to do for the rest of the night. Des wanted music. "It feels like a year since I've heard music that wasn't cranked out of a Midway ride. Wouldn't a couple of hours of live music be great?" There was no response from the group. Bruce wanted to get some decent food at a restaurant. "Even a pub, just something that isn't out of this fucking deep-fried shit on site," he implored in a whiny, utterly dismissible voice. Trish wanted to get back to the motel and "just sleep. I just want to sleep." The hum-haw went back and forth for several minutes, the collective paralysis setting in, when Greg appeared at the edge of the gathering.

"Jonah…" His voice was, bright, sharp and pointed, piercing the circle and stopping their digression cold. They turned to him as one.

"How's it going? Looks like you've got your crew working like a well-oiled machine; both joints up before most everyone else. Wondering what you're up to now. BillyBob is having a little gathering and was hoping you could make it. Maybe with your people." He gave an all-encompassing nod to the group. Wyatt saw the Ray-Bans hanging from a string around his neck, the Polo sweater, the leather deck shows and designer jeans and was sure he'd not have a lot to say to him. They looked at each other, the grounds, the Ferris Wheel catching the last of the scarlet sunset off its top seats, and waited for Jonah to make the call.

"Well, that's mighty kind of BillyBob, Greg. Honestly, I don't think I've even talked to him since we left Florida. Mighty kind. I've got a tired and hungry bunch here. Not sure if they're game…" Greg climbed over top of Jonah's voice, insisting. "He's got the barbecue on and some cold ones on ice. Seems to think you've got an interesting bunch with you this year, and I'd have to say I agree!" He looked directly at Trish and Des. "And it's not often that we get barkers of such… quality." Wyatt hated how he let the word drip off his tongue and felt himself wanting to rise to the defence of the woman until he saw Des flash him a coquettish smile.

"I don't know. What do you guys think? Are we gonna resort to the tyranny of democracy and take a vote on it? Sounds more like BillyBob is making us an offer we can't refuse. Food, beer and collegial discourse." Des was nodding her head; Trish was staring down at her cowboy boots while the rest of them waited for a decision to happen.

"Alright, sure. Thanks," said Jonah. "Give us a few minutes, and we'll head over." Greg nodded and walked towards the RV area. Silence umbrellaed the group until he was past the candy apple concession, well out of earshot.

Jonah spoke first. "Well, that's a wow. I've been working for the Clown for seventeen years and I rarely make it backstage. That's the high-rent district, the gated community, the other side of the moat. Not that it was ever on the agenda anyway, being in with the puppet masters, but still…" He lit a smoke, which got them all digging into their pockets, and looked from Des to Trish.

"Call me old fashioned, but I think BillyBob's noticed I may have upped the genetic quality of my staff this year. It's not just the ride guys and marks hanging around watching to see if January is the winner on the next roll…." He looked at the two women over the top of his glasses before continuing.

"There's more than BillyBob lusting after you two going on here, though. I get a feeling they—not just him, but the twins and Greg and the rest—may have noticed something different in our joints. More the Milk Can, I guess; the interest in the Birthday Game is self-evident." Des and Trish curtsied on cue. He turned to Wyatt.

"When we were in Winnipeg and you were doing your dervish bit, Greg was watching you the whole time. He never does that. I could have sworn there were times where the ball looked like it was going directly in, and it would…move a bit. By the force of your focus or something like that. It looked like that to me. Greg was more intrigued by one guy whipping up a tip like that than by how he was doing it, but still… And that night at the Stampede with the Miss Cow Patty… the twins saw that. Greg was there too. So, we're on the radar for whatever reason." He shared a maniacal smile around the horn "We're going in!"

40

The group dissolved their circle and walked to the end of the line, then formed single file to slide between the reefer barricades. They came out the other end into a quieter, self-contained world. The lighting was lower, muted. Patio lanterns loosely strung above makeshift decks like multi-coloured teeth, smoke and smells from barbecues curlicuing. The guy who managed the rides, Joe, looked up from his sizzling sausages as they wandered past, grunted a "Hey" to Jonah. Wyatt caught him eyeballing the women out of the corner of his eye. They tightened up their group knot as they came closer to the high-rent district, where the twins, Greg and Bob, had the largest RVs. Taking it all in, no one said a thing.

BillyBob crashed the screen door of his trailer open and greeted them in a loud, barker voice with a syrupy Southern drawl.

"Well, there y'all are! Alright. Fantastic! C'mon in! Don't be shy now, that's it. Watch your step. Come right in!" Jonah led them up the steps past BillyBob's mile-wide smile and into the huge RV. The group clustered in the kitchen area. Jimmy Buffet's "Why Don't We Get Drunk and Screw" was playing in the background.

Greg was sitting at a small table against the wall to the left, a Budweiser in front of him. He sat back in his chair, its front legs off the floor, and nodded as BillyBob ushered the group towards the long, leather, semi-circular couch at the end of the room.

"Sit. Go on now, y'all grab a seat. What'll ya have? Beer? I've got beer, bourbon… whatever you want. I'll get some steaks on in a bit, once we're properly introduced and such." They dominoed onto the seat while Greg took a pull off his beer and started talking.

"Good to get out of Calgary, eh? That was a good run, mind you. We're up eleven percent from last year, which is great, but I don't know about you guys—I've had my fill of Stetsons for the year!" They all laughed dutifully, awkwardly.

"It looks like you had an even better run, Jonah. Your joints are up over twenty points from last year. We're dying to know your secret! I'll take twenty points over eleven any day of the goddamn week!" Jonah shifted in his seat, took a drink and sat forward, elbows on his knees.

"Well…hard to say, Greg. I'd like to think it's a result of my motivational leadership, but truth be told it's got a lot to do with the crew this year. A cut above for sure. Have you met them?" He went down the line with the introductions, Greg and Bob nodding to the guys and smiling big *hello nice to meet you*'s to Des and Trish. Jonah shrugged. "Sometimes the stars align, don't they?"

Greg agreed. "Oh, I hear you. I've been doing this a lot longer than you, and I've had every combination of skill, work ethic and incompetence you can imagine. You work with what you have." BillyBob fell into the seat across from him and lit a Marlboro, then absently peeled the label off his beer bottle.

"The thing is, these numbers are outside the margin of error, to quote the pollsters. I think I understand why the Birthday Game is up." He tossed his head towards the women; BillyBob let a greasy laugh slip past his lips. "No doubt having a couple of beauties in the joint helps. Don't take that the wrong way, girls. Just calling a spade a spade. And no reflection on how you do the job—you've both gotten good on the mic and the hustle. I like to watch, you know…"

Trish rolled her eyes and grinned. Des let a knowing smile part her lips. "Guess you're into being there, eh?" she chuckled.

Greg looked confused, then continued.

"It's more the Milk Can... I can't attribute the bump in margin there to the stunning good looks of your crew haha, but there's *something* going on. Can't quite put my finger on it, but..."

Bob jumped in.

"For fuck's sake, Greg. Y'all just missing the bright light for the interrogation, man. Where were you on the night of the eighteenth and all that shit. Relax! They just got sat down after a long day setting up. Let 'em have a drink and chill, that's all we wanna do, right? Just hang out and have a good time. And just call me BB; that's what my friends do." He reached around to the counter and grabbed a framed mirror, one with a weed leaf in it that was one of the prizes in the Shoot Out the Star joint. He put it on the table in front of them and tossed a couple of folded packets onto it. "Help yourself, ya'll. A little pick-me-up after an honest day's work. You won't hear it called that very often around here!"

Des dug in first, dumping the coke onto the mirror, carving out a couple of large lines with a credit card. BillyBob peeled off a hundred-dollar bill from a wad he pulled out of his pocket, rolled it up and passed it to her.

"Not your first rodeo, is it honey?" She gave him a perfunctory smile and snapped the two lines back hard and fast, chasing them along the shiny surface. Got every grain. The mirror and the bill made its way around the horn, snorts, gum rubbing and sniffing animating the small talk that accompanied the ritual; observations on the quality of the product, heartfelt thanks to BillyBob the provider, deep nasal inhalations, slow blow exhales. One packet down and the conversation resumed, shiny-eyed and intense.

"I know what I saw, Jonah, and I haven't seen that before. You..."

he gestured towards Wyatt, who was still revelling in the cool, clean clarity opening up in his head. "You caught my eye in Winnipeg with that tip you manufactured at the end of the last night. We get new blood here all the time, not just every year but every town. And then the night at the Stampede…. What the hell was that all about? How the fuck do you make it so someone can win the Milk Can. That's sure what it looked like from where we were standing. Balls flying, crowd smothering the joint and you—well, all three of you, actually; acting like fucking puppeteers in there! Marionette, marionette, take your money and place your bet haha! Maybe I'll jump into the joint next time!" He wheezed out the last of his laugh, finished with a cough that landed some spittle on the table, wiped it off with his elbow. "You got some 'splainin' to do!"

41

Things accelerated.

Wyatt tried to rein in his focus but there was a lot going on. In the kitchen area, BillyBob was leaning back with his butt against the stove, arms wide, regaling the girls. He heard "invented it man, made money, millions! Got the idea from a Japanese guy…" and Des rocking back and forth on her cowboy boots, hips shimmying slow like she had done this thing before. Trish, a little further off to the left, brow furrowed, eyes bugged, twisting her long blond hair into a knot, taking slow sips off the long neck and nodding. Bruce, tight chopping another line off the mirror as Petr sat beside him, trying to pull it away, spit-whispering "that's not yours…" but Bruce pulling it back it towards him, hissing "they don't mind, not at all, indeed they set it out for us, of course." Wyatt took a long haul of fresh-faced air through his nose and went eye-to-eye with Greg.

"I dunno, Greg"—it felt strange calling him Greg, having never had a conversation with him—"it's hard to explain but I'll try, of course I'll try. Or, better yet, we'll try. Petr, c'mere; Greg wants to know what's happening in the Milk Can! The secrets of our success haha." Petr pushed himself down the length of the bench and joined them.

"What's that, Greg? Looking to learn about the dark arts of Midway manipulation?" He popped his Marlboros out of his shirt pocket, lit it and spoke expansively.

"Well, you see, it's both simpler and more complicated than meets the inquiring eye. To the casual observer, and you're that and more, having watched you watch us from the far side of the Himalayan, it might look as though it's all odds and chance, right? Of course, that's how the company—the Clown—sees it! Empirical analysis and breakdown of the minutiae of transportation, infrastructure, lights, camera and action to arrive at a foregone conclusion. Something you can count on, and then count. Stack 'em high and watch 'em buy— think I heard that in a marketing course I took once. God, I hated that course. Enrolled in first year at U of T, just knew I had to get out of the shitty town I was shackled to and got a scholarship. Tiny town, I used to call it, living on the fringe in a place on the fringe. It was one of the ones for the poor kids that show some...promise. We were poor, Dad being all fucked up from the accident and Mom trying hard to make it all normal, make it work, right?"

Wyatt knew that was bullshit from the monologue he'd heard in the cafeteria days before.

"I sure didn't help once I got old enough to know didn't belong there, being how I was...contrary, Dad used to call me. Not...ordinary. Landed in the big city...where was I? Oh right, the course with that shitty prof—he had weird thick tufts of hair growing out of his ears, never saw anything like it. And out of his nose. Jesus…." He paused for a minute, reforming his thoughts while Greg and Wyatt waited for him to line them back up on the track. Greg's lips were parted slightly, hanging on to the roller coaster rambling.

"Yeah, so the thing is, Greg, there's more going in the Can than meets the eye. There's more going on everywhere than meets the eye, for that matter. I'm an artist, you see. I…we"—a nod to Wyatt that warmed him unnaturally, made him feel as though he'd been elevated to artist status, something he hadn't realized he'd aspired to until that moment—"have a job to do, and important contribution to make. Boil it down, get the meat off the bones and expose the essence. And the essence isn't…visible…to the naked eye, but it's there if you know how to gain access." He opened his hands in front of his chest.

"I had a show in Toronto before I was recruited. You weren't there, Wyatt, but no doubt you've heard from the others…"

Jesus, he's pretentious, Wyatt thought while maintaining nodding-head complicity.

"…Rave reviews by the faculty, I can assure you. Shot to the top of the pops, at least until chaos theory entered the fray toward the end of the event"—leftward tilt of the head towards Des, who was busy wrapping BillyBob around her finger in the kitchen, all wily, flirty, Mata Hari—"It was an event, to be sure, conical constructs I created calling down the thunder, so to speak. The Can…. Right, you have a question? What is the question, again?" Petr's words were running away from him. Bruce sat bug-eyed and Jonah watched all the balls flying, leaning back, hands behind his head, a cigarette burning down in the ashtray in front of him. Wyatt unexpectedly heard himself talking.

"What he…we… are getting at is the idea of energy, Greg. Not to sound all new-age-y on you here. I got spit out here after being in California for a bit of a rip and spent enough time with the crystal academy to last more than the several reincarnated lifetimes I have apparently lived according to a Tarot reader I met." He gave his head a little shake, refocusing.

"Not that it can be owned, or syndicated"—Petr let go a soft snort—"but from what I've seen, and what I've heard about Petr's show and how we all ended up in the place in time, Jonah being the catalyst"—and he thought of words and how catalyst was phonetically cattle-ist and perfectly described how Jonah had somehow herded them onto the Midway but just as speedily banished the thought and got back on track with his talk.

"If you pay close enough attention and let go of the idea of control, you can get some of what you willfully abandon, understand? You can manipulate the moment, be a part of the coalescence. Like here, on the Midway, with what you do. You create this environment that pulls people in from the four corners and watch it all unfold. Line up the games, the rides, the trailers in exactly the right place to maximize the potential, then let nature take its course. But there's more than just the physical world interacting, you know? More than fat fathers pulling twenties from their wallets, tired mothers smiling wearily when their kids get in line for a third run through the House of Horror. More than the money flying from hand, to game, to ticket, to ride. The sum of the parts is greater than the whole, Greg. That's the thing in the Can; we're manifesting this…essence. Thought precedes form kind-of-thing." The wind slipped through the sails of his thoughts as they tailed off. Talking about it seemed like the opposite, where the sum of the parts was less than it could be. The three of them looked from one to the other, unsure how to reboot some conversational momentum. Greg stepped up to the plate.

"Sounds a little bit outside my field of expertise, to be honest, and a carny is nothing if not honest, right? I started out as ride-rat thirty years ago and have seen it all on and off the Midway, but this is the first I've heard of this shit. I think you might be reading too much into your own experiences. Echo chamber kind of thing. I mean, I'm no philosopher and sure as fuck am no artist, but what you're talking about, or at least what I think you're talking about, doesn't add up, the way I see it. What we do here on the asphalt is create a fun factory. An illusion that anyone can have a piece of if they have the price of admission; an admission statement is what this is haha. There's nothing esoteric about that. It's a controlled environment; a closed system, as it were. I did go to university eventually. Did you know there's a scholarship fund for the show set up by the old man back in the seventies? I got in on that; did a couple of years of courses. Didn't get the piece of paper but took a physics course along with some arts and business. See? I'm not just another pretty face! Learned enough to know I knew enough already. Closed systems. They're all closed." He gave them a tight-lipped smile that he seemed to feel settled the debate.

An impasse for a moment. The air in the trailer had tightened up considerably, three distinct ecosystems operating under the flat metal roof of the RV. Bruce yammering on to an impervious Jonah, who did the simultaneous nod and blow-off as he monitored the other two knots tying themselves up, not unlike keeping a finger on all the pulses of a joint. BillyBob, gut in and chest out, performing for the women, thick, hairy forearms bulging below rolled-up sleeves, the gold Rolex prominent and flashing in front of Des's dark eyes. Des in her element, having done that dance around the circuit so many times before, assured and unimpressed as Trish wobbled to her left, the accumulated powder and whisky taking a toll.

"Self-made man, that's me," he barked, jabbing a thick thumb into the thick, black chest hair at the V of his unbuttoned Bermuda shirt. Des laughed in his face, a dismissive chortle that managed to remain in bounds, BillyBob oblivious to her derision.

"I've met a lot of self-made men in my day, BB. Every one of them either had a good woman by their side or screwed someone out of something…which one are you?" She gave him a playful poke in the chest, laughing.

"I don't see any woman around this place so it must be the latter, huh?" Wyatt could see how much BillyBob loved that, thinking he likely wasn't used to anyone on the Midway talking back, challenging him.

"Oh, there's woman around here, honey, I can assure you there's woman. Not too many good ones, but some of them are getting screwed for sure!" A loud, cringe-inducing guffaw blew out of him, rattling the window casings.

Fucking Americans, Wyatt thought. *Why does he have to be such a fucking American?*

42

BillyBob took charge of the room, bringing Des and Trish in from the kitchen, an arm around each of them. Trish was the colour of drywall, smiling wanly as she collapsed onto the couch. Des scooted her in closer to Jonah and patted the seat beside her for BillyBob. He grunted his way onto it, planting his elbows on the table. Wyatt and Petr pulled a couple of chairs up to the other side, and Greg completed the circle on the end. All their eyes snuck expectant glances at the unopened packet on the mirror. Bob grabbed the bottle of whisky in the middle of the smokes, ashtrays and mirror and graciously spread his arms, mimicking Mickey Rourke in *Bar Fly*—"All my friends!"—and hacked out a laugh as he poured two more finger shots. "I fucking loved that flick. Crazy!" Petr adopted a lecturer tone.

"That was about Bukowski. Charles Bukowski, the poet. You know that, right? You know his stuff? Find what you love and let it kill you." Bruce seemed to find this hilarious and oinked out a laugh from the corner, saying, "But I don't wanna die…I'm too young to go! My parents will miss me!" Jonah withered him with a look. He sat back, head on a tilt, sad puppy-eyed behind the Buddy Holly frames. Wyatt slammed his drink and spoke before thought had a chance to interrupt.

"No no no. That's not the best one for BB. He's more a 'I wasn't much of a petty thief. I wanted the whole world or nothing.' That's more your jam, right BB? It's not 'The less I needed, the better I felt', is it? I mean, take a look around. You're big time, BB. Big time!" BillyBob grinned, not even taking a swing at the sarcasm he was missing. Petr picked up the Bukowski gauntlet.

"What about 'The nine-to-five is one of the greatest atrocities sprung upon mankind'? Got to love that one, don't we? I think it's safe to say it's something we all …. subscribe to. " He casually pulled the mirror towards him, squaring it up perfectly as all eyes watched closely, and cracked open a folded packet of powder, shaking it gently out onto the surface, tapping the edges of it to get every last grain. BillyBob seemed amused at this brazen occupation of the distributor role, looked at Des with raised eyebrows and a half smile. She gave him a wink and a nod that redirected his gaze back to the task at hand. The kitchen light sizzled, made a popping sound, and went dark.

The remaining light in the RV living space tractor-beamed down from the lamp that hung over the table. Eyes shone around the perimeter. Bruce's voice cracked from the corner: "Where were you on the night of the seventh? Haha—it's like an interrogation scene." The silence of the rest wrapped around his tittering until it wound itself down. "Who the fuck is this guy?" Bob laughed. "We ought to stick him in the Fun House!" A few chuckles and then renewed focus on the mirror as Petr began to speak.

"Speaking of the seventh, or more specifically...seven," as he tap-tap-tapped the pile of powder with a razor blade, cutting, re-piling and cutting again. "Ever see the way they do it in Europe?" He divided the coke into three large lines. "They have a horizontal line through the seven, so you don't mistake it for a one. Like this. Lucky number seven. But you can do whatever you want with three lines—make them parallel vertical or horizontal, make them into one long line..." Bob laugh-talked, "Those are the ones I like haha" to mandatory chuckles; it *was* his blow.

"Or," continued Petr, "you can make a cup waiting to run over" *tap tap tap* "or, and this is the best one, the only one for me..." He carved the pile into a triangular shape and grabbed a dollar bill off the middle of the table, Wyatt grudgingly admiring the performance art taking place before him. Des had a wide, approving smile. Out of the corner of his eye, he could see Jonah's large-knuckled hands flat on the table, index fingers drumming. Trish was leaning on Greg, then Jonah, and back again, head lolling, trying to stay in the game. Greg was all ears, head resting on his folded hands. Wyatt felt the air in the room tighten up, the way it did in the joint when they had a good tip going. You could feel it if you paid attention, and it would have its way with you regardless, if you weren't. This was the same. Now.

Petr snapped an American dollar open between his hands and continued, spreading it tight and angling it around the table.

"See the pyramid? See the eye? There's a lot of myth around who or how this ended up on the back of the green. Most of it bullshit. But it always caught my eye, ha, even when I was a kid, and we'd go across the border in the States. I didn't think of it as a pyramid, though. It reminded me of an upside-down funnel. My grandfather used to take strips of birch bark off trees when he was working in the woods, fold them into funnels to pour gas into the chainsaw or tractor. Funnels. I've been fascinated by the shape forever. How liquid corkscrews its way down through. Movement, you know what I mean? A propensity…"

BillyBob cut him off.

"What the fuck is propensity? 'Nuff with the big words, just get to the point. I want a line, not a lecture!"

Petr exhaled and continued.

"… propensity…a, uh…" Des, in a low, silky voice said, "Focus, Bob. He means a concentrated focus. But yeah, cut to the chase, Petr. We've got a line lineup happening here!"

Petr cleared his throat and went on.

"Anyway…. Funnels, cones, pyramids. The shape of things to come, right? Trish and Des, oh yeah, and Jonah all ended up at my gallery show. The twelve stations of the cone, remember? Things get channelled through the design, somehow. That's what we're talking about in the game, Greg. You were asking about how we were doing the things we were in a carnival game. It's got to do with…calling down the thunder, as it were. Locking into a grid…Who knew the Milk Can was going to be the manifestation of all those years of fascination?" A paralyzed, awkward moment hung over the huddle. The clock on the wall ticked.

Bob broke the impasse. "Fuck this. We ain't got all night kids. Time's a wastin'…" He snapped the greenback out of Petr's hands and rolled it into a tight tube, bent his head down over the mirror and snorted the thick, three-inch line at the bottom of the triangle. He snapped his head back joyfully, a wet-lipped smile widening as he exhaled. Des refused the tube when he passed it to her, silently shaking her head with her nose crinkled, instead tightening up a Canadian twenty, slowly hoovering the next line into her face, scything the tube back and forth on the mirror, not missing a grain of the blow. Then Wyatt.

Then another three-sided pyramid carved out by Petr, and around and around with more packets tossed on the mirror by Bob, more shots poured from the bottle and slammed. The battery in the clock died.

Synthetic talk swirled and surrounded them. Smiles that never made it into the eyes were stuck to their faces, save Jonah, whose lips were sealed, and Trish, who had fallen back from the elbow-leaning circle to rest her head on the wood-panel wall. She was mouth-breathing, eyes slowly opening and closing. Bruce, who was a leg thumper even in the quiet times, had his right leg pumping under the table, his wrinkled fingers drumming on the black tabletop.

"You have to stop that right now!" The first words in a while from Greg had the desired effect, both stilling Bruce and re-establishing the hierarchy which bubbled on the back burner.

"Or get out. I can't stand a leg thumper. My stepfather was a leg thumper…all the time. Kitchen table…when the hockey game was on…even when we were driving, when I'd be in the back seat watching his goddamn left leg going nonstop when were going down some back road he'd haul me and my mother out to looking for deals on whatever he was trying to flip to make a buck as long as he didn't have to work for it." Greg turned angrily towards Bruce.

"Who are you, anyway? Why are you here?" Bruce blinked a couple of times, opened his mouth, closed it again, like a fish in an aquarium.

"I…I work here. I'm supposed to be here, right? I'm …I'm …" He looked at Jonah, who continued staring at the mirror, hands now folded in front of him. Greg continued.

"You're what? A carny? A bad boy? And adventurer, slumming it for the summer? I've seen you on the Midway a thousand times before, man. You think this thing is a little kick, a bit of little rebel without a clue sticking it to your parents, eh? A real bad boy, aren't you?" He had leaned in closer to Bruce, who pulled back into the bend of the rounded couch as all eyes pinned him to the fake leather.

"No. I mean, yeah, my parents aren't... I haven't talked to them in weeks..." But Greg had him wriggling at the end of the line and wasn't cutting him loose.

"Here's what I see. A skinny little leg-thumping rich kid hanging around. Playing at it, with an exit strategy for the end of the summer, right? Off to university with tuition paid by Mom and Dad. You can hang out at all the freshman activities and pretend you're more worldly, more experienced... cooler than the rest of them? Maybe that'll get you laid if you somehow manage to meet a girl who can handle a leg thumper. That's just repressed truth, you know, the jumping fucking leg. Something that gets way down inside but has to find an outlet or will blow like a pressure cooker." Bruce clenched his hand on his knee to keep it still and tried in vain to make eye contact with an ally around the table. Greg kept rolling.

"Tell you what. Show me I'm wrong, and that you're not a fucking ...voyeur... and you can stay. Otherwise, it might be time for you to leave."

Just as Bruce began to babble out a largely incoherent line of defence, Trish jack-knifed herself up from the bench and let out a long, low groan that sounded part human and part cat. Bob was in mid-laugh as she collapsed sideways onto Bruce. Her back arched. Gagging, pitting, spewing sounds were muffled for a moment in his lap while the rest of the circle recoiled from the table en masse, a "*fuuuucckk*" slipping from Des's mouth. The sour smell of vomit rose from below and filled the air of the RV.

Greg was unbothered. "Timing, eh? The key to comedy...and so many other things. Best that you follow this directive...Bruce? Is that your name? Since we're talking about 'energy'"—the word was wrapped in sardonic intent – "it's pretty obvious where this moment is going, right?" The faux levity in his tone shifted gears, lowering in tone.

"Get her the fuck out of here, along with yourself. Pathetic…" Bruce opened his mouth, right-hand index finger raised to make a case for her being allowed to stay, and then thought better of it, reluctantly nudging Des to the end of the seat so they could get up and let them out. Little chunks of spew clung to Trish's uniform and Bruce's shorts were soaked dark blue. His wet thighs glistened as he wobbled by the table, holding Trish as upright as possible. A couple of whispered "sorrys" made it out of his mouth, an apology that was all encompassing; for Trish, for himself, to Greg, to Jonah, to his parents… He waited in vain for an acknowledgement, but instead got a nod toward the door from Jonah.

"See you back at the motel—make sure she sleeps face down." Head low, he slunk away, supporting her weight across the kitchen tile. The room was silent until the screen door clicked behind them.

43

Des had slid back onto the bench beside BillyBob. "Now. Where were we? Oh right!' She started humming Johnny Cash's "I Walk the Line" as she carved several more lines on the face of the mirror.

"More for the rest of us, more for the best of us ha!" It was a joyless titter that belied the dark-eyed intensity with which she regarded the coke. It made its way around the diminished group once more. The cheap talk picked up its momentum, surface-skimming platitudes and observations that succeeded in negating the awkwardness of Greg's aggression and Trish's messy exit.

"Should be a big one tomorrow; provincial holiday…the fireworks should be good, they always are here…you'd think they'd have been able to come up with a better way to do this than a rolled-up bill, ha—what if you only have change? How do you do the deal?" until the mirror came back to Des. She held the rolled bill between her fingers, right elbow resting on the table, stared at her hand for longer than was comfortable until the chatter slowed and stopped. She turned to BillyBob.

"Any idea what I do for a living? Not this, not the Birthday Game. What I really do?" She said it slow and sultry, in black and white, channeling a femme fatale in a film noir from the forties. Wyatt watched the transformation in fascination. The conical light over the table returned, shadows hemming them in on all sides.

"I was a dancer, *Bob*. An exotic dancer. A very good one. A gypsy stripper on the circuits that spread out into the boonies from the cities in Ontario and Quebec. Paid for everything, school, the whole shebang."

BillyBob let a dirty laugh slide out.

"Shebang? Don't you mean 'she bangs'? Get it—she bangs? Just a joke—no offense." No one laughed. Des continued.

"Hilarious. First time I've heard a joke about strippers, poles and sex. "

She took a deep breath through her nose."Yeah, heard 'em all, seen 'em all and done 'em all, Bob. And please don't say, "You can do me" okay?… But what I'm getting at… what I wanted to say, is I met a lot of interesting and…different people out on the dance circuit. This carnival thing reminds me of those days in a way. The 'can't hit a moving target' constant motion. The being on display for all who wander by. The sense of being on the outside, on the edge of all the normal lives." She opened her palms to take in the group around the table. "And this. Late nights trying to hold back the dawn, with whatever you can get your hands on…" The low hum of the AC was the only other sound as Des held the floor.

"And speaking of hands… I had a co-worker when I was out there dancing. Rose. She was good, but getting a little past her best-before date, you know? Mid-thirties but still gorgeous. Lebanese, I think. She was amazing. Knew how to 'grab 'em and hold 'em', as they say, getting the guys. We didn't call them 'marks.'" BillyBob interjected "Johns?" to no laughter, which elicited a withering look from her before she continued.

"Marks. Though I think I might use that if I ever go back. Rose was the best at getting money from the men around the edge of the stage, the ones that believed what they were seeing. She could seduce more cash out of them than anyone; get a twenty halfway through and then another at the end, with a few of them thinking she really wanted them. Those would be the ones who lined up outside the room after, waiting for us to come out after we'd changed. I was never into that, but she didn't mind. She had a side hustle she'd pull off with some of the more smitten, which was incredible. Because she could read palms. The future; she really could. She'd get another fifty or hundred bucks from these guys to tell their fortune at a table in the bar, one on one. They were more than happy to part with it, if it meant a little more time to prolong the fantasy." She paused and furled her brow.

"She taught me a lot of things. No need to go into all of it, but…" She took BillyBob's left hand and spread it palm up beside the mirror on the table.

"I can read palms. Seriously." BillyBob snorted and tried to pull his hand away, but she held it down. They all leaned in. Wyatt saw some of the low light halo itself around her dark hair, her irises widening. He felt the air in the room cool down. Jonah was smiling at the end of the table. The way he cradled his chin in his hands reminded Wyatt of when they'd met way back in the distant, eastern winter. When Jonah seemed to know what was coming down the line.

"No charge for this BB, okay? You've been more than generous to us tonight, sharing your space and your goodies. Let's think of this as payback for your hospitality." Bob began to sputter something about the old days of freak shows and fortune tellers, but Des hushed him with a finger to his lips.

"*Shhhhh.* You need to relax now, let your hand lay flat. That's right." She ran her index finger up and down all of his fingers, slowly, back and forth. Then over the lines on his palm. Even in the conical light, Wyatt could see BillyBob's face reddening. His ears.

"It's called chiromancy. Not to be confused with necromancy." BillyBob snorted again, but the laugh that was meant to follow retreated instead…

"Not necrophilia. Give it a rest." She loomed large now, occupying the space in the shadows as well. For Wyatt, it felt like those moments in the Milk Can when you couldn't put your finger on the change but felt it. Des was holding court.

"But it's an odd thing, how the dead and the living can sometimes share some space…time….The old saying; if you don't learn from the past, you're doomed to repeat it." She hovered her head above his hand, all else darkening.

"There are five lines. One each for life, heart, money, head and marriage. Let's start with…money." BillyBob blurted, "Don't need a fortune teller to tell me about my fortune…" from his spittle-shined lips and was again silenced with a look from Des. She traced a crevassed crack that ran from the base of his thumb nearly to his index finger.

"This has been with you for a while, hasn't it? Looks like forever. I've never seen a money line like this, so pronounced. It's been what you've wanted and done for all your life." She lifted her head and looked around the table, stopping at BillyBob.

"And the proof's in the pudding, isn't it? Whac-A-Mole King, and all the other games. More money than you'll ever spend, but no sign of slowing down. Even when you were poorer than dirt in Pensacola, when your mother had to do what she had to do for a buck..." She held BillyBob's widening eye with hers.

"You knew, didn't you? Knew you were going to rise above all those bastards that kept you awake at night, the ones you heard through the thin walls of your mobile home out there on the edge of town." BillyBob nodded, eyes tractor-beamed to hers. She broke the beam, returned to his palm.

"No problem with the money, then. It was always going to be this way for you, though as I said, haven't seen a line like this. Too much of a good thing is always a possibility; such a focus on the material.... Let's take a look at marriage." BillyBob laughed, his hand jumping off the table. 'Which one haha!" Des silenced him again with a look.

"Let's see. Looks like... I can see where there are breaks in the line...looks like... two? That can get expensive, can't it? Might help explain the money line running up the entire length of your palm." She ran her finger back and forth along the base of his little finger. "I don't think you're done on the marriage front, BB." She closed her eyes and continued.

"The first one involved a shotgun, didn't it? And the second one... I see a redhead, and...more kids. Three kids in total..." BillyBob turned his head towards her, unsmiling, eyes now hooded. Des's eyes remained closed as she went back and forth along the marriage line.

"There's going to be another one... soon, it looks like. Blonde. Golden hair, young. Much younger. Tattoos. She looks like...she's going to be in your life for the long haul, Bob." He leer-laughed. "Gotta love having a young blonde around! Unless she's puking all over someone, that is haha." Silence around the table again as Des opened her eyes and resumed. Wyatt noticed Greg shifting in his seat, opening and closing his hands.

"The heartline. Different from the marriage line. It's about love, you see. The real love, the kind that takes over you and makes you…crazy." She drew her finger slowly across the breadth of his palm, closing her eyes again. "Mmm…It's been a long time, hasn't it? Since you've let yourself fall in love. These little breaks along it… kind of like one of your Whac-A-Mole games. It looks like every time it reared its head it got knocked back down… three or four of those there, but none for a while, right? But there's a tiny one there right at the end. One more chance, maybe. It's hard to say how long, or when. But definitely one more." BillyBob interjected, "The young blonde, I bet! How could she resist?" Des gave him a wan smile.

"The headline. Read all about it!" She allowed a small chuckle to rattle around the room.

"This one is about intelligence…how you process the things. Your ability to understand how things work, at least here in the material world." She traced the line slowly across the middle of his palm.

"It's interesting. There's a little bend at the start, where it connects with the lifeline, then steady right through. As though something happened way back that was a catalyst; propelled you towards your path." She turned to look at him with a tenderness, a softening that to Wyatt seemed incongruous.

"Probably right around the time your mother had the trailer, right? It can't have been easy for you. Even kids, on levels they aren't aware of, are absorbing things, trying to figure them out. Trying to get out…" BillyBob's shoulders dropped as he nodded several times. Wyatt watched his eyes fill with shine until he rubbed it away with his right hand. Des's voice resumed, recalibrated.

"You have an impressive amount of focus, that's clear enough. Figured out what you wanted and how to get it. Didn't take a lot of prisoners, didn't have time for much else other than accumulating.…

things. All sorts of things. You're surrounded by things, aren't you? Like a moat, right? Meant to keep you safe. They have, I guess. Though there's a price. Always a price. After a time, it becomes harder and harder to lift the gate and let the things you need pass through."

Wyatt was watching Greg, whose eye-rolling and lip-curled head shaking were increasing. Still, he was surprised at the slam of his hand on the table and the force with which he pushed himself up and away from it.

"Oh, for fuck's sake. This is bullshit. C'mon BB, time to move these people out. It's 3:30 in the goddamn morning!" He pushed the screen door open and stood with his hands on his hips, left foot tapping its deck shoe. Wyatt averted his eyes, fearful he might inadvertently chuckle at the caricature Greg had unwittingly become. There'd be consequences. Taut silence as Des held BillyBob's hand in place on the table, looking at him rather than Greg. He could see thin smiles on Jonah and Petr's downturned faces.

"Nah, not yet, Greg. Hang on. Man. We've got one more line to do. Haha. We've done so many tonight, what's one more? Stick around for the big reveal, man!" Greg was twenty feet past the slamming door by the time BillyBob got his last word out. They listened to his leather shoes scuffing away. Des picked it back up as though nothing had happened.

"Hmm.... Like you say, BB. One more line." She took a deep breath and bent over the table.

"The lifeline... The lifeline..." They watched her stare at Bob's hand for a minute, then another... The ticking of the clock kicked back in, metronomic. Des began clicking her tongue off the roof of her mouth in time.

"Down here, at the end. Do you see that? It's kind of faint; you have to look closely." She picked up the bill they'd been using for the blow, tightened it back up, and pointed to the end of the line on his palm, tracing over a faint circle.

"That's something, for sure. Like a little island, right? But no man is an island. That's John Donne, by the way. Donne like dinner, by the looks of this." BillyBob started to laugh, but a different kind than before. A slightly nervous giggle that had no air pushing it out into the room.

"C'mon now, Des, I'm healthy as a horse. Just had the big physical from my doctor before we headed back up to Canada. And he's the best; not one of your socialist hacks! Joking.... just joking!" Des continued.

"That's not what this is. Not at all. There's a small line cutting through at the end there—see that? And then that little circle." Her brow furrowed, she shook her head back and forth, for long enough that it reminded Wyatt of his aunt with Parkinson's. Minute movements that made it seem as though she was reading off a page. They waited for her next pronouncement beneath the ticking clock. When she finally lifted her head back up from his palm, her face had transformed. It was a mask from a museum, taken off a wall from an indigenous exhibit on a faraway coast. Elongated. Her nose appeared larger and wider to Wyatt, her ears hanging, gravity flesh on either side of her head. Her raven hair thickened and knotty. The air had cooled, the charge had changed. He crossed his arms and rubbed his hands up and down his biceps. Jonah and Petr leaned back in their seats, watching.

She spoke, a vibrato fluttering under her words.

"There's something...no...someone. On their way. I can't tell from where. It looks like it's been building for a while; the serrations along the edge of the cut-off line get longer as they move towards the middle. A slow burn, I'd say, a gradual build-up of... anger." She pursed her lips.

"Definitely anger. They're deep. And the circle is the end of things, of current patterns. It seems like it's someone you know or knew. Can't tell if it's a man or a woman, but it's someone who has revenge on their mind. Know anyone who'd want revenge?" She turned towards him and pulled her hair back with both hands, but the spell that had enveloped the room remained.

BillyBob laughed nervously, belying the words he spoke.

"There's a goddamn lineup like the Doppel Looper on coupon day, honey. You don't get to be someone in my position without busting a few heads and breaking a few hearts over the years. Fuck 'em all, I say. If you're gonna play the game, play to win. I learned that early. Whoever thinks they'll get even with me doesn't know me very well."

Wyatt watched the muscles in his neck tighten, little bulbous knots of blood sticking out at the top of the tendons. Petr nudged Jonah's arm with his elbow, nodded towards BillyBob. Des's voice broke in loud and harsh.

"There are things you can't control. It's like your games…" Her voice filled the room, came from the ground up.

"Whac-A-Mole. This is one of those. You try to hit it, but it ducks down then reappears somewhere else. Over and over. I…uh…I have a feeling this circumstance is not something you're going to be able to… defeat." She closed her eyes and let her head loll around in circles for three, four, five rotations. Wyatt could hear the grind of her vertebrae in the clock-tick quiet. Her breath became skipping pond-shallow, shortening as she pulled BillyBob towards her, hair falling forward gain, face buried into the side of his head. The rest of them leaned forward, tilted, trying to decipher Des's whispered incantations. Bob's creased forehead was a field waiting for seed, glistening.

"Uh huh. Uh huh. No!" He was shaking his head slowly back and forth while Des kept up with her fervent whispering, as though dancing while sitting down. It took on a circular motion after a few minutes, in and out, around and around, her words winding, arm on his shoulder, both guiding and steadying him. BillyBob's eyes widened; his colour bled out. Small, incoherent mouthings trickled off his shiny lower lip. The room barely breathed. Des disentangled herself, head and hair back to what they were once again, pushing herself up from the bench and stretch-standing taller than seemed possible, exhaling from her depths.

"I think it's time to go. Tomorrow is now today!" She broadcast a wide, white smile, tilted her head towards the door, motioning for the others to follow. Chairs scraped across the creaking floor. They processioned themselves out, silent funereal, leaving BillyBob with head in his hands, slumped at the table over the remaining grains of promise left on the mirror, looking like he'd seen his own ghost.

44

The faintest tinge of light was creeping over the eastern horizon as they staggered toward the main gate. The city still slept, soundly enough that the scraping of the bristle brooms of the clean-up crew could be heard between their footsteps. Zombie-walking, no one acknowledged what had happened in the trailer until they had exited the Clown mouth, breaking through the membrane into what Wyatt had begun to think of as the other world. Jonah was grinning as he walked away from them to get the truck.

"What the fuck was that? Seriously. What the fuck did you just do in there?" Petr's voice was amplified in the silence, awestruck, giddy, the words riding out on a laugh-cloud.

"What did you say to that moron, Des? He went from sixty to zero faster than anyone I've ever seen. It felt like my show in Toronto in there! Brilliant!"

Des didn't respond with anything other than a faraway smile, a subtle shake of her head.

"C'mon. What were you whispering? That was the most ... syndicated thing. We should have left a card on the table for him, something to remind him every time he cuts another line. Lost opportunity. I get the sense it's going to be a bit...awkward on the Midway here on in. You must..." He was cut off by the lights of the truck coming around the corner, spotlighting them in front the Clown mouth. Like prison-yard spotlights, Wyatt thought. They climbed in, Petr and Wyatt in the back, Des sliding confidently into the front seat, beside Jonah. Crash and burn, up-all-night silence descended.

45

Wyatt woke, not because of the alarm, but because of the knotted-up blankets wrapped around his torso, a result of tossing and turning for the three or four hours available before the carnival curtain call at ten. He wasn't sure what time it was when they'd fallen out of the truck and made their way to their respective beds; they'd driven in silence through the dead streets of dawn, Petr rubbing the stubble on his chin and Des up front sitting close to Jonah. Wyatt was too frazzled to care about what any of it meant. His right arm was asleep from having been trapped under him, pins and needles coursing down it as the blood returned.

He stumbled into the kitchen to find Des already up and about, running water into the coffee pot and whistling "Parker's Mood" to herself.

"Early bird gets the worm, I guess!"

She turned from profile, big smile, fresh shirt and painted pink toenails on her bare feet.

"What? Oh, haha! I see what you did there. A little wordplay on

Charlie Parker. Clever." She poured the water into the top of the coffee maker. "That's what I like about you...well, not the only thing I like about you; you're pretty funny. But you're quick and clever with the words. Wyatt. I like that."

Wyatt had to admit it felt good to hear that coming from a woman, and, as he often forgot but was reminded of as the northern sun shafted into the kitchenette, a beautiful woman. Des was glowing, beaming, shining. On three hours' sleep.

"I can't think of a lot of people who would have picked out that tune. I used to play it in the dressing room before shows. It calmed me and got me into the zone. Pretty sure I was the only exotic dancer doing that...." She lit a smoke, bent down to check the level of the coffee in the pot.

"Almost ready. They'd better get moving if they want some before we head to the grounds. Grounds. Coffee. Grounds *ruck ruck ruck!*" Even her voice was brighter, lighter. Wyatt felt like he'd been hit by a truck, nose clogged, head pounding, the coating of the dream still on. As she turned back to pour the coffee, it dawned on him. She was happy.

Bruce had slept through it all, curled fetal on the hide-a-bed couch, a tick twitching his cheek while his legs jerked in the sleeping bag. Wyatt thought of a dog he used to own that slept like that.

Jonah came into the room frowning, adjusting his glasses as he sat in a chair at the table and reached for the pack of Drum.

"Trish isn't doing too well this morning. A little too much of nothing last night. She's gonna get a taxi later." He lit his smoke and cleared the night from his throat, tossed the pack of Drum at Bruce, hitting him on the side of the face. "Hey! Let's go, Bruce. Twenty minutes."

Des placed a cup of coffee in front of him and slid the carton of cream over from the other side of the table.

Bruce sounded like a child, a high-pitched moan-yawn escaping.

"Fuck. What time is it? Jesus… We were at BillyBob's last night, right? When did we get back?" He was sitting up now, head in his hands tussling his curly black hair, the Buddy Holly glasses on the coffee table looking like they belonged to someone else.

"Fuck. I can't remember the last part of the night.… I've done blow and shit before, but I can't recall.…" He shook his head, kicked his cocooned legs off the side of the bed and wormed himself out of the bag and into the world.

Petr's voice slid around the corner of the room before he entered.

"You had to leave so the adults could have some quality time. Both of you. What a mess the two of you were." He sneered his way in, sliding into a chair across from Jonah. He tapped a smoke out of a pack of Marlboros and pointed it at Des.

"I'll take a cup of coffee too, if you're still…serving." His eyebrows arched over the wire-thin crease between his lips.

"Can't believe the service in this joint. Jesus H. Clown, you were up early enough to have a full breakfast set out. Rise and shine, eh? At least Jonah has his. Lucky Jonah…"

Wyatt's words rose out of him.

"Leave her alone. It's a bit early for this bullshit. At least let us get to the Midway, for fuck's sake. That was a strange enough night without having the morning go south." The words he spit were his but came from a place Wyatt wasn't prepared to admit to or understand. It was the first time his dislike for Petr had manifested itself. The rest of them stopped. Waited. Petr spun the Bic between his fingers like a drummer with a stick, before returning the volley.

"Now, Wyatt. It was a long, strange night. But there's no need to take it all so…seriously. I was just joking, of course. Just having some fun with Des. We go way back, don't we Des?"

She was leaning against the counter, unsmiling, nodding her head.

"Oh yeah, nothing but fun."

It felt like a Mexican standoff to Wyatt, everyone gathered in a circle waiting for the next shot. It didn't come. The air slowly settled back into itself, waiting for the sound of a spoon in a cup or the flush of a distant toilet to signal the return to the surface world. Jonah spoke instead.

"Okay. Time's up. We've got to get going."

He rose and went back into the bedroom while the rest of them got ready. Des called into him.

"I'll stay here and get Trish moving if you want. Then we'll come down."

Ten minutes later the four of them were in the truck, making their muted way to work, avoiding each other's eyes. The five to-the-hour news came on as they pulled into the parking lot behind the trailers, warning of possible thunder, lightning, hail and even tornadoes in the afternoon. Wyatt thought of apocalyptic horses riding over the horizon.

46

Hot. Heavy. Humid. Swollen, silent summer lay heavy over the Midway. Wyatt's grandfather used to describe these kinds of days as 'full as a tick', way back east, when the dust from a vehicle would hang over the dirt road for what seemed hours after it had passed, a brown ribbon reminder. Eyes down, Wyatt figured it must be the red-brown dust sticking to his Chuck Taylors that made that memory slip out of its slot. The sounds of the waking Midway were muted: test runs of the Doppel Looper sliced briefly through the air before fading away. Grunted greetings between carnies creaked like the cranking of awnings on the games up and down the sides of each line. A cough rattled out of a thin, bony chest inside a still unwrapped joint. Plastic trays crashing onto metal racks in the cafeteria seemed further away than they were. Things seemed closer, right on top of each other in this muted mid-morning light, yet the sounds were far away, hard to isolate.

Jonah wasn't himself, or at least not the person he'd known up to this point. The snap, the vigour, the focus, were somewhere else, stuck between last night and now. He stood smoking, eyes to the ground, while the rest of them looked anywhere but at each other. Wyatt noticed the bumps of his spine at the top of his collar. They waited for a plan. Who was going where? With the two women late, they'd have to split up to get both joints open. It was almost eleven, and Greg would be giving them grief if they weren't open on time, even though there wasn't even the usual smattering of gawkers shuffling around yet. Jonah spoke.

"Fuck. I've felt this air before. Every couple of summers these strange days land in places on the prairies. Meteorological phenomenon, of course. Nothing but that involved, though some say the rainmakers knew what was going down. Way before the white man. You can feel it building, sense the ions getting recharged up there somewhere." He gestured up past the Doppel Looper, cigarette between his fingers.

"See that, way over there?" He turned towards them, straightening, stretching his neck back. "We had a wicked storm here about fifteen years ago. Hail. Tornadoes. I think four people died in the city…" He took a drag from his smoke and tossed it.

"Oh well. Here's hoping, right! Let's get open before Greg shows up. Bruce, you come with me to the Birthday. You guys get the Can." He turned away and headed down the line. Bruce scurried after him, like Chester chasing Spike on Loony Tunes; "Hey Spike, wanna get some cats Spike?"

47

Petr and Wyatt worked in silence, the late night and early morning mixing in with the humidity so that everything was heavy, sticky like the Cotton Candy that was now spinning behind the glass up the line. Canvas up and cotters pinned. Plush hung heavy on the hook, Wyatt's arms shaking with the effort to get them arranged up high.

Fucking elephants. I'm hanging fucking elephants with this asshole. Petr kept his back to him. He could hear him counting out the float in his irritatingly efficient way, bills snapping as he faced them. He turned to Wyatt and passed him his. "There you go." Even that sounded smug and condescending.

The Midway began to get populated, but not to the degree you'd expect on Bracelet Day in the first week. A few marks bit on his half-hearted hustle, but Petr was managing a steady stream in his half of the joint, pulling in some decent dough for early in the day. Out of the corner of his eye, Wyatt could see him pacing, cat-like, beckoning them in out of the butter-sun with a wave of his cash-hand, barely speaking until he had them. Wyatt hated the sound of his own voice, the "Come on in and you can win, one in wins, one in wins" patter falling to the ground like failed attempts in the ring toss game. Chatter. Clatter. Doesn't matter. He started to slide into the memory vault. Where'd you go? Why'd you leave? Where are you now, why couldn't we be? Cooling off in the back winter room of old lonely December, hanging onto a pillow for fear of flying away, silhouettes profiled through the glass of the sliding door. "Is it her coming back for me was it all just a bad dream I can remember how it was with us the last time when you rose up and beckoned me from behind…"

"Hey. Hey!" It took a second for Wyatt to retreat and re-emerge.

Glasses, a moustache, hairy nostrils, in his face.

"I wanna play. Are you deaf?" Wyatt stuttered, sputtered and grabbed three balls off the counter. "No. No. I was just thinking about… something. Here. Five bucks." He turned away just in time to hear the familiar tight pop sound that meant the first ball the moustache had tossed had gone in. A winner. The hoots behind him lashed his back. He couldn't even pretend to celebrate with the man and his family, waiting impatiently while they debated which animal to pick. Petr smirked as he hauled down the elephant with a hook. The family shuffled away happily, the elephant on the shoulders of the father. He found some solace in the knowledge the idiot would have to carry it around for hours.

They patrolled their sides of the joint as guards in a castle. Wyatt did his best to not look at Petr whenever they met in the middle, but he could sense him waiting for a chance to say something clever. He was slipping too far into his own head, back to the ratchet of the heart he'd run from. Had tried to run from. Air so heavy it felt hard to walk through, metaphors running wild. A membrane that had been wrapped around him for how long now? When? When had that been, when he'd been able to just be where the fuck he was without his thoughts riding shotgun. The end of the innocence, when does that happen? To go from being in the scene to watching yourself in the scene. Degrees of separation. Isn't this what it was supposed to be about? Reclaiming the moment, breaking the rules about what is and isn't?

Wyatt watched his hand pass balls to another set of hands, felt the money slide into his apron, knew that Petr was conjuring up marks, many more marks, on the other side of the game. He was barely there. Swore he could smell the fresh-air scent she used to wear hiding in the thick, still; smell the other her on his fingertips as he ran them under his coke-clustered nostrils. Was I with her again, right? For real, this time. Which one is the dream, anyway? I am with you. I know I am. Once again, the gut-punch pop of a ball hitting the hole in the can, the "Ha" from Petr, put a pin in the balloon and drug him back down to the bottom of now. The winning couple scurried away, heads bent into an invisible wind.

"I dunno, Wyatt… you're blowing out the margin early today, eh? Not in the game? Well, you're in the game, but not, right? More than a little off, I'd say. What have you got, less than fifty bucks in your apron? I've got …" he pulled a neat pile of bills out of his apron and fanned them out… "maybe a hundred here and I haven't given one out yet." He smiled joylessly. "With that kind of performance, you won't make the syndi-cut haha." Wyatt hated him.

Two hours of heavy humidity had left a sheen of sweat on them. Petr's face looked like a glazed donut; Wyatt's arms were shining. Their light blue uniforms had dark stains under the arms and down the middle of the back. Even the sounds of the Midway, the cacophony of metal and music, screams and chatter of the endless stream of people passing by, had lost its separation. A world low to the ground. Petr had just begun a self-righteous soliloquy, whiny and aggrieved at the lack of relief in the joint ("Where the fuck is Bruce? We've been in here almost three hours. Fucking idiot. Did Des and Trish stay back the motel with a purloined pile of blow?") when Wyatt felt the change in the air. A sudden breeze brought some coolness in under the canvas. It didn't feel good, though.

48

The temperature dropped quickly, fast enough to harden the sweat on Wyatt's forearms. Canvas started to snap and heave in all the joints down the line. The awnings over the trailer games were creaking, and on the rides, the rivet-metal groaned, swaying high above the ants' nest that the Midway was becoming. People were scurrying in all directions. Mothers hauled bawling kids by the arm, fathers led them through kaleidoscopic knots of people, hanging onto candy apples, mirrors and stuffed animals. Shouts were swallowed and redirected by gusts coming with more frequency and intensity.

Greg's voice cut through the human and metal noise. Wyatt's first thought was "Where the hell did he get a megaphone?' when he heard the thin, metal shouts coming closer and louder from the far end of the line. A tracheotomy voice box imploring people to "keep moving, let's go everyone, get to the gates, get to your cars!" And seemingly concurrently, but separately to the carnies, a harsher, more demanding order to "Get this shit shut down! Tie down the joints, kill the power, c'mon, let's move!" He came towards them at the Milk Can, chewing up yards of asphalt at a time, his leather deck shoes managing to step around the garbage littering the Midway. Shot them a derisive look as he went by, hissing "Hurry the fuck up and get that joint tied "as he leaned into a gust down the C line. His voice got smaller and smaller. Wyatt and Petr finished tightening the knots. Jonah, panting, Lennon specs slightly askew, ponytailed hair barely hanging in the elastic at the back, got there as Petr cinched the last rope.

"Good. This is good. We just got the Birthday closed. Bruce was fucking useless. Where is he? He was going to the bathroom and coming here. This is a big one; we gotta get out of here now." Petr stood up and let go of the end of the rope. He was smiling.

"Don't know. Haven't seen ol' Brucey since uh …this morning. God only knows, eh? God only knows…" He popped his cigarettes out of his shirt pocket with a snap of his middle finger and offered them around.

"Smoke? Anyone?" Wyatt could sense his satisfaction but had no clue as to why. Jonah took a smoke without looking, then hunched over, cupped his hands, lit it and stood up scanning the grounds. He took a long haul and flicked it high into the wind; Wyatt watched it until it disappeared over the Himalayan.

"Fuck it. We can't wait for him. Hopefully Trish and Des haven't left yet. Let's get out of here."

The three of them put their heads down and ran towards the exit, dodging paper plates, cotton candy and broken prizes as the slate-grey sky began to scream.

49

The truck's lights swept the side of the motel as they turned in. Darkness at the break of noon, thought Wyatt, wondering why the door was open to their suite in such wind and rain. Jonah muttered a "What the fuck?" from the front, jerked the truck to stop, shut it off and tumbled out in one motion. Wyatt and Petr followed him into the darkened doorway. The door slammed behind them unbidden, a blast of cold wind sealing them in.

Des was at the kitchen table, chin cradled in her hands. Smoke rose languidly from a cigarette in the ashtray. Serenity emanating, black background, lights down, white teeth gleaming. There was a smell in the air, just beneath, of burnt hair. There was a dark stain on the knuckles on one hand, the red revealed when Jonah snapped on the light and called for Trish.

"Not here," said Des, leaning back in the kitchen chair and slowly stretching her arms up and back. She clasped her hands behind her head and cracked her knuckles. A few blond hairs hung off her watch strap. Jonah had gone into the other room, her words following him in. "She left about an hour ago. A bit of a mess after last night, to be sure. She wasn't herself at all this morning, you know? I tried to get her up and going, of course, so we could get down there on time, but she was… basically fetal on the bed. Rough shape. Compromised." Jonah had come back in by the time the "P" in "shape' had popped from her lips. He pointed to a busted cup on the kitchenette floor. "What happened?" His voice was low, soft. "Tell me what happened. Where did she go?"

The same self-satisfaction Wyatt had noticed earlier with Petr had wrapped itself around her. There was a smirk, a smile not quite hidden.

"I'm not sure, Jonah, but I think she might have left for good. Gone home. It took me forever to wake her. To try and get her up. She'd kept telling me to go away, hanging onto her pillow like a life preserver. Honestly, I knew we had to get to the grounds and kept telling her that—that you needed her—but she was fucked up. Pulling at her hair, screaming. She threw a cup at me when she finally came out. Saying crazy things. Accusations. Threats. I tried to calm her down. I really did. She wasn't having any of it. Pushed me away. And was calling me all sorts of crazy things. You, too. All of us. She didn't even call a cab, just grabbed her bag and ran out the door." She paused and took a drag off her smoke. "Thankfully, the storm hadn't started yet. Crazy out there, eh? Where's Bruce?"

Wyatt had taken the seat across from her. Petr had folded up the pullout Bruce had slept on while she spoke. He curled up on the end, catlike. Wyatt heard a throaty purr between the hauls on his cigarette, a quiet "mmmm" as she finished each of her sentences. Jonah stood in the middle of the kitchen floor, arms crossed, watching Des with his head tilted to the side. "So, she just left. That seems a little out of character, doesn't it? Not like her to do too many things on her own." He turned to Petr. "You know her from school. Ever see her do anything remotely independent?"

Petr smiled. 'Well, she came to the carnival, didn't she? Went against her father on that move. So, maybe there's more, or less, there than you know. Women, right?"

It got quiet. Hear-your-blood-pump quiet. Tap of a knuckle on the Formica table. Shuffle of Jonah's shoes pacing, circular and slow on the creaky, cracked tile. Wyatt got up, walked to the window and parted the curtain. Rivulets of rain ran down the mottled glass. Beyond, the trees along the road were vertical and calm. A blade of light sliced through, a bloated black cloud, a bit of blue behind it. The road shone.

"Looks like the worst of it's over," he said. "Rain's let up and the wind has died. Let's go get some food and then head back, see if things are still standing. C'mon. Maybe we'll find the MIAs."

It was moving past dusk now, but the air that had nose-dived in temperature when the storm hit was warming back up. A few lonely cars were scattered around the parking lots. Jonah pulled into the staff lot behind the trailers and everyone got out, the four doors of the truck slamming in unison. Jonah stood looking at the jagged metal horizon of the Midway. The rest of them waited. He took a deep breath.

"So clean, isn't it? The air gets recharged after something like this. Renewed. You can feel the change." He breathed deeply again.

"It's as though the edges of things are sharper." He started towards the Ferris Wheel. "Let's see what the damage is."

There was enough ambient light to see their way down the line towards the Milk Can game. One behind the other, Jonah in the lead.

"Hopefully they're there." A few people were cleaning up, setting garbage cans upright, pushing broken glass into piles with heavy-handled brooms scraping the asphalt. Most of the carnies attending to their joints had stuck around and toughed out the storm, their light blue shirts dark from the rain. They rounded the corner past the Himalayan to see Bruce leaning against the corner of the Milk Can, smoking. He didn't see them coming.

"Hey!" Jonah's voice had a bark to it, startling Wyatt and causing Bruce to drop his smoke into a puddle. It sizzled out. "Where the fuck did you go?" Bruce's face went from shocked to puzzled to smiling with relief.

"Oh, yeah. Yeah. It got kind of crazy, didn't it? I mean, you left, and the wind was getting wild. Honestly, I've never been in a storm like that. It got so dark and cold so fast. I kind of lost track of things with everyone running back and forth. Umm, I didn't know where you were. I figured the Can but because it's just canvas you wouldn't be staying there so I was going to go try and find you, maybe get some shelter in one of the semi-trailers, but then BillyBob came along, right out of the blue. Grabbed me by the arm and …yeah, he took me to his trailer to ride it out. That's where I was. Have been. With BillyBob. At his trailer."

Bruce was surrounded by them, his eyes darting back and forth as he talked, craving contact. Which had the opposite effect. As usual. They all looked anywhere but his eyes. After a bloated, awkward moment, Jonah relented and took him up on the offer.

"You've been with BillyBob for three fucking hours? Last night wasn't enough?" He stared at him, scanning his face, lips, hands and back to his eyes. "What'd you get up to?" A question that sounded more like an accusation. A conclusion. Bruce babbled.

"Nothing. Well. Not nothing. We rode out the storm. I was coming to the Milk Can—just had to run off to the other can for a minute for a piss, and when I came out, he was there. It was starting to hail! Did you get caught in the hail? Size of golf balls. Nuts. So, we ran for it. BillyBob had an umbrella we shared."

The group collectively crossed their arms and waited for him to continue. Bruce had no choice.

"So, yeah. It was nice of him, you know? I mean, who am I? Just a minion working a game on the B line, right? He put on some coffee and got me a housecoat because I was soaked, right. So…mmm… we relaxed and rode it out. Not gonna lie—there may have been a line or three involved haha but that's okay, got me back into the groove after last night. Great guy. And oh yeah, he's offered me the spare room in the RV for the rest of the run here, which beats the fuck out of sleeping on that pull-out. My back is still sore from that bar that runs across it. Why do they put that in there? A real design flaw…. So, the rest of this run, I'm staying with BillyBob. Never thought I'd be back there in the high-rent district, but we really hit it off. He likes me. Says I've got a lot of potential." He stopped for a minute, caught his breath. Wyatt noticed the red raw rings around his nostrils. Bruce ramped it back up.

"Don't look at me like that, Jonah! I'm not abandoning ship or going over to"—he put up finger quotes—"the dark side. I'll still be working for you, doing the syndicate magic back in the Can! Can't leave you hanging high and dry, right? The three of us are a well-oiled machine now, all thanks to you. Sorry, all of us! All of us. Don't mean to leave the ladies out. I mean lady out!" He paused for a minute, a quizzical, puppy-dog look coming across his face.

"Where's Trish? Still messed up from that session at BB's? Man was she wacked. You wouldn't believe the shit she was babbling while I tried to get her home. Crazy. Saying she knows something's coming… we should just leave … plus she puked in the back of the taxi. Had to give him an extra twenty…"

Des spoke. She had the same near-smile on her face as when she'd broken the news to them earlier.

"Trish seems to be gone, Bruce. She left. It all got to be a little too much for her, I think. Obviously. I don't doubt she's on a plane back to Toronto by now. Good luck getting that twenty back." A snicker from Petr.

"Too bad. I liked her. We all liked her, didn't we?" Des's eyes scanned the circle and landed on Jonah's. "But we carry on, right? Our mission is not yet complete!" She laughed longer and louder than Wyatt could recall her ever having done before. Jonah took over.

"So, you're going to stay in the RV with BillyBob for the rest of the run? Seriously?"

Bruce nodded.

"And he's just doing that why? Why do you think? The size of his heart? Your wit and charm? Coming and going around here is a bit different than you might think, is all. Of course, you're free to do what you want. Free will. Free Willy. Free the pandas. Stop continental drift…whatever. I do know it's easier to get on a ride than to get off it."

Petr took a step into the middle of the circle.

"Ah, Jonah, give the kid a break! Don't you remember when you were a fresh-faced young lad, looking for adventure out there in the great big world? I know *some* of your stories! When BillyBob offers you a house on a hill, wouldn't it be less than gracious to… decline? You sound maybe a wee bit jealous you've never had that carrot dangled. Or have you? Haha! Just joking…."

Bruce was smiling and nodding, the centre of much more attention than he was used to.

"Jeez, Jonah, it's not like I'm going to be on the other side of town. I'll be closer to work than any of you. I always get stuck with the couches and hide-a-beds… Don't get me wrong; I'm not complaining, but boy oh boy the thought of my own room with a fucking door for a few nights sounds pretty good to me. Not even gonna mention the other accoutrements that come with the place." He sniffed a couple of times to make the point more obvious.

"It won't be a problem. I promise. I'll even get the joints opened in the morning before you guys get here, just to save some hassle." He looked at Jonah, far too bright-eyed for the waning light.

Jonah slid a smoke from his pack and lit it. It stayed quiet but for the ambient Midway sounds.

"Bruce, you don't need my permission. And no one needs to be your advocate or defender. Big boy pants, right? I've already had my say and you've already decided, so let's go with that. If Trish doesn't come back, maybe one of you two"—he looked at Petr and Des—"can grab the hide-a-bed and get a break from each other. For rest. Talking that long into the night must be tiring, right? Little change will do some good, maybe." He tossed the smoke onto the ground.

"See you in the morning, Bruce." He lit towards the parking lot, the rest of them slowly slinkying into line behind him. Wyatt saw BillyBob leaning against the Whac-A-Mole joint at the other end of the line, watching them. "Okay…" said Bruce in a plaintive, little boy voice. "I'll see you in the morning." It sounded like a question.

50

Wyatt pushed open the door to the dark motel room, pawing the wall to the left for the light switch. Trace elements of Trish dusted the air, the light, springtime scent of her perfume mingling with the decades of cigarette smoke that clung to the wallpaper. He ran his tongue along the roof of his mouth and swallowed the smell. Petr pushed past him, brought his hands together in a slow clap.

"Alright. Whole new situation in here now, isn't it? *Lebensraum*. We can sort out the sleeping arrangements in a bit. No need to rush things. I'm calling first shower though!" He goose-stepped down the hall to the bathroom, tittering to himself until the door clicked shut.

Down to four from six meant a quieter space, but there was more to the less than Wyatt could articulate to himself. After showers and pizza, they sat watching TV, sharing the smallest of talk. Sentences tiptoed around each other. The mundanity of "So, anyone know the weather for tomorrow?" from Petr, or "I guess we can just soak our uniforms in the sink and hang 'em to dry" from Des were less conversation as much as they were fillers. Ways to deflect from the defections. Only Jonah avoided the surface noise, smoking one Drum after another, rubbing his thick knuckles with the smoke-holding hand. When he finally got up and wandered off to bed, the rest of them did the same. For a long time, Wyatt lay awake to the sounds of the hissing of tires on the main drag outside, the occasional headlight slicing through the crack in the curtains.

51

A north wind kept the bright morning cool the next day. They got out of the truck and slammed their doors shut in unison again, Petr commenting on how nice it was to have them all in sync, saying it but not meaning it; still with the sardonic undertone tone that got under Wyatt's thin skin. He was fonder of his own sarcasm. He and Petr split away from Jonah and Des down the B line to the Can and were pleasantly surprised to see the sides up on the joint. Bruce sat on the boards smoking, elbows on his knees, staring at the ground. He lifted his head as they got close, finding a smile.

"Hey. What'd I tell you? Got the ol' joint up and open ready for action. All good! All good staying on site, get the three squares and a place to put my feet up. A headboard to call home, amirite?" Crickets.

"Umm…yeah, me and BB just sorta hung out, you know? No big deal hahaha…a few lines, maybe more than a few, haha, but that's about it. Not much to write home about. Maybe up a little late…" The way the late morning light hit his glasses made his eyes look wet to Wyatt. Petr stopped in front of him, looking down.

"Good. Very good. Glad it…worked out. BillyBob certainly has his charms, especially when the crowd goes home. So they say. I've no doubt you'll be well served during your stay." He smiled the whole time he spoke, pushing some flesh up onto his angular cheeks. His pupils sat back in his eyes, shuttered. Wyatt thought how a cat can sit so still, watching a mouse. Relaxed, because it knows the mouse never gets away. Wyatt decided to leave them to it.

"I'll take the first break. Jonah said a half hour is what we get now, then we take turns pitching in at the Birthday Game. It's too late in the run to hire a local. I'll grab a bite and go down there for a couple, come back and spell you off."

52

Leaning on the corner of the House of Horrors, Wyatt stood with a Styrofoam plate, finishing his BLT. He had an unobstructed view of the Birthday Game and could watch Des and Jonah pace the cage, adjusting to the new "Trish-less" dynamic. They had a decent tip going. The Birthday Game always had a decent tip going because, as Jonah said on the mic several hundred times a day, if you've got a bellybutton, you've got a birthday; there was no skill involved. Jonah's patter got mixed in with the bells, whistles, slams, smashes and screams from the rides until it was lost to Wyatt's ears. He lit a smoke.

Des had her hair in a ponytail, so you could see the high-cheeked, wide and steady smile on her face, even from a distance. She moved smooth and quick up and down the three sides of the game she was covering, spinning on the corners, slipping the money off the counter into her apron with grace and subtlety, giving a wink or a word to each mark. The personal touch. Wyatt was reminded again of how Des had made her money before the carnival. It was still performance for her; she was wired to move with rhythm.

Jonah was sticking to one side of the joint, pacing with the mic in one hand, the other sweeping bills and coins off the counter or tossing the ball from the middle of the game to the next player. He'd catch their eye, ask if they want to give it a try, managing to make it sound like a new and unique opportunity every time. Laughter and smiles before the ball was thrown, followed by "C'mon March" or "Let's go, November!"; Jonah building up the suspense as the rubber ball bounced inside the plexiglass square ("It's gonnnnnnaaaa beeee Octo…oh wait…. November for the win! November bringing home the bacon!") before the tension of the toss was released with cheers, or groans of disappointment.

Jonah kept his back to Des most of the time, angling away from her even when retrieving the ball from the far side, her side, of the box, reaching his arm out but still leaning away. Wyatt watched Des watching him in between cash scoops and entreaties to the steady stream of people slowing down as they passed by. Wyatt could see Jonah was always in the corner of her eye, and she kept that smile on the whole time. A serious smile. Strategic. He tossed his smoke and went to the game. Jonah welcomed him on the mic.

"There he is folks, a late, great addition to the Birthday Game family, all the way from the Milk Can on Line B, give it up for Wyatt!" A couple of confused claps as he climbed over the boards and grabbed Trish's apron, stashing his under the boards. Important to keep the cash separate. He took his place on the far side of the game. Even in the fifteen minutes he'd been watching them the crowd had gotten noticeably larger. Two deep around the game now, so they locked in hard and started grabbing peak-hour cash.

Up close, he could sense it. Des magnetized in her high shorts and cheekbones, cowboy boots and choreographed movements. Despite the confined space, sliding her way around the game, there was a patience that emanated; muscle memory of a thousand dances. He thought for sure that she winked at him at one point before tossing the ball back over to Jonah. A conspiratorial, smug wink. Or, maybe I'm projecting that, Wyatt thought. *Maybe this is all in my head.* Jonah would know. He'd recognize. Manipulating circumstance was one of the core takeaways from his time here so far, and Jonah had a black belt in how that worked. How energy could be guided, if not controlled. Surely, he'd not be a mark.

Jonah kept the patter rolling. Wyatt had marveled many times at his ability to keep the "if you've got a belly button, you've got a birthday" thread winding through the long, neon nights on the tarmac. With a raised eyebrow, or a wink and a nod he'd dial into the eyes of an unsuspecting mark. "Hey now! Come on in and win. Winner every time, turn it on a dime. And hello there! Yes, you with the dazzling and radiant energy coming off you! In from out of town for a big night, I see!" And the mark would nod demurely, self-consciously, embarrassed and loving the attention. Respond with a smile, or laughs with the group she'd come to the Fair with, everyone happy thinking what was going on was what was actually going on, that the man up there with the microphone was a permanent fantasy fixture. "Well come right over—that's it. Don't be shy; not asking you to take the collection plate around in your church tomorrow morning! You know the good lord gives and the good lord can take it away, but I'm just here to give you this ball to toss in the bin and make a dream or two come true!" Giggles and 'aw shucks' laughs gathered around her as they moved en masse towards the boards.

While Jonah was working the mic and building the tip, truly charming the folk with a big smile and open arms, Wyatt was at the other end scooping up cash off the counter. Des was doing the same on the other side. She had her back to him, sliding money off the polished wood into her apron. Her left hand was in her back pocket. Wyatt finished his sweep and watched her left hand move towards a pack of Marlboros and a lighter tucked under the corner. Her fingers felt around while she faced out towards the Midway. Like a crab, he thought. Curled around the lighter and pulled it up and slid it into her back pocket. It struck him as odd, and odder still when she pulled it back out once the crescendo for the toss of the ball was building—'What's it gonna be March, April or May, or the old November grey?"—and tossed it hard and low across the Midway, hard it enough that it went way under the House of Horrors façade. It made no sense to him.

Twenty minutes of a busy tip flew by like a thought, and the three of them came up for air before the next wave. Jonah went to the corner to grab his smokes, fumbled around for the long-gone lighter. Bent down and checked the ground. "Shit... must have put my lighter somewhere," he muttered. He turned to Wyatt and was about to ask for a light when Des came over to his side of the game, got out her Zippo and snapped back to the top, lighting it in one very smooth motion. She cupped her hand around it as Jonah leaned towards the flame.

53

At this point in the summer run, differentiating between days of the week was not so much impossible as irrelevant. Wyatt had truly lost count of how many days they'd been here. "Here" mattered even less than the day of the week. The name of the city was only useful in telling someone where you were. The horizon of office towers meant nothing. Life existed somewhere in the in-between, midway as it were, warmed by asphalt, cooled by a rare bit of breeze that came down from the north, blowing past the tar fields, skimming over forever-blue lakes, scarping through the boreal forests till it found its way to cooling the back of a neck in the humming summer heat. Aching lower back and feet, watching the watch for 11 p.m. so the sides could come down, the lights could go off and the ants could make their way in under the hill until the cracking dawn.

Wyatt groaned his way up off the bed. Lights still on in the kitchen, the smell of cigarette smoke coating his nostrils. Another day. Three more here? Or two. He couldn't remember. Fog all around, feet finally on the floor, toenails too long, more of an effort than it should be to force himself vertical. Finally, up, walk sliding off the carpet onto the dirty linoleum tile of the kitchen area. He remembered putting coffee in the machine right before bed. Was that last night? He pressed the button, reassured as it began to percolate. He went for a piss.

They came out of their rooms within minutes of each other, the smell of the coffee cutting through the stale air, slipping under their locked doors. Wyatt felt like he was watching a B movie zombie outtake, Des with her hair hanging down haggard, still with a bit of that glow from the day before lifting her cheeks and lighting her eyes. Petr, ponytail untied, sallow and pale under the one-track light, and Jonah, least and last of all. Wyatt could see the remains of Trish still clinging to him. Not much was said beyond passing of coffee and lighters. Once the pot was empty, they got up and headed out. Des closed the door behind them.

54

Metamorphosis. Not like a chrysalis, Wyatt inner-corrected. Nothing beautiful happening here. Might have been Grade Two, or somewhere thereabouts, when they'd watched a film in class about Monarch butterflies, strange, sticky cylinders. Globbed up, then drying, cracking open with the Super 8 slow motion going *tickity tickity tick* in the dark, blind-drawn room, young, eager eyes wide watching the orange-gold creature pry open the crinkly casing of its former self and emerge into the world. A miracle, the teacher had said. But this was not that.

Bruce looked like…hell. It was too easy of a thing to say, too trite and not what he would have chosen to come coursing into his thoughts; he'd have used far more florid language, even to himself, had he been more prepared for the sight. But…hell. There it was. Bruce was a fucking mess.

He was waiting for them in front of the Milk Can, whose canvas flaps were still down. Pacing as they approached, little smoke signal puffs from his cigarette visible, rising in the dead morning air. An attempt at a hale and hearty good morning fell flat, falling from his lips and disappearing.

"Hey ho! Yeah, here we are again. Here we go again. How's it all going? Morning. Morning. No one thought to have brought me a coffee huh, haha. No worries. Not a problem"

So different from yesterday, Wyatt thought. What was going on? Was this day three since he'd taken up residence at the BillyBob luxury suites? Looked like thirty. His knees. His surreptitious scan started with his knees. Red, raw. A gash opened on the top of the kneecap blinked wet as Bruce shifted his weight from one foot to the other. A couple of welts on the inside of the other thigh appeared to be blistering. His non-smoke-holding hand was balled up in the pocket of his shorts. The veins at the top of his wrist were the colour of blue cotton candy. His stained clown shirt was tucked inside his underwear band in the front and hung half out on one side. Blue and red stripes. Further up, past the clockwork clown face and Marlboros in the pocket, a sunken throat and jagged trachea, mottled skin stretched tight over it like a turkey at Christmas. Wyatt hadn't noticed that before. To the chin, again red (From shaving? Can't be from shaving because the stubble was still there on his cheeks), one of which was as red and raw as his knees. The ear on the same side looked swollen.

But it was the eyes. It's always the eyes, thought Wyatt. They had a curtain over them, or more to the point, a Venetian blind that might open a crack if there was a little light to let out or in. Behind his glasses, Bruce's eyes had changed colour. Definitely. Lighter, paler. Not baby blue. Closer to the cotton candy blue of the veins just under the skin of his arms. Irises like the tip of a Bic pen, as tiny as could be. Wyatt couldn't imagine how any light got in there. He seemed to be someone else. His lips were as cracked and dried as his old-man hands. Smiling had to hurt. The big, dumb grin was MIA.

Petr hop-scotched his way into the space between, whistling while he snapped the yellow rope knots loose on the canvas.

"Up and at 'er, big guy! The sun is high, nearly as…umm… high as you are. Or were. Did you even look at yourself in the mirror in BillyBob's bedro…. I mean bathroom. Haha."

Light, nasty little whipping of joyful words. Savouring the sight before him. Wyatt hated that Petr was loving it.

"Getting much sleep over there, or up all night…talking?" Bruce was trying to respond, trying to be cool. He swallowed hard and his Adam's apple seemed to nearly poke through the pale, under-the-chin flesh.

"I, uh, yeah, I'm fine," somehow made it through those papery lips, but the words were low to the ground, hard to hear and didn't convince.

"Really? If you say so, but I have to say, from way out here, you look like you've seen better days. Either way, let's get the rest of the sides up. We're open." Petr turned towards him.

"We've got this, Wyatt; you might want to go see if Jonah needs any help."

Wyatt hesitated. Petr was moving around the game with methodical intensity, polishing the mouth of the can, rearranging the plush, tying his apron on, lighting another smoke, counting his float. He appeared happy, which was incongruous with the person he'd spent the last month with. Cynical, sarcastic, caustic, cutting and insightful in a sterile, soulless way. Certainly never genuinely happy, but that was the vibe. Even whistling. To take such joy from someone's pain… obviously messed-up situation…. Wyatt didn't want to leave Bruce with him. Wanted to protect him, which at the same time struck him as ridiculous. Hadn't he had a lot of fun at Bruce's expense? Hypocrite. But he still didn't move.

"Maybe Bruce could…" He couldn't think of much Bruce could do.

"As if! Look at him!" It was like Bruce wasn't there. Or he was some little kid.

"I've got control here; you just go and make sure Jonah and Des don't need anything. This guy"—he gave a derisive tilt of his head towards silent, sunken Bruce—"is no good to anybody right now." Wyatt walked away, hands like rocks stuffed into his apron, stopping to look back several times until he rounded the bend onto Line A.

They were up and running at the Birthday Game. There was a young blond kid, maybe fifteen, in the game between Jonah and Des when he got there. Jonah was animating with his hands the way he did when he was explaining something, the kid locked with his eyes and nodding up and down, Des smiling benevolently. He must have managed to recruit a local. There was always ballast hanging around by the rides and trailers over the course of a run. The kid would have a couple days of work, a few bucks and bragging rights with his friends, if not his parents. Wyatt caught Jonah's eye long enough to be waved away. Things were under control at the Birthday Game, the new kid tying on his apron as Des looked on indulgently, then helped him with the knot behind his back like a mother would. Wyatt left them to it.

55

As Wyatt stood by the edge of the Himalayan, watching the Milk Can from about a hundred feet away, he felt as much a voyeur as someone involved in the guts of what was unfolding. Sinead O'Connor was blasting "Emperor's New Clothes." Again. He had no lipreading skills, especially from so far away, but the body language…

The crowd had begun to overrun the Midway, the screams were as high as the rides and most of the games down the line had begun to grab some marks, but the four sides of the Milk Can were empty real estate.

Petr was standing over a sitting, fetal Bruce, his arms folded across the clown on his shirt, a cigarette sticking out of the corner of his smirk. He was talking and shaking his head, short pacing back and forth in front of him, hectoring, lecturing, laughing, finger-pointing. Bruce, sitting on the boards with a couple of softballs in his lap, had his Buddy Holly glasses off and kept wiping his eyes. He looked half the size of Petr, even though he was taller. No one was going anywhere near whatever was going on. When he saw Petr casually swipe the glasses onto the ground with his foot, Bruce blubbering and getting down on the ground to find them, he pushed himself away from the speaker stack and started to walk over, his blood beginning to bubble. That's when he saw BillyBob, on the other side of the line, watching them. He made a beeline round to his blind side.

56

The ether entered his head as he rounded the backside of the Funhouse, triggering the out-of-body. Watching himself from somewhere else, not unlike the lucid dream trails of the past. Closer, in fact, to his more recent revelations in the Can, where the space/time inexplicably shifts. The sounds of the Midway had begun to elasticize; teenage-girl screams from the roller coaster wrapped around the ding-dong of the hammer smashing the iron to the bell. The *tickity-tack* of the Money Wheel rolled in and out of the cotton-candy blowers, *sloooowwwwinnng* to one final snap like a tongue off the roof of the mouth of the Clown at the gate. A singular shout of victory and the low, collective drone of loss, followed by the sound of more money snapping down on the various, varnished colours on the counters. Money all around, flying from hand to hand to hand. Money metastasized into "unlimited ride" bracelets hanging off bony, pre-pubescent wrists, darts held point-down in bundles of three in calloused, thick-knuckled man hands, cheap plastic rings tinging off Coke bottle necks reflecting the blinking, blinding kaleidoscope of lights. In and out and all around, infinite roiling variations, the same and opposite of the forever replicating image manufactured in the House of Mirrors.

BillyBob remained fixated on the scene of transferred abuse unfolding in the Can as Wyatt floated up beside him. Even in his faraway fugue, Wyatt somehow separated the sounds and smells from the surrounding Midway and was able to silo himself beside Bob, gaining access to the specific, nuanced vibrations emanating from him. A weathervane, he thought. Am I that, or just vain to be thinking I'm accessing this shit? He could see the pockmarks that crept from the back of Bob's collar around and up his neck to his cheek.

Must have been bad when he was a teen, Wyatt heard himself think. He saw flakes of makeup wedges in the tiny craters, meant to smooth out the pockmarks; make them less visible. Hidden. Flecks of dandruff clung to the collar and were scattered onto the shoulder of his striped Polo shirt, belying the slicked-back hair. (Brylcreem? It couldn't be Brylcreem making the dyed black shine, as perfect as that would be given the location! Location! Location! of this silent observation.) The crinkled corner of his eye in this two-dimensional profile might have been lifted off the wall of a long-hidden, uncovered tomb in the Valley of the Kings. Oh, how he'd loved those books when he was a kid, cradled in his bony-wristed hands atop the quilt his grandmother had passed down.

The smells, though. That's the real trigger of memory, isn't it? That's what all the experts say. You can go back to a specific place in time with just one whiff of a relevant scent. He'd experienced that, more than once. A smell of rye and ginger once transported him back into his six-year-old skin, waiting in the back of a brown sedan outside of a small town Royal Canadian legion for what felt like hours because it was hours, screaming inside the car with the windows rolled up for them to come out and go home. More recently, a thin waft of the same perfume she had used to wear, maybe still wore, arms around a new love, had been left behind in the hall outside the bathrooms at a lonely, lost American night truck stop off the interstate in northern California. He'd walked back outside, into the mosquito-speckled fluorescent humming night, looking for her in the space between thought and time. Then, the comedown, as though waking from an impossibly beautiful dream.

This thing, this sideview... The eye in front of him was not laugh-crinkled, knowing without knowing how he knew. They were different crevices, deepened by squints and curses and unholy demands. He concurrently thought of Des reading Billybob's palm in the trailer way back there somewhere, lines in eyes, lines on hands. Fortune. Telling. Everything following a fissured trail, leading to something. Wyatt felt himself being pulled in closer to the bas relief of Bob, until he could smell only him, becoming overwhelmed with whatever the scent was that enveloped him, tried to recall the name on the bottle in the bathroom of BillyBob's RV. 'Eau de Owe', he thought, smiling somewhere at his unbearable cleverness, and that being the last sense of self he had until he emerged from the search for lost time in the vapours.

57

He was walking down a dry, reddish-dirt midway. The dust had risen and coated the cuffs of his dungarees, a makeup foundation on the heavy blue cotton. The surrounding sounds slowly came into focus: a distantly familiar ring of a lead bell hurtled with a hammer; hurdy-gurdy melodies cranked up and unleashed into the dust hanging in the hot mosquito air; barkers belting out their wares to the slow walking, eyeballs-wide shufflers, continually feeding the evening sundown haze with more dust-matter from the ground.

"Over here, over here, all the way from the dark, mysterious lands where the Romanovs met their maker at the hands of godless communists, the one and only Bearded Lady. A quarter gets you in to see for yourself, and yes, folks, you can poke and prod and pull that beard! Find out for yourself if this freak of nature is a real woman, a Siren of Siberia!"

Dreamtime Wyatt kept walking past, the bearded lady hustle leaking air behind him, supplanted by a black top-hat-clad man with a megaphone in deep cylindrical tones beckoning the window-shoppers to dare to come behind the striped exterior and see a "genuine wonder of the world, the Lizard Boy!"

He sidled up to the little knot of people peering into the tent through the gap in canvas. The barker on the platform caught his eye, gave him a one-sided smile and continued.

"You won't believe your eyes, ladies and gentlemen. On a scale... haha, *scales*...of one to ten, this freak, this abomination of the laws of God and man, is an eleven! A thirteen! A six hundred and sixty-six!" The people involuntarily recoiled, then moved closer together, Wyatt included. He could see the sheen of sweat on the barker's upper lip, the dark stains under the arms of his white-as-a-knight shirt. Little bits of spittle sprayed those up front as he hissed, hollered, cajoled and convinced. He finished his pitch and majestically stepped off the platform towards the dark hole in the front of the tent, the megaphone left on the lectern, his open hand accepting carefully folded and crinkled bills with equal magnanimity, deftly stuffing each one into the pocket of his razor-edge-pressed black pants. To his surprise, Wyatt had a one-dollar coin with a seven with a line through it in his outstretched hand, shining silver in the late-day sun.

The sweat on his neck cooled quickly once he followed the little line inside the dark confines of the tent. The sounds of the carnival were muted, replaced with a cool, shadowy, canvas-stretched quiet. His eyes rolled upwards to a hole in the top of the tent where the roof beams met; he could make out a lone star in the darkening sky of the outside world. Without the megaphone, the barker's voice was softer, wrapped in vocal velvet.

"Thanks for being here everyone. Come on in now, don't be shy. Come a little bit closer, towards me." Feet shuffled through the dark and dust to the far corner of the room. Other shuffling could be heard once they all stopped—quicker, back and forth and back and forth. And wheezy, laboured breathing. Blond, abnormally tall twins stood on either side of what Wyatt's dark-adjusted eyes could make out as a red curtain, a conical, tornado shape woven onto it in thick, gold thread.

The barker's voice now sounded as though it emanated from the bottom of a well.

"Now is the time, ladies and gentlemen, for your notions about what is and isn't possible on this mortal coil to be shaken (the voice got louder, began to surround), to be questioned, (louder, the twins standing taller, growing taller, candle shadow trickery!) to be changed forever! Witness the Lizard Boy!" The twins pulled either side of the curtain. It scraped dry on the rod, herky-jerky. The knot of people loosened and pulled back.

There was too much to take in at first. Undulating greenish scales, like the deep phosphorescent green on a dragonfly wing, rising and falling quickly with the short, panic-breaths. Upright but slumped, it looked old and young all at once. The arms, if you could call them that, reminded him of mockup pics of a T-Rex, blended with the horrifying photos of thalidomide babies from *Life Magazine*. The feet were webbed, wet looking. Through the red-rusted bars that separated it/him from the gawkers, it was the eyes that Wyatt's own came to rest on, despite the freakshow body on display.

They were blue, blue as a finger-flicked marble that finds its way to a hole on a playground, and a thin, dark ring of black around the edge. They shifted, quick, feral, fear-filled, though God only knew how many times this curtain had been pulled. A woman in front swooned and dropped. The barker took charge.

"There, there now. That's right. Move her to the side. Right there. Prop here up against the pole. She'll come around soon enough. Happens a lot. The shock of it, you see…" One of the twins slid towards her, moving without lifting his/her feet. It was hard to tell if it was a man or a woman; there was an alien androgyny to the gaunt facial features and thin, elongated body. It leaned down and wiped the woman's face with a wet white cloth. The harsh, razor voice of the barker brought their attention back to the cage.

"Look! Just look at what you've done!" He was spitting the words at the now cowering creature. "You know better! We've been over this. No eye contact with the women. You're vile. Evil. Wicked and wormy. I can't have you doing this with fine, upstanding, paying customers, can I? You must learn. You must be punished…again!" The repellent reptilian attraction was fetal in the corner of the cage, back turned, pathetic. Choked sobs escaped through the nostril gills. The barker's voice softened, took on a weary tone of resignation as he turned back to the people.

"I am so sorry. Truly. I thought we'd been able to amend the behaviour enough to prevent this sort of thing from happening. The Lizard Boy does and *should* know better." He paused for a moment for effect.

"You know, maybe another intervention is needed. Some discipline to communicate the severity of his transgressions." The barker's voice transformed again, morphing into a Midway version of a Southern Baptist fire-and-brimstone thrower.

"Why yes! Yes, brothers and sisters. He must be punished. Only through punishment can true change, dare I say, transformation, be achieved." His voice ascended, filling the room.

"Will you, good citizens of this fine town, help me bring it back to its place, to knowing its place?" Slow shuffling silence.

The barker, now louder, more urgent and demanding: "I ask you again; will you help me?" A "yes" squeaked out from the back row, then another. A hand on the end of an arm beside him went up. Then another. Soon, everybody, all fifteen or twenty of them, were in. All except Wyatt; he watched himself watching.

The twins on either side of the cage seemed taller and thinner now, and backlit. Luminescent, the light from their bodies allowed Lizard Boy to be seen more easily. The residual noise from the other world outside was long gone now, overridden by a metallic hum that filled the tent. It had replaced the bangs and laughter and shouts surreptitiously, Wyatt determined, with no one inside even noticing. There was a hypnotic effect to the noise that wound itself round and round the inside of his head. The barker's now metallic voice was the only sound that cut through the ear-drowning drone. That, and the rat-a-tat rattle of a shiny, silver triangle of keys on the bars of the cage. The barker beckoned the crowd closer with his free hand as he hurled verbal darts at the Lizard Boy.

"Get up! Right now, get up and get over here." No movement, only the rise and fall of the scaly, shiny chest and the opening and closing of the gills.

"I said get up! Don't make me come in there. You know what happens when I come in there!" The gathering tightened up, leaning forward as one. The Lizard Boy turned over on the pile of straw so that one dark eye stared unblinking. Another loud, violent clang of the key triangle on the bars sent a ripple shock through the body of the Lizard Boy, who slowly rose to his elbows and knees and crawled towards the front of the cage. The woman in front of him backed up, stepped on his toe, turned and whispered "sorry." Wyatt responded with the same.

The twins had moved towards where the barker had been standing, their eyes casting beams like stage lights on the vacant space. His shadow preceded him into the light, arriving way before his body, hunched over from carrying great weight. His arms were tight around his torso, clenching a black box. His knees cracked as he knelt down and set the box on the rough dirt in front of the cage. The air above the box shimmered, mirage-like. The bars of the Lizard Boy's cell began to bend; Wyatt could feel the fierce heat on his face, even from the back row. The top of the box was radiant red-orange.

The barker's voice sounded like crinkling tinfoil as he addressed them. The triangle of keys had been replaced with a metal stick he waved in the air like a conductor as he spoke. It had a square shape on the end of it, perpendicular to the rod.

"You know, people, I've tried and tried to…civilize the Lizard Boy, to no avail whatsoever. Rescued him from the swamps of Amazonia where his own family rejected him outright and left him to die. Brought him north across many borders, fed, clothed and provided shelter and protection, and this is what I…what *we*…get for thanks." The brittle voice got louder, the twins nodding in unison as the barker continued.

"Just when you think everything is good, all the lessons have been learned, everyone knows their place and life can go on as it should, there's another …situation." He turned to the Lizard Boy, who was watching warily, his shiny body sideways, head turned so that both black, lidless eyes beheld them.

"I don't know, ladies and gentlemen…I just don't know. It can get so wearisome. Truly, all we…all I… ever wanted was the best for him. But he appears to think none of that matters. That he can crawl into a corner and sulk instead of putting on a proper show for you fine, hard-working people. You paid your money, did you not?" Silence. Louder. "Did you not?" Grudging, tremulous muttering of "yes, yeah, right."

"Well, if he won't listen to me, maybe he'll pay attention to someone else. Who wants to teach the Lizard Boy a little lesson?" He was wielding the metal rod more menacingly now, waving it in the air as he spoke, making his verbal points with violent, jabbing motions. When he finished, he held the thick, heavier end over the red-hot box. He looked around the crowd, held each person's eyes for a moment, before settling on Wyatt. He smiled knowingly.

"Awww, yes. You. You in the back there. Come here now." It wasn't a suggestion. Wyatt felt himself pulled past the bodies in front of him, the barker hauling him through the front row with his free hand.

"We have a volunteer, folks. This young man will make things right and show the Lizard Boy the error of his ways. "His voice was softer now. Warmer. Wetter. The heat from the box felt like it was blistering Wyatt's face. The twins on either side had morphed into tall, white-robed vaporous number sevens.

The barker passed the metal stick to him. Up close, Wyatt could see what it was now, a cold-as-ice brand, the kind he'd seen in cowboy movies on the black-and-white TV. At the bottom, hovering above the coals, were three lines, like a European numeral seven, but connected to a silvery, cylindrical cone. He stuck it into the red box without being told, and watched the metal gain the colour of the coals. The shaft remained cold.

"There ya go son, that's it! You know exactly what needs to be done. I knew I picked the right guy." He turned back towards the Lizard Boy.

"I said"—he was spitting it, the spittle sizzling on the coals below— "get over here now!" The Lizard Boy obeyed and shuffled through the straw closer to the bars. He looked up at Wyatt sideways, the black eye so shiny and clear that he could see his own face in it, shrunken and backwards. The barker reached into the cage and grabbed the tail of the Lizard Boy, flipping him around so his other side faced the cage. The crowd gasped, inhaled; someone thudded to the ground. The entire side of the Lizard Boy was a grotesque pattern of brands from the iron Wyatt held in his hand; circular symbols one on top of the other on top of the other. There were dozens of them, giving his hide the appearance of old wallpaper. Wyatt felt bile rising. The barker was grunting, groaning, cursing while the two twins hovered ever higher on either side of him.

"Go on! It's ready. Go on. Let him have it. Sear him! Sear him! Save him! Save him! Nothing can save him; nothing can save him now!"

58

BillyBob's voice? The barker's voice? The scene went up in an ethereal, smoky mist, wound around twin towers of light. Wyatt's ears popped. He felt the paralysis of the vision wearing off, clenching and unclenching his hands to be certain. The cloistered sound of the dream was punctured, overcome by harsher, harder sounds of the Midway that had reappeared in front of him. BillyBob's face was six inches from his, sneering, sweating, smiling... accusing.

"You think you're gonna save that kid? Seriously? Just look at him over there. A pathetic fucking mess? I have to admit, we've...I've haha...had a pretty good time with him the last little while. Up all day, up all night, am I right? But his time in the trailer would appear to be coming to an end. There's an expiration date with all good things. They get predictable after a certain point. Fuck; just look at him." He gestured towards the Milk Can.

Petr's razor-thin smile looked a mile wide, even from a distance. He had a cigarette pinched between the tips of his fingers, waving it about like a conductor's baton as he harangued the prone, all-alone body of Bruce. Every few movements, he'd bend down close to his downturned face and yell. Wyatt could tell it was a yell because he could see the tendons and veins in Petr's neck swell from the effort, before standing up straight again and pacing the side of the joint. The marks making their way past moved further out from the game, eddying around it the way you do with a canoe and rock-rapids in a river. It was nearing dusk, the golden hour when tips begin to manifest, but the only action in the joint was Petr and Bruce. Wyatt turned back to Bob; there was a thin film of sweat shining on his grossly fat lower lip.

"I don't know what you've been doing with him, BillyBob, and, honestly, I don't want to know. I think everyone was cool to let sleeping dogs lie, for a while at least. More room for the rest of us at the motel. But Jesus Christ, man! Look at him over there. He was fucked up before, but now he's a mess." Bob's fat smile-smirk triggered a gut rage.

"Oh. Funny, right? Just a mark, just a game. There's blood on the back of his shorts, Bob. What kind of a sick fuck are you, anyway?" The smirk died with Bob's eyes as he turned to face Wyatt.

"Okay. Listen to this thing I'm about to say. Listen good." The air changed its charge; Wyatt felt it way down deep where a few butterflies began to swoop and dive.

"I've been running with the carnival before you were a wiggly little sperm at the bottom of your old man's nutsack. Before he was one at the bottom of his father's, for fuck's sake. I grew up here. I'll die here. You've been here, what, a couple of months? Don't think I don't see what's going on with you…with your little group of artists. Intellectuals. Adventurers." He held up his hands and made quotation marks with his fingers as he voiced the words.

"You look a little surprised. Seriously, you think I'm fucking stupid? You think no one notices how special you all think you are? Guess what, asshole. I do. A few of us do." He paused, wiped some greasy sweat off his face with the back of his hand, and continued.

"Here's the thing. I know you feel so bad about little Bruce over there, so far in over his head, such a victim of the bad, bad man. Haha! I didn't even know I could be such a bad, bad man until he showed up, to be honest! Kudos to the dark-haired gypsy for calling that one! But... where was I?" He pulled a smoke out of his pack and lit it.

"Yeah. Been doing this a long time. Seen more water...and bodies... under the bridge than you could possibly imagine. And I know this. It's the same fucking thing you see when all the marks are walking by the games. What makes them pick one game over the other? Why the Water Gun instead of the Crown and Anchor? The Fun House instead of the House of Horror? The Doppel Looper instead of the Ferris Wheel? You wanna know what I think? Doesn't matter one fucking bit; people just make their choice. You pick it, you live with it. Watch your money get pulled off the table into an apron, watch your ball" he jerked his head towards the Milk Can—"bounce off the edge and hit the ground. I don't care. No one really cares, other than the ones with their hand out, waiting on the cash. People make their choice and pay the piper. Bruce over there, poor, weak, pale Bruce? Is he a part of your little gang? He made a choice. He's a big boy."

Whatever words Wyatt may have hoped to use in response circled the drain and went back down his throat. Disgust could not be discussed as the heavy, hard truth of what Bob had blurted descended. They had all set him up for this; any thoughts or feelings to the contrary had to be outed for what they were: self-serving and antithetical to the cumulative results of the past couple of months they'd shared. He and Bob turned towards the scene in the Milk Can. A lonely mark stood on the far side of the game with a five-dollar bill in his hand, head at a confused angle, watching Petr standing over Bruce.

59

Something snapped around Wyatt's head like a neon elastic. A switch flipped, a string of lights migrated from the Himalayan, blinking, blinding. His palms started tingling, getting wet the way they did right before a migraine came in for a landing, but this wasn't that. BillyBob's voice sounded so far away he couldn't make out any words; it had more of a distorted radio frequency to it. He felt himself drawn further away from it, from BillyBob…towards the Milk Can. He approached the game tentatively, tenderly, how one would approach the known scene of a crime, tiptoeing, careful not to disturb any evidence. Whatever had tethered him to BillyBob frayed and fell to the ground. The sounds of the Midway, of a bumping, humping Friday night, the ding-dangs, screams, laughter and curses enveloped him, brought him back into his own skin. He surprised himself when he heard the force of his voice cut through the shiny plastic din.

"Leave him alone for fuck's sake! Get away from him!" The slow-motion montage he'd made his way through picked up to real-time, with Petr turning towards him, the tip of his cigarette glowing beneath an arched eyebrow. Bruce's head emerged from his fissured hands. There was blood on both palms, and red residue on his temples. He made eye contact with Wyatt and tried to smile.

"Hey Wyatt. How's it going? Uh…not…not quite getting it done here uh right now. Not quite. No. Me and Petr are just kinda talking, you know? Figuring some things out. Whew…not quite feeling myself, you know? Tough. Tough coupla days indeed…"

Petr had moved to the corner of the joint, was now leaning against the boards.

"Well, there he is! Just who we've been waiting for; the cavalry. It's the cavalry, Brucey. Coming to save your ass. Ha! Your bloody, battered ass. Get the fuck up, man. Show a little respect." His voice became barbed. "Enough of the wallowing, we've got to get some money in the aprons!"

Wyatt climbed over the boards, standing between Bruce and Petr. He felt himself filling with an alien energy, enervated, elevated. He made magnetic contact with Petr's opaque blue eyes.

"Back the fuck off, Petr. He's a mess, man. What the fuck is wrong with you? He's hurt, can't you see that?"

Petr snorted.

"Hurt? Well, yeah. Did I do that? Did I force him to spend his nights in the… Whac-A-Hole? Haha, I'm fucking hilarious. God only knows what prizes made their way up in there, eh? One in wins indeed. Actions. Consequences. Weakness, Wyatt, more than any other thing, he's weak, amirite? You know we can't abide any weakness in the ranks, can we?"

Wyatt felt as though they were acting this out on a stage, despite the fact the only audience member was the guy across the other side of the game, who still held his fiver in his hand but had stopped waving it. His mouth hung slack, waiting for a June bug. The rest of the marks continued to eddy around the joint, a few looking in with bemused curiosity. An elbow nudge to a companion. A wink and tilt of the head. Teen girls in packs of three, tittering as they skittered past. A play within a play. Bruce had become a prop, like a desk, or a wig, or a lamp. Heat rose through Wyatt's throat, filling his head. His words were far away, somewhere above the roller coaster, hissing through the gaps in his teeth.

"This isn't a goddamn game. Petr. This isn't some shiny anarchist concept. I know how you love those big ideas, where you're high above it all…where we're all a part of this cabal, this silo of superiority for fuck's sake. He's gotta get out of here, get to a hospital or something. He needs help. It's not funny anymore. None of this is a joke. I'm taking him…somewhere. We gotta get him out of here now."

Bruce tried to object, coming between them.

"No Wyatt, I'm alright. I'm good. Indeed. Starting to come around now. Just needed a breather, maybe ha." He pulled a Marlboro out of a pack and tried to light it, but his hands were shaking too much. Wyatt reached out, held his wrist and helped him get it lit.

Petr agreed, gloat-spitting at them.

"See, Wyatt? You can tether your horse, the cavalry"—he dropped into a southern slang—"don't need to come to no rescue. A smoke, maybe a slurpy and a line or two and our boy will be as good as gold. Staying power, I tell ya, that kid's got staying power!" He wrapped his arm around Bruce's shoulders.

"We've all got the best interests of the company at heart. When the going gets tough and all that. You're tough, right Brucey? Tough as a Timex, taking a licking and keeping on ticking!"

The two of them stood on either side of Bruce, who remained halfway between sitting and standing. They only needed to have a hand on each arm for it to be a full-on tug-of-war. Back and forth with accusations, Bruce's head pinging left and right like he was watching a tennis match. Wyatt unwilling to concede the point.

The whip-crack of Greg's voice broke the impasse, a harsh hissing whisper.

"What. The. Fuck is this?" He jerked his head to the left. "You've got a guy there with money in his hand and…?" He gestured around the periphery. "I don't know what's going on, I don't care what's going on, but it stops now." He leaned low, coming eye-level with Bruce.

"Stand up, motherfucker, and start grabbing some cash. You two as well. Trouble in paradise, Jesus Christ. Where the hell is Jonah?" Petr spun on his heel and slid to the other side of the joint, started barking out the mantra to the marks.

"Here we go! Here we go! Helluva a game we got going on here folks! One in wins! One in wins! We've got the big ones!" Wyatt turned his back on them, made eye contact with the mark standing with the bill in his hand, slamming three balls on the boards in front of him in a wordless exchange.

60

It was 8 p.m., peak time on the line. A tip began to coalesce around the joint. Bruce was incapable of doing much other than smiling wanly, smoking one Marlboro after another, rust-red stains on his hands, useless to the point that Petr offered him as a prize to an East Indian family who gathered in a knot to try their luck.

"You can take this one home if you get one in! Not much to look at, but only requires minimum care; he's on a powder-keg diet haha!" They smiled and backed away slowly.

Wyatt and Petr took care of three sides and split the fourth if it got to be tipped. Their hustle accelerated, making up for the time that had been lost, quickly becoming a battle of wills. Petr was facing his bills like a Vegas dealer, snapping the accumulating paper in the palm of his hand, sending smokeless signals to Wyatt, who felt the carnival air beneath the canvas and plush become lighter, the colours sharper, the sounds clearer, separated. *Locked in. Stay locked in. Bury this prick...* Plush, cash, Bruce...all had metamorphosed into high stakes. The accumulation. The big deal, the reason for the season. He saw it for what it was and vowed to win.

The peak hours flew, tips three deep, the roar of the rides all around and overhead. Money and balls flying back and forth, inside out, yelling, laughing, groaning as balls tinged off the edge and fell to the tabletop or ground, deep screams of girl-on-the-arm triumph of the rare but requisite winner that served to recharge the Milk Can battery. Wyatt whipped his tip into a frenzy, waves over and over, subtle wrist-twitches, coughs or head nods to the side influencing the trajectory of the ball's flight, making it just miss, so close, or collide in midair with one from Petr's side of the joint. No laws-of-physics defying action like the night with Miss Stampede, but the full application of the skills he'd honed; the focus, the distraction, the manipulation, the 'being ready and reading the air'. He was on fire, grabbing the fast and furious cash. He knew Petr was doing the same, the joint having become a coliseum of sorts, the two of them a mutation of gladiatorial competition, the prize being less a thumbs up/thumbs down from the emperor in the stands as it was for control of the soul, bragging rights, bagging the game rights. The emperor was absent, MIA, the clothes slowly peeling off him over in the Birthday Game, à la Salome. A birthday suit, of sorts.

61

Over the past couple of months Wyatt had experienced long dry deserts of late-afternoon entropy in the joint; tire-kickers sloughing by, ignoring the imploring bark of hopeless desperation, both barker and the barkee going through the futile motions. "Hey there! Yeah! You! Wanna give it a try? Free shot, c'mon, free shot. One in wins!" Hating the dumb-ass shrugs and smiles as they keep on walking, loathing the lean-into-each-other whispered laughs, at his lowest points taking it on, wearing the loser label, the tables turned. He had also been swept up in the high of co-creating and maintaining tips of intensity and duration that defied logic, physics, explanation, the scene with Miss Stampede being the most memorable of the run. This one, though…

The money was flying, both of their aprons swelling with coinage, their hands holding ever thicker wads of bills. Normally, Jonah would have swung by the game by now to grab cash and get it to a safe place, but with the carnival in full tilt, he was too busy. Bruce dawdled and dithered his way through it, the intuitive sentience of the crowd keeping them away from his side of the game. Fear and failure are things that can be felt, even smelled.

There was nothing here that threatened the spacetime continuum, merely the manifestation of an epic battle of Good vs Evil. Wyatt was convinced that he was representing all that was honourable in this world. It was a battle for a soul, the sense solidifying in him with every self-assured smirk from Petr when he faced another bill in his fist. But Bruce wasn't really the one he was competing for. He was merely the conduit. This wasn't about Bruce at all, and even in the flurry of balls and lights and sounds and sense, he felt it rising. The way-back sense of who he had once been.

Wyatt was in it and beyond it simultaneously. Here and there. He was beside a gurgling brook with speckled trout lingering beneath the sun-dappled pool, the moment frozen as the baited, weighted hook hovers upstream before tumbling in the current towards them, punctuated by the ding-pop of a ball landing on the metal edge of the milk can top. Lingering laughter in the kitchen of a camp in the summer, snug and sure, curled up under sheets as the adults on the other side of the wall smoke and drink and tell jokes that don't quite make sense, while the mark in the game digs deeper into his front, right pocket to get more cash to try and win the elephant for his little girl in the wheelchair, her eyes dancing with diamond-ringed hope. The smell of an adolescent fort in the potent-pungent forest floor autumn woods, before the beginning of the end of the innocence, mingling with woven-wafting cotton candy, deep-fried mini-donuts and cigarettes in the flat western air. The self who he remembered, the one who he trusted, coming back into focus.

62

As they manifest, so do they dissipate. The nature of the beast on the metaphoric Midway. Among other things, they all knew this. The clock had ceased to exist for them during this timeless two hours, wave after wave of humans drawn in, filling the spots around the joint as they became available, the departing shaking their heads, cursing their luck, blaming the game, the occasional winner holding their bounty straight-armed above their head to avoid stains, cigarette burns, sticky candy apples, thievery. The kaleidoscopic, continual reconfiguration of the tip was a murmuration, a coral reef of swirling schools. Wyatt caught sight of Greg and the twins standing together by the Himalayan, arms crossed, mouths moving, heads both nodding and shaking.

When the tip finally dissolved, he and Petr stopped, coming up for air in the metallic forest silence of the stopped rides. It was somehow eleven o'clock and it was over. In the corner of the joint, Bruce was holding the electrical box on his lap, running his old hands over the inputs.

"Hmm.... yesss. Must be...sounds like...well, now, there's no sound at all out there now, is there? Indeed, indeed. Must be time. It's over, isn't it?" He turned to them; sad, blue eyes in Buddy Holly frames, fading away.

"Is it time? Are we done? Can I pull the plug?" Wyatt let a small smile seep, gave him a nod, exhaled. Bruce did as he was allowed. The fluorescence sputtered off.

Petr kept his back to them, his shoulders hunched, while he counted and faced the bills. Wyatt began to do the same, trying to match the snapping, number-whispering efficiency of his rival with his "five, ten, twenty, twenty-five" mantra. Wyatt worked his way through the pile, the largest he'd had in his hands since he'd begun. Usually, Jonah's cash grab every few hours kept the amount down. The wad had gotten so thick in the heat of the tip, he'd stuffed some into his apron. The two of them were engrossed enough in their accounting that they missed seeing Jonah approach the game, alerted to his arrival with Bruce's "Hey boss! How's it going?"

"Sorry I couldn't get here. The new kid was useless. And a thief. Caught him pocketing an hour in and gave him the boot. I couldn't leave Des there on her own. Really busy night." He glanced at the thick bundles in their hands.

"Not bad here either, I see. Jesus, you'll get carpal tunnel hanging onto that all night." He extended his hand to take the money, which they both ignored. Petr stepped in front of Wyatt.

"We're just getting it all counted for you. A bit of a…competition here in your absence, you see. Kings of the castle, dirty rascals… Maybe you can start with Brucey boy—he doesn't have too much going in the plunder department. More plundered. It's down to me and"—he tilted his head towards Wyatt—"him. Gentleman's bet. See who gets bragging rights, spoils of war…that sort of thing."

Jonah was nodding.

"I see. We're down to it, eh? Alright. Gimme what you got Bruce. We'll let Spassky and Fischer here gather their pieces. Come on, we can do it over in the cafeteria. You should probably get off your feet." He offered a hand and helped him over the boards. Wyatt watched them go. The bloodstains on Bruce's shorts were rust-brown now, his bony shoulders slumping, shuffling feet gingerly baby-stepping over the trash. Jonah had a hand across the middle of his back, guiding him through the closing Midway towards the cafeteria tent.

Some minutes passed, punctuated by the slamming of stanchions, clicking of locks, scraping of thick, wide brooms and the dropping of game fronts up and down the lines as the neon night waned. Petr finished the counting of the change from his apron on the counter, stood up and lit a Marlboro.

"Alright. Big fucking day in here. Whatcha got?" Wyatt sat down on the boards, lit a smoke, looked up and gave him the phoniest smile he had in his quiver.

"You first, Petr. You were in the game longer, so it's a seniority thing. I wouldn't presume…" Petr snorted.

"Right. Technically, of course, this is a game of trust as much as it is of chance, wouldn't you agree? Now, I know you don't trust me…" He held up his hand to silence Wyatt's response.

"No, that's fine. Day one, Wyatt, day one I knew you far more than you knew me. That's why I trust you with your count…so you're gonna have to accommodate my…proclivities. Can there be honour among thieves? Only the shadow knows, right? And we both know the shadow."

He put both hands in his apron and smiled.

"Marquee total here. Top of the pops. This day in history, at the end of the prairie run, I was able to liberate a grand total of $2315.00 from the fine folk of the flatlands. A new land-speed record…." He folded his arms and waited.

Wyatt knew before he heard. He'd kept a rough count through the day as he always did and knew he hadn't cracked $2000. Still good—amazing, in relative terms—but he knew Petr was always going to win the war of this world. An unexpected sense of relief descended. He took his first deep breath in memory, savouring the expectations of Petr; slowly exhaled as he spoke.

"Yay you! You won. You win again." A line from the Hank Williams tune. "The news is out, all over town… congratulations!"

Petr had a quizzical look on his face. "Again? I know I usually grab more than you, but am I missing something?"

Wyatt laughed. "Oh, come on. Cut the fuckin' shit. It's not about the money. Never was or is. There are prizes and then there are prizes, and you must be sittin' on top of the world now. You got the big one, right? I get that you can't let things take their natural course in this place. Everything gets a bit of a boot in the ass…. Bruce has been broken, and that's what you really wanted. Don't fuckin' smirk. I was with BillyBob—fucking Whac-A-Mole BillyBob—watching you standing over that poor bastard. That grim fucking grin of yours… I don't want to know what the fuck happened. Honestly, Jesus. He needs some serious fucking help. Medical and otherwise."

Petr just sat on the boards during the diatribe, smoking and smiling. Silence descended, blanketing the tension.

63

They were finishing taking down the canvas sides of the joint when Jonah returned. He had an empty apron folded across his forearm like a waiter.

"Well, we're down to four now. Bruce is done like dinner." He popped some smokes out of his pack and passed them around.

"We just had a meeting of the minds; went like clockwork haha. The Clown is concerned. Wipe the smirk off your face, Petr. He's in bad shape, way worse than I thought. Greg's taking him to the hospital now, then getting him home. They're concerned about lawsuits, the law, his parents; everything. His old man's an oil exec for fuck's sake. I think the plan is to get him back home in one piece and hope the scandalous nature of this condition will preclude any legal action. Consenting adults and all that shit…" He grabbed Petr by the arm.

"I'd love to send you on that fucking plane. You could be the male escort getting him back to high ground. You get so much vicarious joy out of his situation, it's a shame to see it end. I've never seen you so happy. You always struck me as asexual, to be honest. All these beautiful women around; on the Midway, Des and Trish; and never batting an eye. Even Wyatt sneaks a peek every now and again, but not you. Something different lurking in there, something distant. But, alas…. lawsuits…" He put his right hand out, palm up, fingers beckoning.

"I'll take it now. Whatcha got?"

Petr untied his apron and tossed it to him. "Twenty-three hundred and change. More than Wyatt. That's the main thing, right? Winning. I won. I always win."

Jonah spit.

"Really…all Darwin now, is it? What happened to the collective? You're putting the 'sin' in syndicate, eh? Lone wolf from the Canadian Shield. Shield… better keep that up." He grabbed Wyatt's proffered apron.

"So, just the two of you to tear this down. We'll get the Birthday packed up. Try and get along; see you in a couple of hours. We leave in the morning"

64

A thin line of dawn slivered the horizon. The last load of the joint to the trailer was done. Wyatt and Petr had worked in silence, unsnapping, untying, unplugging and lugging for over four hours. They made their separate ways past the Midway detritus to the Birthday Game. Only the orange Xs from Greg's spray can were left to indicate something had once been there. Empty everywhere. Metaphors pinballed around Wyatt's worn-down mind.

Jonah had brought a truck over from the parking lot and was sitting in the driver's seat. Des had her feet up on the dash. She was turned towards him, smiling, hand outstretched towards him, open-palmed, explaining something, or maybe pleading. *The fifth*, Wyatt thought. Absolved, or seeking absolution. Wyatt remembered seeing the same leaning forward, the same smile, in BillyBob's trailer. The phrase "Night of the Long Lines" skipped across the pond of his mind.

He thought of prone, bloody Bruce, the hollow man, and felt guilt for the first time. He could have done more. Could have done something. Anything, but nothing might have made a difference. He couldn't hear what was being said in the Clown truck. His anger got redirected toward Des, moving his sense of guilt to a back burner. He needed someone to blame.

Jonah creaked the door open and climbed out.

"Jesus. That took a while, eh? Helen Keller might have been quicker."

Wyatt and Petr stayed silent, stung by the reprimand.

"Slight change in travel plans. I already talked to Greg. He needs a couple of trucks commandeered, delivering games to Winnipeg for storage; they're not going back to the States. We can grab another game there and head to Toronto. I volunteered us." He looked at Wyatt.

"You drove quite a bit from Winnipeg, so you'll take one. I don't think it's the best idea to have you two"—he pointed his finger at both—"in the same space at the same time right now, so Des'll go with you, Petr with me. It's an ass haul: fourteen hours at least driving these pigs, likely longer. F250's hauling two tons of broken dreams, winging back and forth in the wind. Gotta take your time or you'll jackknife. Greg left the keys at the office. Go grab a truck, get your shit at the motel. We'll catch up with you in Winnipeg; no need to be paralyzed by vehicle co-dependence. Stay awake on the highway."

Des, who'd been leaning out of the driver's-side window, pushed open the door with her cowboy boot and stepped down onto the asphalt.

"Perfect!" she gushed. "Finally, some quality time, away from the madness. I'll be good company, make sure you stay awake and get the game to the station on time, don't worry!" She put her arms around Jonah and gave him a dramatic kiss, left leg cocked like a woman from a VE-Day photo. His arms hung at his sides. She held out a hand, which Wyatt reluctantly took, and led him towards the office.

65

It was radio-quiet in the truck on the way out of town. Classic rock. Wyatt's armpits were stinging from sweat. He kept a tight, two-handed grip on the steering wheel, aware of his triceps bulging below the shirt sleeves, hoping he didn't fuck up right out of the gate and have an accident. The weight of the trailer made it feel like the front end of the truck might lift.

Bare feet up on the dash, pink toenails catching the mid-morning light, Des leaned back with her eyes closed, rocking gently to the rhythm of the stops and starts, the turns and twists of the roads leading to the forever prairie highway. They finally arced off the ramp onto the Trans-Canada highway, the staccato of the diesel morphing into a whine when Wyatt put the pedal down, getting them up to a cruising speed of 120 km/h. He dropped his right hand off the wheel and exhaled. Des lit a smoke, passed it to Wyatt, then did the same for herself.

"Are we there yet? Are we there yet?" she whined in a high-pitched voice. Wyatt played along in a stern dad voice.

"I'll tell you when we're there. You keep quiet and enjoy the sights. I have to concentrate here; I can't have you distracting me while I'm driving. Read your book." They laughed a little until the hum of the tires wrapped itself around them again.

Fence posts, barns and tractors; hay bales, wrapped in white plastic, dotting the fields like marshmallows.

"Sooooo… that was …interesting, eh? Did you get a chance to see Bruce before he left?"

Des shook her head.

"It was pretty fucked in the Milk Can, to be honest. I don't think a standard goodbye scenario would have registered with him. He was a fucking mess," Wyatt said. "If I hadn't seen it…. He looked like a Sodomized sacrifice. Blood stains in all the wrong places, a sort of stigmata on the palms of his hands. Just hollow, Des. He could barely get a word out. Hollow man in a wasteland. Down and out. Airlifted out of the combat zone."

"Yeah, I know. Jonah and I talked about it a bit in the joint. Honestly, I never thought it would get to where it got…. That night at BillyBob's RV feels like a million years ago. Jesus…what a shit show. Fellini couldn't have filmed a more surreal scene."

Wyatt nodded solemnly, didn't speak for a minute.

"What the fuck was up with that night? It was …consequential… the end of the line, as it were, for Trish. And to be backstage like that…. Fuck, felt like I needed a shower after. But you had something going on, right? A different kind of VIP access from what I could see. What was up with that, Des? You bent BillyBob's ear out of shape, Des. For a guy who claims to have seen it all, I'm pretty sure he'd never seen whatever it was you showed him. I'm way beyond curious."

Des chuckled, gave her head a little shake, brushed a few strands of black hair back off her cheek.

"Oh Wyatt." She chuckled indulgently in a way that made Wyatt feel childish, naive.

"I barely remember that night. You know how it gets, when you're far enough into the zone that you speak a kind of flickering truth. I was kind of fucking with him, I'm not gonna lie; it wasn't too hard to pick up some useful information on BillyBob. His backstory is pretty common knowledge on the Midway; I was down the rabbit hole enough to embellish. A few clues in the RV helped with the fortune-telling! That's the main thing I learned from my friend on the dance circuit: get a few facts from appearance… clothes… and run with it. People want you to know their story on some level." Des took off her seat belt and turned towards him.

"There's always some…flakes of flesh on the memory bone when I have these kinds of nights. These kinds of experiences. I get them every now and again, I'm sure you've heard. It's strange. We've been locked into this scene for a month, and there's way more we don't know about each other than we do, and yet… Even backstory. Sure, we know where we came from, or at least claim we do haha. It's like we're all cardboard cut-outs of ourselves until the cards are dealt, the chips are down…the die is tossed. Running out of gambling metaphors here, but you know what I mean. Until we're down into it. Then you see the real stuff, right? Ya see what you're really made of."

The prairie sky had opened even wider. The horizon seemed to run off in every direction, giving no point for Wyatt to fix his attention on. He wanted something to concentrate on beyond her words. The coffee he'd cradled in his hand on the way out of town was cold now and had nothing left to offer. Judging by the height of the sun it was high noon.

The west. They were still in the west. Smoking gunslinger movie poster memories laid themselves over the landscape unfolding past the dash of the truck. Des's voice cut into his matinee, bringing him back to it.

"Hey Wyatt. Hey!"

He straightened the wandering wheel back into the lane.

'Sorry. Fuck. Drifted off for a second…" He shook his head, cranked the window down for some air, letting the adrenal butterflies swirl back to a landing in the pit of his stomach. Des laughed, calm and comforting, not bothered at all by the jerking of the truck.

"You must be exhausted. I caught a nap waiting for you during teardown. Look up there. That silo? Pull in there. We can get out and stretch. Reboot!"

She held up one of her cowboy boots and raised an eyebrow.

66

Wyatt slowed the truck down gingerly, decelerating rather than pumping the brakes, to avoid jerking the trailer too much. The crunch of the gravel under the tires blended with the high whine of a transport blowing by them. He stopped and killed the ticking diesel engine. They stepped out into the sudden silence.

Des spread her arms wide and high and did a slow pirouette at the front of the truck. The shadow from the rust-red silo split her in two, light and dark.

"Don't you love the great wide open?" She took a deep breath and yelled, "If you've got a bellybutton, you've got a birthday!" and laughed way too long, as Wyatt saw it.

"You can watch your voice run away for days haha. I bet that makes it all the way to the mountains! It'll trigger avalanches in the Rockies.

What a concept, what a world!" She finished her spinning and walked to the far side of the silo.

"Gotta go to the little girl's room, Wyatt," she said, her voice an octave lower than her pan-prairie bark.

Wyatt touched his toes a few times, took a piss by the non-highway side of the truck and climbed back into the cab. A moment for his thoughts to ungather, going off with a mind of their own. Awareness for the first time in a long time of the shoulder shadow. The fear. The wondering what the fuck he was doing here in the middle of nothing, nowhere with…who? He had no idea who. He had some clues regarding what, the way everyone does. "So, what do you do?" as though that's a window into anything at all, other than choices made back at the beginning of the falling of the domino tiles. Lonely, it occurred to him. Why am I so alone? Who was this person sharing the ride with him? He'd seen her shining in the Birthday joint, smiling and strutting her undeniable beauty beneath layers of prizes. Cleaning cups as the warm, morning sun yawned into the Winnipeg kitchen where they'd stayed so long ago. Wound up tight at the cafeteria tables in conspiratorial conversations with Petr. Oddly both mother and sister. Whispering dark and disturbing predictions into BillyBob's ear. Did she call it? Bruce's demise? Dark gypsy dancer of the Midway, a flashback to the dirty Thirties of rigged games, freak shows and unspeakable liaisons inside tightly tied tents. Wyatt wondered how he was going to make it to their destination with this degree of exhaustion rearing its head. The pinball associations stopped careening when Des got in and shut the passenger door.

"Well, that's much better. Whew. Needed that." She turned to him. "Whaddya think? A little pick me up before we hit the road? You must be beat." Wyatt nodded.

"Sure. What the fuck. Whaddya got? Caffeine isn't cutting it."

"Well…this might work haha." She held a folded packet between her thumb and index finger, shaking it back and forth.

"Though it may or may not be cut ha-a. Joking. Got this from last night. Or was it this morning? It all feels the same." She pulled the driver's manual out of the dash. She set it on her lap and poured the contents of the packet onto it, cutting a couple of large lines with the flap of her cigarette pack. She nodded to Wyatt. He rolled a twenty-dollar bill, bent down and hauled it deep. She took the bill and did the same. And again. They smiled at each other, feeling the familiar lift kick in. She poured the rest back into the packet. Wyatt turned the key, and they re-entered the highway.

The powder was doing its work. The edges of sight lines became more defined. Wyatt took vast expanses of air through his nostrils, filtered and filled with possibility. This wasn't going to be a problem at all. A Grateful Dead tune—"Truckin'"—landed in his cerebellum. Chips cashed in, what a long, strange trip it's been. He took it up to 120 and clicked the cruise control on. The road was smooth.

"Kind of crazy, isn't it?" Des was musing more than asking. "We've been living and working on top of each other for a couple of months now. It just dawned on me, just occurred, just landed on the wire. All I know about you is whatever Jonah has mentioned. Well, not all I know, don't take that the wrong way; I've seen you in action, as it were. I get a sense of who you might be from that, but far be it from me to presume. You're good in the game; you've got a good intuitive sense of what's happening there, and really, with all the games, if you know what I mean. Emotional intelligence, right? No shortage of brains flying around this crew, but you've got that other thing. Or maybe it's more than a derivative DSM-5 diagnosis. Maybe the other thing is a conduit. Tapped in. I don't wanna say psychic, but…"

Wyatt was buoyed by her words. The last time he could remember being complimented by a woman was a lifetime ago. He liked the sound of her voice, liked how it felt in the cab of the truck right now. Out of time, out of place.

"Same here. We're probably all the same, speculating, assuming, even judging without having the shoes to walk the mile in. Gotta say, the Midway petri dish might be both the best and worst way to get a sense of who someone is; Dickens and all that. Best and worst of times. Schrödinger's joint, you know?" He was aware of the boost to his thought, speed, clarity and articulation. *Cooking with the coke.*

"We've all formed opinions and impressions, eh? We've got nothing but time between here and there, Des. A real opportunity to clear the air, isn't it? Get to know each other, exorcize all those negative thoughts and impressions that have gathered up into a ball over this run. A snowball, right, rolling down a hill, getting bigger and bigger until it crushes whatever gets in the way. Fuck that, Des." Des broke into the Tom Cochrane tune, "Life is a highway!" They kept up the patter for a half hour or more till Des pointed ahead.

They pulled in alongside another silo, did a couple of huge lines each to finish off the packet. Des flicked the cardboard out the window. "There's more where that came from! Left turn, Clyde! Wyatt wound the truck and trailer back onto the road.

"So, Wyatt. You show me yours and I'll show you mine. Ha, relax now. I'm joking! We've got miles to go before we sleep. We can fuck around and waste this glorious one-on-one opportunity, or we can spend actual time saying actual things, get to know the back line. What makes the clock tick, what force through the green fuse drives. That Dylan Thomas, eh? You think you know someone… nah, we don't. We've been basically inseparable for the summer. Sleep, eat, work, travel…. imbibe together… and yet, what do I know? Bright enough, fancy yourself some type of creative human, sensitive to the point of paralysis. Judgy. I've seen the way you look at me, caught you out of the corner of my mind's eye more than once. That's okay. That's fine. Seriously. I've got a black belt in being judged…you have no idea. But here we are, just the two of us. Let's dive in. Tell me something. Fuck it; tell me everything." She produced another packet for her purse, pulled the driver's manual out of the dash and poured some coke onto it. "You talk, I'll listen." Hummed as she carved up a couple of lines.

"Jesus, I'm jacked…" Wyatt's heart was thudding, pumping buckets of thinned-out blood. He imagined auricles, ventricles, capillaries speeding the red gold to every cell in his body. He breathed as deep as he could, gathering oxygen to send to the troops. The sun blazed, bathing the prairie fields in swirling Van Gogh amber.

"Walk the walk, right, Des? Seekers of …something. The common ground for us, isn't it? Looking left, looking right, round the corner, on the horizon. But isn't it always right here, right in front of your face. I mean, look at the colour of that waving wheat." Des was nodding and smiling bright. She placed a rolled bill up to his nostril, held the powder-laden driver's manual under his chin, and imitated him— "Right in front of our face!" He snorted the line back, pushed the gas down. The two of them rode along the white line for the rest of the day, telling a new version of their story to each other while the sun spun through the sky.

67

It was dark now, the sky like old ink but for the moon, a few stars and a chunk of glimmering light up ahead on the highway. Wyatt wondered if Des heard his words the way he heard hers; staccato sentences pinballing round in his head, leading him down alleys of thought and image that had a life of their own. Ripple effect, domino effect, up too late and long with nostrils caked with speedy coke, antiseptic fresh to every breath. Yesterday? When was that? Bruce had been spirited away. Saved. It had been so important, to rescue him from the dark. Not the sky dark; the sinning heart dark. How had it happened? Had it happened?

Des was still sideways towards him, legs folded under her on the seat. Who she had been, or he thought she was, had mutated over the course of the exodus from the Midway in the morning. Broken Bruce being spirited, the harbour in Wyatt's head filled with thoughts of her anchored in fear and loathing. What kind of person…? The Jezebel label, the sorceress label, the bitch label. He applied them all to her at one point or another since the night in BB's RV. How to reconcile that projected judgement with the warmth between them that filled the cab of the truck. Together, hurtling through ecstatic sunset insight in the warm womb of the night. Sharing. Vulnerable. Naked but for the skin wrapped around their bones. Wyatt wondered if he was thinking or speaking this. His jaw was beginning to ache from his clenched teeth.

68

The chirp of the tires and the jerk of the truck brought him back into focus. The trailer did a slow, snaky weave in and out of the oncoming lane before righting itself. Wyatt's heart hit another gear, banging the cage of his ribs. The adrenal rush that followed overrode the chemical confusion.

Shit. Wide awake and dreaming, he thought.

Des put a hand on his arm. "Whoa there, Wyatt. Not ready to cash it in just yet." She squeezed. "I think it might be time to drop the silo stops and find a place up ahead. Let's grab a room, get a drink. You go like the Energizer Bunny until the batteries can't take any more charge. We may or may not have reached that point haha!"

The speed limit went from 120 to 80 as they made their way into the town. The highway didn't run around the edge, instead it suddenly became a single lane bending into slow and then sharp turns through the middle of it. Down to 50. People on the streets, Dollar Store culture club, gas station mini-mart, colonial outpost branches of a couple major bank chains.

"Same as it ever was," Wyatt snarked. "What the fuck do people do in places like this? Big night out, bowling in the summer, curling in the winter. Waiting, wanting, wishing? What would they wish for? Jesus…"

Des laughed. "Wish for Jesus for sure! Upon a star. In a well. Who knows, Wyatt. Silos all around, right. The beauty of just passing through is you get to pass judgement with no repercussions, no challenges. Safe and sound, all around, on to the next town. Midways as far as the eye can see!" They slowed to a crawl to make a right-angle turn, dead in the middle of town. The sign in front of the flat-land hotel made the decision easy.

"Midget Wrestling—Tuesday Night!!!"

"Pull in here, Wyatt. Looks like our kind of place. It's what, Sunday? Damn!" Des enacted a high-pitched, redneck voice. "What I wouldn't pay to catch me some live midget rasslin'! Takes me back to the good ol' carny days of peep shows, freak shows, burlesque tasseled-tits and Fearless Freep and the High-Divin' act. Yee-fuckin' hah!"

He signalled, and guided them in, taking it to the far end of the parking lot where there was more room for the trailer. The high beams swept along a low, ranch-themed entrance, complete with log front, hitching posts and Old West saloon-style swinging doors. He killed the engine and lights. They sat in the silent cab, and exhaled in unison.

Wyatt spoke first.

"Holy fuck.... That was a bit of a burn, eh? We just made"—he checked the odometer—"over a thousand kilometres. Looks like Amarillo by morning here. Gunfight at the OK Corral. Time and space fly when you're having fun." He opened the door and slowly stretched himself out of the cab. Des did the same on the other side, groaning dramatically.

"Oh, Jesus. I haven't heard my hip joints in a while! Sitting like that can't be good for any part of you. My kingdom for a hot shower." They grabbed their bags from the back of the cab and waddled their way to the lobby, pushing through the swarm of summer bugs and swinging doors.

A Stetson-sporting clerk at the front desk checked them in. "A double good for you, I assume?" elicited no-no-no's from both of them.

"Two single beds please. We're not together. I mean, we're together, but not shared bed together. Two singles for sure!" Awkward laughter, a couple of keys on a large key ring and they careened down the long hall to room 113.

69

Bags on their respective beds, Des sat down and opened another packet, carved a couple of lines and snorted hers back. She offered the rolled-bill tube to Wyatt.

"I dunno...Not sure I need another blast right now... A beer or six might take some of the edge off, you know?" Knots were cording around his shoulders and neck.

"Come on, might as well. Do this one and we can take a break, grab a shower and head down to the bar. At least there'll be mental midgets there to entertain us, right?"

To Des's satisfaction, Wyatt complied. She lay back on the bed and slid her cowboy boots off.

"Pink toenails, hands all dirty with money," a Dire Straits lyric, popped up in Wyatt's jangled brain. The room somehow felt smaller than the truck, less intimate but more revealing. He moved to the end of his bed and sat, grabbed the remote and clicked the TV on. "You go ahead, Des. Grab your shower and then I will."

"Thanks. Won't be long." She took her bag into the bathroom and closed the door. He listened to the little noises inside, the clink of glass, the soft falling to the floor of jean shorts, shirt, bra. He looked at the remote in his hand and couldn't bring himself to press the power button. Passively regarding his pumping right leg, he realized he was holding his breath and listening to his heart pound somewhere back behind his ears. He opened and closed his lock-jawed yap while he judged the quality of the Louis L'Amour pastel art prints on the wall and exhaled when he heard the explosion of water in the shower and heard the honk of her feet on porcelain as she stepped into the tub. He fired up the TV, hit the mute button and paced back and forth in front of the beds, wishing his heart would slow down.

The faucet slammed shut. Wyatt kept pacing, listening to Des's post-shower rituals; the snap of a towel off the rack, a blow dryer activated, teeth being brushed for an inordinately long time ("Must agree with the crystal-clear clean feeling of the blow," he speculated), the slurp of still wet soles on slippery tile. Back and forth, back and forth, he was awkwardly in front of the bathroom door when it opened. They faced each other, eyes locked. The smile on her face wasn't the one she'd shared with him on the way here. Even the eye contact was… off. She was smiling at him, but through him. It was the same with the eyes; they had changed from green to a mottled mix of black and hazel, almost camouflaged. She kept the smile painted on her face as she angled sideways past him. "Your turn, Wyatt. Pitter patter!"

The shower provided no relief from the end-of-the-world palpitations. He ran the water hot, then cold, hoping to head off at the pass the sense of dread that was taking up residence, but to no avail. The pale, skin-tightened rack of bones he saw in the steamy mirror bore no resemblance to his memory of himself.

Des was at the edge of the far bed when he emerged. She'd moved the end table from the corner, and a huge white line laid out on it in the shape of an 'S'.

Wyatt thought of tapeworms.

"Almost ready, Wyatt? One more before we head down?" Her voice sounded deeper, with a bit of reverb. He'd heard it before, knew it wasn't just the shape of the room, the thin walls, the lack of bodies to swallow the sound waves. Thoughts raced around his cranium, and a vacuous, distant smile was taped on his face as he kneeled on the floor in front of the table and dutifully did the line. As the powder slammed into the back of his nasal cavity, he realized both that this was a different concoction, and that he'd heard that timbre in her voice the night in BillyBob's RV. He came up for air like a snorkeler.

His heart hit another gear. He didn't think there could be another one.

"What the fuck, Des? What's in this?" He took several deep breaths. "This isn't the same shit!" She towered above him in a blazing white t-shirt and cut-off jean shorts, looking down with the same joyless smile cracking her face.

"Not to worry, Wyatt. Not to worry. It's been… a hard day's night. A little speed to carry us through, to get us over the finish line. Just enough to keep us going for a bit; the coke isn't cutting it, right? Come on, let's get down there and get a drink, take the edge off everything!" Des spun on the heel of her cowboy boots and strode out, Wyatt high-stepping to keep up, shadowing her down the hall to the bar.

70

The swinging doors creaked like Wyatt expected them to when Des pushed her way into the bar. He felt like an afterthought in the wake of her entrance. A subtle head-down, eyes-up scan of the joint revealed a couple of guys at a pool table, a few sets of elbows resting on the bar, a couple of tables with people at them. All men, and Wyatt noticing them noticing her. How couldn't they? There was something different, something that had changed in her. Even the way she walked. It was performance.

A slow Sunday night on the Levelland. They chose a table in the corner underneath a massive set of steer horns.

"Ye Olde West," she laughed. "Shouldn't this room be in black and white, just to complete the picture?" She dropped her voice an octave. "You have now entered the Twilight Zone!" The bartender ambled over and took her order of two double scotch and two beers. Des didn't bother asking Wyatt what he wanted. When the drinks arrived, she took a long, slow sniff of the peaty amber and raised the glass for a clink. Wyatt dutifully responded.

"To the Clown. Send in the clowns! Long live the Clown!" Her voice was loud enough to draw surreptitious stares from the patrons, a couple of guttural chuckles from one of the tables of guys. Wyatt could see she was aware she'd drawn some attention, setting her glass down hard on the uneven table. He forced his scotch down and reached for a beer chaser.

A couple more rounds made their way to the table, Des's beckoning hand ensuring their arrival. Wyatt welcomed the warm, curative alcohol buzz that he hoped would take a bit of the jangle off the powder in his bloodstream. He was aware of opening and closing his mouth (*Stop it—you look like a fucking guppy*), trying to unlock the tension that had come to live in it, trying to get more air down deep. He tried distracting himself, taking in the myriad cliché Western paraphernalia—saddles, stirrups, Route 66 signs (*That's in the States for fuck's sake*) and horns. A rack of branding irons stood by the massive, dormant fireplace.

The bartender turned the volume of the music up, to Wyatt's disdain and Des's delight. He liked country music, had grown up with it back east: kitchen parties, guitars and foot stomping and fiddles, Export A cigarette smoke and booze and George Jones and Johnny Cash. The racket accompanying the video on the screen above the bar was anathema to him—shitty pop with a cowboy hat. Des responded to it much differently, shoulders moving to the beat, lips pursing and cowboy boots keeping time under the table. Wyatt felt the air thickening between them, the table lengthening. Murmurs from the others in the bar were getting louder, bee-hiving around the ceiling fans. It took some effort to push himself back from the table. He wasn't sure he said something out loud about needing to go to the bathroom. Des just looked at him, with a different kind of smile, one that he had seen before. At BillyBob's.

Wyatt walked as straight a line as he could to the bathroom. His heart had made it to his head, hummingbird beating in his throat, vice-gripping his temples, popping his vision. He careened through the doors, caught a glimpse of a shadow of himself in the mirror before dropping into a stall and locking it. He sat on the flush, arms wrapped around his knees, still wondering if sounds he heard in his head were making it out of his mouth: "too much, too much, too much of nothing can make a man ill at ease. This is no good. Fast faster fastest. Na na na na na na na na fast man, fastest man alive ladies and gentlemen see the high diving act bring on Freep. What the fucking fuck? Breathe. Breathe. You gotta breathe, boy! You gotta breathe!"

He wasn't sure how long he stayed in the cubicle. A couple of guys had come in for a piss; he held his breath and stayed quiet both times. His armpits were stinging from speed sweat, rivulets on the side of his face now dry, salted like the edge of the tide on a shoreline. He thought of the Bay of Fundy, heard the call of distant seagulls, wheeling high above the froth. To be there…to be anywhere. Wyatt took a long, deep breath, went to the sink, splashed cupped handfuls of cold water on his face and slowly made his way back into his body. *Jesus,* he thought, *how long have I been in here? A half hour? An hour?* He went back through the doors towards the bar.

She was gone. He scanned the bar left to right, one hand on his chair to keep steady and cool in the eyes of those who were staring at him. No sign of her but the empty glasses, including the other glass of scotch that he'd left on the table. The bartender was watching him intently, tilted head, bar cloth hanging from his left hand. He had a knowing smile on his face as he pointed to the door.

"She left about fifteen minutes ago, while you were in the can." He gestured to an vacant table along the wall that still had a collection of beer bottles on it. "With those guys. You might want to hurry haha." The chuckles and hoots of those remaining in the bar followed him through the swinging doors.

71

Their voices clung to the carpet, slid along the wallpaper, reflected the hallway neon, made their way out the open-a-crack door at the end of the hall. Des was loud, laughing, reacting to a muted male comment, a low drone. Wyatt did the tiptoe walk to the doorway and stood outside, leaned and listened.

One of the cowboys: "How could you know that? Lucky fucking guess! What are you, a travelling gypsy with that carnival? Part of the freak show with the Siamese twins and the bearded lady? Or do you get up to the good stuff, the striptease and what-not that goes down with the sun?" The other guy laughed a complicit, idiot laugh. Weak, conspiratorial. Gutless.

He hated them, and hated them more when he heard the smoke in Des's voice seep a "You never know, do you? It's not so far from the "guess-the-birthday game to Salome." "Salami? How did you get on salami haha" and more Neanderthal chuckles. Wyatt felt the same protective rising rage he'd had in the Can with Petr and Bruce.

He pushed the door open.

The three of them were perched on their knees around the end table, several lines of powder cut onto the glass surface. They turned their heads simultaneously towards him, a bit of choreography that he wasn't in on. The words that he'd expected to issue forth stayed wherever they were. He wasn't a part of whatever this thing was. Des looked at him like a stranger, an intruder even. No acknowledgement. Black cowboy hat guy snorted derisively.

"There he is! You okay? You look a little pale there, buddy. We waited for you, but hey, a half hour is a long time to spend in a goddamn toilet stall. Had to get this show on the road, if you understand. She got tired of waiting. Insisted we leave without you and come on up to the room. You're a little late to the party."

Des looked out from under a sly smile.

"Here Wyatt, you can play catch up. If you want. These guys are just starting to hit it. Kevin and Josh, right? Couple more might get you back where you belong. It's just starting to get interesting." The words belied the lack of enthusiasm propelling them. She turned her attention back to the table before she was done speaking, retubing the twenty-dollar bill in her hand and knocking back a thick line. The cowboys joined in.

It descended upon Wyatt quickly, took him back to the tornado winds on the Midway. His body, his thoughts, his sense of self sucked away from him as quick as coke up a nostril. Wind-tunnel howling began to roar in his ears, the room elongating, stretching away from him. Dust-Bowl sepia, theme song from *The Good, the Bad and the Ugly*, memory of a memory of a behind-the-tent-flap gathering to witness a freak show, "step right up folks, don't worry, it can't hurt you" in a metallic voice. His head was leaving his body, riding above the hotel room, roof lifted off, watching him watching the Ouija Board coke lines on the glass reconfigure into parallel lines, arrows pointing up at him, European sevens, horizontal tapestries. There was laughter, at him, all around him. The words were from someone, somewhere else.

"Gonna take my bag, Des. Just take it out to the truck so it's there in the morning. So it's safe. Safety in numbers. You can't be too careful. Out to the truck... going out to the truck. Right back. Be right back." He watched one of his hands pick up the keys off the counter, the other hoist his backpack off the bed. He backed away what felt like very slowly, thought of how they leave the bank after a robbery in the black-and-white movie world of the past. Bonnie and Clyde. The fangs of cruel laughter followed him down the hall, out the door, dissipating when he slammed through the swinging doors of the lobby.

He stumble-ran to the truck, crashing against the passenger door, keys and backpack falling to the ground with a clink and a thud. The whine in his ears waned, the swirling world slowed and stopped. Overhead, the full, magnetic moon brought him back into his skin, into himself. He looked at the veins on top of his hands, saw the slow pump of blood and was reassured. Breathed deep. Let it out. Breathed deep. Let it out. The cool night air stung his raw nostrils. He could make out distant diesel from recent trucks doing the slow wind through town. The scent from a clump of wild roses that had fought their way through the asphalt wrapped itself around him for a moment. The stars were out, a constellation chandelier twinkling. There was a sense of coming in for a landing on a plane, when the plane finally softly comes to a stop at the end of the runway.

He stood as still as a cactus for the longest time, regarding the Clown face on the side of the trailer. The bowler hat, the straight smile, the two black eye-crosses. It was a standoff. He finally picked up his pack, threw it on his back and walked past the Midget Wrestling sign towards the silent, waiting highway. Stood still for a forever minute, looking one way, then the other, waiting for his legs to start moving. Left or right. East or west. It didn't really matter at all.

...

The old custodian stood watching, leaning on the handle of his broom, waiting for the last truck hauling the Ferris Wheel to leave, before he started. The driver gave him a wave, and he nodded in response, leaning his head away from the grey-black burst that choked out of the pipes. It was getting light enough that he could see the expanse of detritus that lay before him; garbage cans overflowing, clumps of French fry boxes and cotton candy containers skidding around in the breeze, tiny key chains, bingo cards and busted cheap-shit paintings and mirrors. The acreage of the grounds undulated. It was built on wetland, he thought. A long time ago. An asphalt ocean smothering polliwogs, salamanders, cattails. It only looks to be on the level when it's covered in carnival, he thought, and chuckled. On the level. As if.... He lit a smoke, leaned over the broom and began to push the garbage into piles.

"Maybe I'll find me some money again. Or something worth hanging on to."

...

Acknowledgments

So many have helped me make the move from guitar and music to the laptop and fiction. Heartfelt thanks to Seaside Scribes, ArtsNB, The Writers' Federation of New Brunswick, Gerard Collins, Beth Powning, Grant Heckman, Julia Wright, Jackson Doughart, James Mullinger, and Jeremy Gilmer; I wouldn't have been able to be able to call myself a writer without your support.

The biggest thanks goes to my family, most especially my wife, Sandra Watt, for indulging, encouraging and enduring my road to the written word.

Brent Mason is from Belleisle Creek, New Brunswick, and lives in Saint John, New Brunswick. He's made twelve albums of original music, writes a column of short fiction for the Saint John *Telegraph Journal* called *Mason's Jar*, and continues to host the longest-running open mic night in the free world at O'leary's Pub every Wednesday night. *Midway* is his first novel.

See www.brentmason.ca